Holding Out for a Hero

Mari Manning

Published by
Crimson Romance
an imprint of F+W Media, Inc.
10151 Carver Road, Suite 200
Blue Ash, Ohio 45242

www.crimsonromance.com

Chapter 1

Seneca Simms hurried down the narrow corridor, scanning the numbers on the office doors as she brushed past them. When she reached number 425, she stopped. Through frosted glass and thick black letters announcing *Collin Atlee, Private Investigator,* she saw the shadowy figure of a man hunkered over a computer.

"Gotcha."

She twisted the knob and pushed. For a moment the door stuck in the frame. Then it gave, banging against the wall with a dull thud, and Seneca gazed at the most beautiful man she'd ever seen. His features were sharply cut, forehead high, cheekbones prominent, nose straight. His mouth was generous, almost sensual, a feature the dark stubble covering his square jaw failed to hide. Beneath blond hair and dark brows, long-lashed eyes glittered like a king's ransom of sapphires.

A few seconds ticked by while Seneca adjusted to the presence of a handsome stranger sitting in Collin Atlee's office. He frowned at her, perfect brows knitting over the sharp bridge of his nose. Concern creased the corners of his mouth.

Seneca hitched up the heavy purse slung over her shoulder and folded her arms. "Where is Collin Atlee?"

Mr. Beautiful's eyes narrowed until the blue barely showed beneath his sweep of lashes. "If you are looking for Richard, ma'am, you're on the wrong side of town."

"I'm looking for the guy whose name is on the door." She jerked her head sideways at the lettered glass. "Collin Atlee."

His head tipped back. His eyes widened in surprise. "I'm Collin Atlee."

"I've met Mr. Atlee, and you are not him. If you don't tell me where he is right now, I'll-I'll . . ." What would she do? She itched to punch him, but from the width of his shoulders, she guessed a jab delivered by a woman barely five-foot-two wouldn't convince him to start talking.

"Who are you?" he asked.

"You know very well who I am. Mr. Atlee put you up to this, didn't he?"

Mr. Beautiful rose to an intimidating height, requiring her to tilt her head to keep an eye on him. As he came around the desk, he fished something out of the back pocket of his desert camo combat pants. He produced a worn leather wallet and flipped it open. An Illinois state driver's license with the name *Collin R. Atlee* stared out at her along with a fairly hot DMV photo.

She gaped at the picture. Red hot anger exploded behind her eyes.

"Are you all right?"

"How could I be all right? A bumbling, addle-brained *jerk* screwed with me. I've been on pins and needles for a month, waiting for his report—"

"Report? What report? Who *are* you? What are you talking about?"

Poppy's voice spoke in her head. *Breathe deep, Sen. Take it one step at a time.* She took a cleansing breath, then tipped up her chin and eyed the genuine Collin Atlee. "I better go. Obviously there was a mix-up of some kind. You are not the man I talked to last month." If she wanted to resolve her problem in two weeks—and what choice did she have—she'd better get cracking.

He slid his wallet back into his pants. "You talked to someone last month who said he was me?"

"Yes."

"In this office. With my name on the door."

"Yes. Just after Labor Day."

"You're sure."

"Of course I'm sure." She stepped back. "I've got to go."

"What did he look like?"

She let her eyes drift down his body, taking in the black T-shirt, the camo pants, the long legs. "The opposite of you. Short for a man, sort of light brown hair, brown eyes, and well-dressed."

One perfect eyebrow lifted.

"He asked me a lot of questions, mostly about myself, but he didn't write anything down except for my phone number."

"I'll bet." He muttered the words under his breath.

"What's that supposed to mean?"

He gestured toward the set of chairs in front of his desk. "I'm sorry for any trouble this guy caused you. I'd like to make it up."

Chicago is a big city, Sen. You can't trust people. She studied his desk. It was cheap and battered, but his laptop looked new. He kept no photos or other personal items on the desk. A Styrofoam cup held a motley assortment of pens and pencils, an iPhone glowed beside the laptop and a white paper bag with the Golden Arches printed on the front teetered atop a stack of unopened mail. In the window, behind a comfortable leather chair, an ancient air conditioner rattled. Spartan, definitely masculine, but it said nothing about the man himself.

"I don't know."

"Do you need help or don't you? From the way you burst into my office I thought you came about an urgent matter."

An urgent matter that should have been resolved by now. Her fists bunched at her side as her temper inched up toward the danger level again. Maybe he noticed because he backed away from her.

"I'll get you some water." He strode around his desk, back ramrod straight, shoulders thrown back, a posture Seneca had seen hundreds of times. Half the boys in her little hometown joined the military after high school, and when they came back they walked just like Collin Atlee.

Relief washed over her. "You're a soldier, Mr. Atlee."

He dug around in a canvas bag dangling from a bent coat rack and pulled out a bottle of water. "Yup. Call me Collin."

"Seneca Simms."

He twisted the cap off the bottle. His long arm, tattooed just above his elbow with a combat knife and crossed arrows, reached over the desk. Familiar ink on the streets of her hometown. He handed the water to her. "Have a seat."

She lowered herself into one of the visitors' chairs. "I don't know where to start exactly."

"The beginning."

She frowned. "That's my problem. I don't know how to find the beginning."

Tiny smile lines creased the corners of his mouth. "Just dive in. We'll straighten the chronology out later."

She nodded and looked down at her hands. "Well, my father, his name was Woodrow Simms, died last May."

"In Chicago?"

"No. Peabody, West Virginia. I was born, uh, raised there. Anyway, I drove down to Peabody over the Labor Day weekend to sort through his papers and clean out the house. I discovered a birth certificate for a Seneca Albers Simms, same first and last name as mine and same date of birth, but everything else was changed, and I don't have a middle name."

"Brothers, sisters, mother, cousins?"

"Just me." She swallowed. "As far as I know."

"You waited three months to retrieve important documents from an empty house?"

She'd come to Chicago because she wanted to play music, but on the eve of her audition at the music conservatory, Poppy died alone in their small clapboard house in Peabody. *Music corrupts. Don't ever forget, Sen.* He'd said those words to her just before she left to go north. If she'd listened, Poppy might still be alive. Being in the house where he died made her nauseous.

She looked at Collin and shrugged. "I was busy."

"I understand. Go on."

"The other birth certificate says a man named Thomas Simms is my father and someone named Sonja Albers Simms is my mother. But Loralynn Simms was my mother. She died when I was three but I remember her. I've never heard of Thomas or Sonja. There must be a mix-up. I was born in West Virginia at the County Hospital just outside Peabody. I know it."

"But . . ."

"But this other certificate says I was born in Los Angeles. I've never set foot in California."

"Did you take them to the registry in your county?"

She nodded. "The clerk told me the California one was a fake. He tried to take it away from me, but I raised a fuss until he gave it back."

"What makes you think it isn't a fake?"

"It has an official California state seal on it. I checked. They're both authentic documents."

"What do you think happened?"

"I don't know. I thought maybe I was adopted, but when I researched online, all the adoption sites said the original certificate is sealed by the courts. The names of the adoptive parents are entered on the new certificate, but all the other information is the same. Mine has a different place of birth."

She paused. "Besides everyone in Peabody says I look like Poppy. He had red hair and mine is darker, auburn, I guess. His eyes were blue not green like mine, but I have his freckles and his quick temper." Her face grew hot. "Plus we're both on the short side."

Collin tipped his chair back and folded his hands under his chin. "Doesn't make sense."

"What do you think?"

"One of the certificates is counterfeit, and if I was a gambler, I'd put money on the one issued in Peabody."

"But why the Peabody certificate? Why can't it be the California certificate?" *What if Thomas and Sonja were alive? How would she explain all this to Michael?*

"There is no logical reason to forge a birth certificate naming strangers in L.A. as your parents."

"What is the *logical* reason for faking the Peabody one?"

His voice gentled. "Come on, think about it. The man who claimed you as his daughter would need a birth certificate to prove it. Why would strangers in California risk arrest or a prison sentence to produce a forged document for no purpose? Or at least not one I can see." He dropped his hands and leaned forward. "Are you all right?"

"I knew the California certificate was genuine the minute I pulled it out of Poppy's box of important papers. I just couldn't admit it to myself. My, uh, father is the only family I've ever known. We had our differences, but he loved me as his daughter. I know it." Bewildered, she shook her head. "I don't understand. Why did he do this?"

"I don't know."

Chirp, chirp, chirp. Her cell phone burst into bird song. *Damn!* She'd forgotten about Michael. Her eyes met Collin's.

One corner of his mouth tipped up. Tiny laugh lines curved around his lips. "Do you need to get your phone?"

She slipped her hand into her purse and fished around for her cell. "Excuse me." She retreated into the corridor, shutting the door firmly behind her.

"Hello? Michael?"

"Where are you?"

She stalled for time. "What do you mean?"

"I went by your apartment after work, and you weren't there. You said you'd help me with my speech tonight."

Firing Mr. Atlee was supposed to take five minutes. She planned to be home before Michael arrived. Seneca glanced over her shoulder at the frosted glass. The shadowy head on the other side appeared to be watching her. She ducked out of sight.

"Seneca. Are you there? Is something wrong?"

Poor Michael. He carried the worries of an ailing planet on his shoulders. Some days the weight nearly crushed him. How could she pile on her own minuscule problem and say she loved him? Next spring he was running for the state senate. *No skeletons, Seneca. It's critical. That's how they kill a political movement.*

"I'm fine. I went for a long walk."

"Did something happen at work?"

"Just walking off a bad day. He loaded up my inbox at 4:30. Tomorrow's going to be hell." Administrative assistant to prominent attorney had sounded like an exciting job. Paper shuffler to cheap, egotistical ass proved closer to reality.

"Are you sure?"

"Of course I'm sure." She raised her eyes to the cracked ceiling. Was Poppy watching her fib from his heavenly cloud?

"You've been walking a lot since you got back from Peabody last month."

The scrape of Collin's chair vibrated through the thin wall. "Nothing is going on, Michael. I just forgot." Her temples began to throb. She pressed her hand to her forehead. "I've had a long day."

"Are you almost home?"

Heavy footsteps approached the door. It opened, and Collin's very large, very hunky body filled the doorway. His eyes met hers. He mouthed the word, *Okay?* She held up a finger. *One minute,* she mouthed back. He nodded and turned away. The door stayed open.

She lowered her voice. "It will take me at least an hour to get back to my apartment. I'd understand perfectly if you wanted to bag it and go home."

"I thought this speech was important to us."

Irritation prickled her. "You're being dramatic. It's almost done, and you still have a week before the rally." On the other side of the door, Collin cleared his throat.

"Sorry. I'm just disappointed." A loud sigh blew through the phone. "I'll get something to eat. See you in an hour."

"Can you make it two?"

"An hour. I can't—"

"Two." She turned off the phone.

Seneca ducked back into the office. Collin wore a grave expression, but that darned eyebrow of his lifted again. It was probably how he asked women up to his apartment. "Trouble?"

Her fingers smoothed the folds of her skirt. "Can you take my case?"

"Depends on what you want me to do."

"I want you to find out which certificate is genuine."

"I already told you. It's the California one."

"Where's the evidence? I want to know why. Who are Thomas and Sonja?" She stopped. The eyebrow hadn't moved. "Who am I?"

His eyes softened. "Of course. I'll start right away."

"I need this done yesterday. I've already wasted a month."

"Did you bring the certificates?" He glanced down at her purse.

"They're in my apartment."

He stood. "Let's go."

The sensible part of her brain nudged her. "Mr. Atlee—"

"Collin. If you would prefer to bring them by tomorrow, I understand." He reached over, grabbed a bottle of water from the canvas bag, twisted the cap off and took a long slug. The muscles under his tattoo rippled. They didn't let psychopaths into the Green Berets, did they? Besides, if they didn't get the certificates tonight, she would have to spend eight hours slaving in her airless cubicle before she was free to return with them tomorrow evening. Another day wasted and no closer to finding the truth.

"I guess it would be okay if we hurry. I have an appointment at eight."

Chapter 2

Collin bent his head and patted his pockets for the car keys. "Did you drive?"

"I took the bus."

"My Jeep's downstairs. You can direct me."

He sensed her hesitation again. Reaching for the bottle on his desk, he swallowed more water he didn't want and tried to feign indifference as she studied him. Finally, she picked up her purse and slung it over her shoulder.

"My apartment is in Lincoln Park."

"Let's go."

Grabbing his jacket from the rack, he ushered her out the door before she could change her mind. In front of the building, his Jeep Cherokee waited at the curb, its rusted bumpers and faded navy paint discouraging would-be thieves.

For the first ten minutes, they drove in silence. He concentrated on the tangled Loop traffic. His passenger sat beside him, arms crossed against her chest, knees pressed together beneath her skirt, eyes fixed on the windshield. Then she stirred.

"The man who impersonated you. Do you know who he is? It just doesn't make sense—" She trailed off.

He frowned at a merging bus and checked his side mirror. "Maybe." He was going to kill Rory. Rory Brouchard was supposed to be his friend—maybe ex-friend. A rusty nail had sidelined Collin's Jeep last month. By the time he changed his flat for the spare and raced back to the office to meet with Seneca Simms, he was an hour late. He found Rory lounging at his desk. As Collin walked in, he waved two Cubs tickets in the air. He'd snagged seats behind home base for the game that night. *Don't know, Bro*, was all he said when Collin asked him what happened to Seneca Simms.

"I can't believe I fell for his act. He called me twice and his phone didn't have caller I.D. Plus he asked me weird questions."

"Weird questions?"

"Where was I? What was I doing? Did I have plans for the weekend? Did I like sushi? Date stuff." She rubbed her arms. "I am *so* gullible. No, just plain ignorant. You probably think I'm a clueless small-town girl."

"It could have happened to anyone." *How she could mistake carefree, motor-mouth Rory for a detective?*

She took a deep breath. "Why me? It doesn't make sense."

An easy question to answer. Seneca Simms was a looker, and whatever Rory's faults, passing on a hot lady was not among them. At five-one, five-two, tops, she was small. Normally not his cup of joe. But everything about her was just right—the curve of her breasts above a small waist, slender arms, shapely legs, hair the color of dark copper and a voice like sweet southern honey.

When she'd burst into his office, her cheeks pink with fury, her hands balled into fists, desire had stirred in him instantly. He liked a girl with spirit. Made everything more interesting.

"Don't worry. We'll get it figured out."

In Lincoln Park, he turned into a narrow side street and found an open parking space in front of her sprawling apartment building. As he backed into a tight spot between a pale blue Beetle and a black Escalade, Seneca gasped.

"Oh my god, don't look!"

She slipped down in her seat, curling her back over the cracked upholstery until she was nearly horizontal. He gazed down at the shiny waves of hair fanned across the seat. A curl rested against his hip. His fingers itched to touch it. Before his brain stopped functioning, he put the Jeep in park and lifted his head to see what caused his good luck.

"Don't look." She hissed the words.

"The windows are up. You don't have to whisper." Ignoring his client's direct order, he glanced over at her building. A slender man in a tweed jacket and jeans, a canvas messenger bag flung across his chest, punched at a buzzer by one of the entryways. Collin's eyes slid down to the passenger seat. "Who is it?"

Her eyes shot green sparks at him. "What sort of detective are you? Don't stare at him. Use the corner of your eye. Pretend you're waiting on someone."

He fought back a smile. "Who is this guy?"

"My fiancé."

She'd caught him off guard. "Your what?" His head swung toward the building again.

"My fiancé. *Don't look at him!*"

His gaze flickered to her left hand. "Where's your engagement ring?"

"We built a house instead. Besides, Michael says diamonds have blood on them."

"Right." If this girl belonged to him, he'd never let her loose in Chicago without his ring on her finger. The young man pressed the buzzer over and over, glancing up and down the street between assaults on the button, as if Seneca would materialize if he just pushed it enough. *He* was her fiancé?

Collin looked at Seneca. "Doesn't your fiancé have a key to the apartment?" Hell, he'd given up his key for a lot less.

Her eyes nearly bugged out of her head. "Don't look down at me!"

He tilted his head but he could still see her. "Well? Doesn't he?"

She grimaced. "Poppy's dog, well, my dog now, took a dislike to him. He goes after Michael every time the poor man sets foot in my apartment. I tried everything but wrapping Michael in a sirloin steak, but those two are like oil and water. She shrugged. "What's he doing now?"

He glanced toward the entry.

"Don't look straight at him!"

"Er, sorry."

Collin pretended to ponder the evening sky through his front windshield while he snatched brief glimpses of her fiancé. The

Chosen One fished around in his jacket, which appeared to have square patches attached to the elbows like the Nutty Professor's. When his hand emerged from a sagging side pocket, he gripped a cell phone.

"What's happening now?"

"He's texting."

More accurately, her scrawny lover seemed to be experiencing a meltdown. As he pounded out a message on his cell, his lips tightened with emotion. But Collin saw no reason to upset his hot client with this detail.

He peered down at her. "He's walking away."

She slid up in her seat. "Where did he go?"

"Toward Clark Street." Collin studied her. "You're engaged to Poindexter?"

"Michael is a committed environmentalist. He started *Action for Environmental Justice* and next year he's running for the state senate. He doesn't just believe in a healthy Earth, he fights for it every day." She pressed her lips together.

He'd fought for a lot of things too, but he let her slight pass. "Sorry. So why are you hiding from Mahatma Gandhi?"

She looked away. "I'll get those papers."

A tree-hugger seemed like an odd choice for a feisty girl with a hot body. "I can't help you if you don't tell me the whole truth."

She dropped her eyes and concentrated on her hands. "Michael doesn't know I hired you."

"Why didn't you tell him?"

"I'll just worry him."

"Why would he worry?"

She raised her eyes. They reminded him of new grass in the spring. "He believes in what he does, Mr. Atlee. No compromises. It makes some people afraid. If one of his enemies discovers my double birth certificates, and it turns out Thomas and Sonja are bad people, there might be a scandal. His career could be finished."

"I can't prevent a scandal from erupting."

"I know." She turned away from him. "If it's something bad, I'll give Michael a chance to back out."

He studied the proud tilt of her chin and her downcast eyes. A girl all alone except for a fiancé too busy saving the environment to worry about her. Sometimes he hated the world. "Would he really leave you?"

"I don't know what he'd do. He loves me. But a lot of people are counting on him." She pushed the door open. "I'll just be a few minutes."

He worked his expression into indifference. "Maybe I should go upstairs with you in case I have questions. Unless you would prefer to answer them out here. On the sidewalk."

Her head twisted, and she gazed at the corner where Michael disappeared. "I don't know."

"I'll just grab the papers and go."

Her forehead wrinkled.

"What's the problem?"

"My apartment is a mess, and my dog might go after you. He's a little unpredictable."

He slid the keys out of the ignition. "I'll wait in the hall."

He followed her at a respectable three paces through the rickety outer door that wouldn't stand up to a crowbar and up a narrow set of stairs. Soot stained the walls. The pungent odor of garlic hung in the air. She didn't seem to notice.

Before she pushed her key into the apartment door, the eager pants of her killer dog drifted into the hall. She twisted the knob and opened the door a crack.

"It's okay, Peabody Hill. It's just me and a nice friend."

One large tan paw managed to scratch its way through the crack in the door, then a black nose and drooping jowls appeared, then another big paw wedged itself into the opening and the door flew out of her grasp. A slobbering bloodhound burst through the door. Collin jumped back as a hundred pounds of eager canine leaped onto Seneca and nearly toppled her over. She knelt on the dirty linoleum floor in the stairwell and let him lick her face as she scratched his ears and laughed. Collin leaned against the door jamb and watched girl and dog reunite and his mood lightened. There were simple joys in life. Sometimes he forgot.

While the hound distracted her, Collin made a quick assessment of her apartment. Small, exactly like her. An open sofa bed sat in the center of the room. Rumpled sheets and tossed pillows were piled on top of a thin mattress. A pair of pink pajama bottoms lay on the floor beside a metal leg of the makeshift bed. Behind the bed, a bright green tea kettle and a mug sat on a kitchenette counter. Opposite the door, a narrow closet yawned with a few blouses, slacks and skirts hung inside. A frugal wardrobe for a pretty lady. A shelf over the clothes held a plain brown box marked *Documents—Save* in black marker. A dark object caught his eye on a high shelf over the box. He stretched his neck and squinted, but he couldn't see what gleamed in the closet's depths.

The dog's eager pants ebbed. He stepped back from the door but as he turned away, he noticed framed posters of dead trees and grease-covered birds and melting ice caps crashing into the ocean. They covered the walls of the tiny apartment. *Action for Environmental Justice* blazed across the top of each picture. No doubt compliments of Mahatma Gandhi.

Seneca pushed the dog away and scrambled to her feet. "Stop, you." She giggled, and her sweet voice reminded Collin of a bell. The hound licked her hands and arms as she dragged him across the hall to the apartment. Then his nose contracted with a loud sniff, and his attention turned to Collin. He slipped out of Seneca's hands with a tack to the left and went in for a few hearty whiffs of the newcomer.

Collin had served with dogs in Special Forces, and he'd learned to respect the disciplined, brave canines who accompanied his detachment on patrols. Eager to meet the dog who sank his teeth into Poindexter's leg, Collin crouched in front of him. Peabody Hill sniffed his hand, then tilted his head and studied him through dark brown eyes. Collin patted the floor.

"Here boy." The hound came to him and sat at attention as if he knew Collin was an officer. Collin scratched the dog's ears and neck. "Good boy." The dog yipped sharply. *Yes, sir.*

"He likes you. I wonder why." Collin looked at Seneca. Her hands rested on hips, her head was tilted as she studied him.

"I like him too. Do you want to get the papers?"

"It will take a few minutes to dig them out of the box." She looked sheepish. "I was actually planning to fire you, er, the other Mr. Atlee, when I stopped by tonight."

His gaze dropped to the dog. "Hey, boy, why don't us guys take a walk and give your mistress time to find her papers."

Peabody Hill wagged his tail, eager for a neighborhood reconnaissance mission, and his mistress favored Collin with a soft smile.

"Would you? He's been cooped up all day, poor thing." She lifted a heavy chain-link leash from a basket by the door and handed it to him.

Out on the sidewalk, a green-and-white Starbucks sign glowed at the end of the block. Collin remembered the tea kettle on Seneca's counter. He'd bring her tea on his way back.

"Come on, boy."

They turned away from Starbucks and strolled around the block. The dog marked sign posts and hydrants accompanied by Collin's off-tune humming of "The Battle Hymn of the Republic." The trees lining the narrow street rustled in the light breeze. Golden leaves drifted downward and fell at his feet. The ache in his heart deepened. He'd walked through so many hellholes in his life, places where an innocent-looking shadow meant death and the enemy waited at every crossroads for an unlucky soldier.

He thought of Alex, his sergeant and friend, lost to a sudden burst of flame beside a pitted highway and how, when Collin turned away from Alex's bloody remains, he saw what Alex saw in the last second of his life—a lifeless land where everything was the color of sand. After Alex died, Collin stopped believing safe, peaceful streets like this one existed, and when he came back to the States and saw them again, he didn't care. That's how he knew he'd left his nerve in the dust of a crossroads six thousand miles from home. He'd resigned his commission and drifted into the detective business to keep his mind off Alex.

He should do something with his life. But what? His grandfather left him a townhouse and enough money to keep a simple soldier in rations for a lifetime so he didn't need money. For the past year or so, he'd floated along, not caring what happened to him until tonight.

This woman—this fierce, small-town girl—interested him. He wanted her more than he'd wanted any woman, *anything*, since Alex died. The idealistic tree-hugger presented a serious challenge, but engagement was not marriage. He had a right to press his suit, didn't he? It was like joining up. You filled out all the paper work, but you weren't really a soldier until you took the oath. Besides, a woman like Seneca deserved to be fought over. He reached down and scratched Peabody Hill's ear.

"We'll fight fair, won't we, boy?"

But it didn't take much imagination to see that the tree-hugger was going to be outmatched by the Green Beret.

Three tipsy, twenty-something girls turned the corner and headed in his direction. Two blondes and one brunette. They giggled and nudged each other, and Collin decided he must be getting old because they looked incredibly young and interchangeable. Tanned, toned bodies, tight jeans, high-heels with sharp toes. "Hi," they chirped in unison as they got a good look at him. "Wanna party?" He was accustomed to this, and until he returned to the States for the last time, never turned down a little impromptu party.

"Maybe another time."

"Your loss." They giggled as they passed him.

He rounded the next corner. Starbucks gleamed at the end of the block. Peabody Hill, nose to the ground, picked up his pace. He was nearly at a full gallop when they reached the coffee shop. The dog came to an abrupt halt and, panting eagerly, gazed up at Collin. He peered inside Starbucks.

Only one table was occupied, by none other than the groom himself. A tall paper cup sat by his elbow, his Nutty Professor jacket hung on his chair. Collin watched him scratch a giant X in ballpoint pen across a sheet of notebook paper covered in tiny scrawl. Lifting his hand, he stroked his thinning hair as he considered the page. He wore a wrinkled oxford shirt, yellowed with age. A pair of red suspenders held up a pair of jeans. *What did she see in him?*

The perfect opening for his campaign to win sweet Seneca. He looped the hound's leash around a bike rack just behind his competition.

"Sit, boy."

The dog, head high, gave him a little yip. *Yes, sir!* What a great soldier. Collin patted his head. "At ease."

He pushed open the door and went inside the shop. As the little bell over the door tinkled, the groom spun his head around. Collin's eyes met the groom's.

"Evenin'."

The groom nodded, then scooted his chair closer to the table and studied his notebook.

"Can I help you," asked the barista behind the counter.

"I'd like a venti tea."

"What kind?"

Collin frowned and bent over the row of colored boxes as if this was his most important decision of the evening. Behind him, a chirping-bird ringtone went off. The conversation was muted and brief. *"But I'm waiting for—" "What's wrong?" "A cold?" "If you'd let your dad's dog go you could move into the house with me—" "Of course. Bye."* Then there was a rustle of papers being gathered and a chair scraping back and a gasp.

"Hey!"

Collin and the barista turned to the groom.

"Is something wrong, sir?" asked the barista.

The groom stared at Collin. "What are you doing with Peabody Hill?"

Collin widened his eyes and tried to look shocked. "What are you talking about?"

"The bloodhound outside is Peabody Hill. He belongs to my fiancée. What are you doing with him?" The groom squared his shoulders.

"He's my, uh, girlfriend's dog. She's coming down with a cold, so I'm walking him for her." Peabody Hill caught sight of the groom through the window and growled. Good dog.

The groom's eyes blazed at him. "That's impossible! There can't be two identical dogs in the same neighborhood."

Collin shrugged. "I guess."

"What's your dog's name?"

"I told you, it's my girlfriend's dog."

"Okay. What's your girlfriend's dog's name?"

He saw Seneca's soft smile when he offered to walk Peabody Hill. "Rory."

"Your dog's name is Rory?" The groom looked skeptical.

Collin painted a weary expression on his face and sighed. "I'll prove it."

Outside the store, he hunkered down near Peabody Hill while the groom watched from inside. "Here, Rory, here." He snapped his fingers. The hound considered him woefully, then lifted his haunches off the sidewalk and sauntered up to Collin. The heavy leash rasped across the pavement as he moved. "Good boy." He rubbed the dog's wrinkled neck vigorously and scratched behind his ear before going back inside.

The groom was apologetic. "Sorry, man. It just freaked me out. Your dog looks like the one my fiancée has."

"No problem."

"By the way, I'm Michael Berger." He extended his hand for Collin to shake. "I'll be running for the state senate next spring. Green Party. If you know anyone who lives in the far northwest suburbs who's concerned about over-development, let them know." He dug around in his Nutty Professor jacket and pulled out a brochure.

"Is that where you live?"

The groom studied him. "My fiancée and I built an eco-friendly prototype house up there."

Score one for the tree-hugger. Collin stuffed the brochure in his back pocket. "I'll keep you in mind. Good luck."

"Thanks." Mr. Nature shrugged into his coat and pushed open the door. Peabody Hill bared his teeth. Backing into the shop, the groom sat down at his table and opened his notebook.

Collin returned to his inspection of the teas. Finally he gazed back up at the barista. "Wild Sweet Orange." He said it loud enough for the groom to hear. He remembered the dog. "Throw in an oatmeal cookie for Rory."

They cruised back to Seneca's. Halfway down the block, the sixth sense Collin developed in Iraq kicked in, and he knew he was being watched. When he turned into the building, he glimpsed the groom staring at him from the Starbucks door.

Seneca buzzed him up, and when he knocked, she opened the door and waved him inside. A bright blue sofa had replaced her rumpled bed. The cardboard box from the closet sat on the cushions. When he handed her the tea, her eyes widened.

"You didn't take Peabody Hill to Starbucks!"

"He waited outside. I thought you might like some tea. I hope orange is okay."

"Michael was there!" She banged the cup down on the counter in her kitchenette. Hot tea spouted out of the sip hole in the plastic lid. She crossed her arms. "Did he see the dog?"

He hadn't considered how Seneca would feel about his mission. Still, it was a fair fight. "He didn't recognize him."

She spun around. "Didn't recognize him? Exactly how many bloodhounds do you think live in Chicago?"

"Not sure."

Her face softened. He noticed a sprinkling of tiny freckles across her nose. "I'm sorry, Mr. Atlee. It wasn't your fault." She held out two documents. "I meant to make copies."

"It's Collin. I'll be careful with them."

She nodded, but when he reached for the certificates she held back. "Would you mind putting the box away for me first? It goes on the shelf in the closet."

"Sure." He pushed a ladder-back chair away from the door, lifted the box up and slid it back where it had been earlier. His eyes traveled to the top shelf. A violin, nearly swallowed by shadows, lay under a gray blanket of dust. He stepped back. "You play the violin?"

Her eyes grew wide. "No. Why do you ask?"

He nodded toward the shelf. "There's a violin up there."

He watched a play of emotions cross her face—pain, fear, wariness. Her mouth tightened with determination. "It came with the apartment. Oh, by the way, I have to resolve my case before Halloween." Her voice sounded sharp, like a knife.

He swallowed hard. "Why?"

"Because it's my wedding day."

She was marrying Poindexter in two weeks? He couldn't think of anything to say.

Her eyebrows rose. "Do you have a question?"

Rousing himself, he slid the papers into his jacket. "Nope." He headed home to regroup.

Chapter 3

Home from another day under the steely gaze of Mr. Prominent Attorney, Seneca dragged a jubilant Peabody Hill back into her apartment. The entry door creaked open, and Collin's voice drift up the stairwell. "Thanks, man." The steps groaned under his feet.

Barking gleefully, the dog tore away from her and bounded down the stairs. Seneca heaved a soulful sigh as she listened to his claws clattering against the linoleum. "Peabody Hill, come back here." The command sounded half-hearted.

Collin appeared on the landing below her looking dangerous and sexy in a black T-shirt, worn jeans, and leather bomber jacket. "Are you okay?" Her traitorous dog panted at his side.

"Of course. Why wouldn't I be?"

"I've been calling you all day."

"I forgot my phone." By the time she left for work this morning, she was tired to the bottom of her soul of Michael's urgent text messages. *Where r u??? Call me!!!*

It didn't take a genius to figure out Michael was in an uproar over sighting Peabody Hill and Collin at Starbucks. But it would take a lot more imagination than she possessed to rustle up a logical explanation that squeezed past the truth. So she conveniently forgot her phone while she considered her story.

Intelligent blue eyes studied her. "Did Michael dump on you about seeing the dog at Starbucks?"

"I haven't talked to him since last night before you left."

"I see."

Below them, the door clicked open again. The bright voices of two girls floated up the stairwell. She stepped back, opening her apartment door wide enough for Collin. "You better come in for a minute." Too tired to set up her bed last night, she'd slept on the sofa so at least the apartment was presentable today.

He brushed past her, the spicy fragrance of his aftershave drifting around her head like a warm mist. When she closed the door and turned, he was lounging on the sofa, legs stretched out, arms spread across the back. The dog lay at his feet.

"Make yourself at home."

"Thanks."

She leaned against the door and crossed her arms. "What do you want?"

He reached into his jacket and pulled out the certificates, setting them on the coffee table. "For starters, I wanted to return the originals."

"For starters?"

He looked at her. The skin radiating from those incredible eyes furrowed. "I tried to call the courthouse in Peabody, but they gave me the run-around. The clerk informed me they can't release personal information. Apparently, identity theft is on the rise in West Virginia. I did find out that the man who signed the Peabody birth certificate still works there, but I'll have to corner him to get answers, and I'll need you with me." The dog rolled on his back. Collin leaned over and concentrated on scratching his belly.

"You're kidding me." She was not driving to West Virginia with the hottest guy in Chicago. Michael would never understand. Not to mention his future constituents . . . or the upstanding citizens of Peabody. "When you get down there, I'll call the courthouse and give them permission to share my personal information with you."

"Seems short-sighted."

"What is that supposed to mean?"

He stopped scratching the dog and looked up at her. "How many people did you say lived in Peabody?"

She low-balled the number. "A few thousand. Give or take."

"Would those 'few thousand' notice a stranger in town asking questions about the Simms family?"

The entire town would be buzzing about Collin less than twenty-four hours after he landed there—even if he didn't ask a single question. "Maybe."

"Maybe." His brows knitted as if he were in deep thought. "So if people asked you about me, how would you explain my presence?"

She narrowed her eyes. "If I went with you, people would still ask."

"I'm a friend."

He was unbelievable. "Look at you! No one in their right mind is going to believe you're my friend."

His mouth turned down. "What's wrong with the way I look?"

"Nothing!" The word echoed off the ceiling. She took a deep breath and lowered her voice. "Which is exactly my point."

Her phone began to chirp. The dog howled at the ceiling. She snatched the phone from the coffee table and turned her back on Collin.

"Hi, Michael." Did she sound too bright?

"I've been texting you for the past twenty-four hours."

"Sorry. I left my phone at home this morning. Where are you?"

"At Starbucks." She closed her eyes. "Hey Seneca, is there another bloodhound in your building? I ran into this guy last night with a dog that looks exactly like Peabody Hill, and he was walking the dog for his girlfriend who was getting a cold just like you, and the dog lived in your building because I saw them go in the front entrance. It was unsettling."

Her forehead broke out in a cold sweat. She glanced over her shoulder at Collin. He raised a perfect eyebrow and mouthed *Okay?* She swung away from him and stared at a poster of an oil-soaked penguin. "Uh, I don't know."

"Whatever. It was just unsettling. Maybe bloodhounds are the new 'it' dog." Michael's voice softened to a suggestive whisper. "Can you get a neighbor to watch Peabody Hill and come out to the house with me tonight? We can eat dinner and go over my speech together. Maybe get to bed early."

"Oh, Michael, I'm so sorry. But I can't."

Michael's mood flipped from amorous to suspicious. "Why not, Seneca? Something is going on. You're avoiding me. I can feel it."

She glanced at Collin. He was bent over Peabody Hill, vigorously scratching the dog's ears, and probably hanging on every word. She considered his bowed head, the closely cropped dark blond hair, the well-shaped hand cupping the dog's neck, the thickly corded arm with a warrior's tattoo. She had to get him out of her life—A-Sap, to quote Mr. Prominent Attorney. "Don't you remember? We talked about this."

"We talked about what? I have no idea what you're referring to."

"I told you I'm taking tomorrow off. I leave tonight for Peabody to, uh, take the dog back home." She'd have to call in sick. The boss was going to blow a major artery in his flat head.

"You said your best friend from Peabody would drive him down when she comes for the wedding? What's her name again?"

"Janie?"

"Exactly."

"Janie and Jim are bringing their two little boys. They'll be a handful on the drive back without throwing a drooling bloodhound into the mix. Besides I want to make sure he gets settled. He's all I have left of Poppy's." Dead silence greeted her. She tried a different tack. "You know how we talked about selling Poppy's house and using the money to build a deck off our kitchen? I have to pack up his personal stuff before the house can go on the market."

Michael emitted a long sigh. "I guess it makes sense. But why now? In the middle of the week?"

She turned around. Collin was studying her while his hand absentmindedly rubbed the dog's back. She met his eyes straight on. "If I do it now, I can move into our house this weekend, and we'll be together every night."

The skin around Collin's eyes tightened, but Michael was appeased. "I guess I can wait three days. The planning meeting for the rally will be over by five on Friday. I'll come over and help you move your things."

"See you Friday." She turned the phone off and dropped it on the kitchenette counter.

Collin patted the dog's head. "Why are you giving away your dog?"

"Not that it's any of your business, but Peabody Hill and Michael obviously can't live under the same roof. I've made arrangements for one of Poppy's friends to take Peabody Hill."

"Too bad. You have a great dog." He stood. "When do we leave?"

"We? I'll meet you in Peabody." She was not spending seven hours in a car with Collin.

"That's ridiculous."

"Really? How do I know you're not a rapist or a serial killer?"

Collin threw back his head and laughed. She watched the smile lines at the corners of his mouth deepen and pressed her lips together.

"Fair question. If I introduce you to a few people who've known me all my life, will you trust me then?"

A memory popped into her head. *If you are looking for Richard, ma'am, you're on the wrong side of town.* "Your father?"

"No." His face hardened.

So her private eye had secrets too. "I was hoping to leave tonight."

"I'll make a call. We can be on the road before eight."

"But you can't stay at Poppy's, er, my house. There's a little motel on the main road. You'll have to get a room there. Peabody is a small town, and everyone knows I'm engaged. It would be scandalous for us to sleep under the same roof."

"Of course." Collin lowered his lashes and nearly melted her with a hot gaze. "Would you be interested in a little fun tonight before we leave?"

Her jaw dropped. "What are you suggesting?"

"Payback."

Chapter 4

Rory Brouchard stretched his head over the bar and tried to catch the eye of a dark-haired hottie sitting a few stools down. She stuck her cute nose in the air and turned her back on him. Damn, he missed DeeDee. She'd moved to Houston because she claimed he couldn't "make a commitment." He *could*. He just needed a little more time.

He settled back on his stool to enjoy the fifth game of the World Series until Collie showed. His long-neck was cool as he rolled it between his palms, and the familiar jumble of voices warmed him. For most people Estelle's was a hole-in-the-wall beer and burger joint, but for Collie and him it was a second home. They'd been coming here since they were kids. Rory was closer to Ray, the owner of Estelle's, than his own sisters. Still, when Collie phoned him a half-hour ago to meet up at Estelle's, Rory caught a weird vibe.

"What gives?" he'd asked.

"Nothing, Bro. Got a hankering for one of Auntie Estelle's cheeseburgers. I thought if you were free we could grab something together."

At the bottom of the third inning, a pretty girl with dark red hair walked into the bar. Rory squinted into the pale evening light washing through the open door. Was that Seneca Simms? It was. He twisted around in his stool and hid his face behind his hand.

"Mr. Atlee?"

Shit!

"Mr. Atlee! I'm so glad I ran into you." She shrugged off her coat and hung it on a hook by the door. Then she came over and plopped herself down on the barstool next to him. "You weren't saving this for anyone, were you?"

His eyes shifted down to his beer. "Um, no."

"Good. You can update me on the investigation."

Ray wandered down and dropped a coaster in front of Seneca. Behind her back, Rory shook his head frantically. Collie was due any minute. She had to leave.

Ray shot him an "I'm-just-doing-my-job" shrug and said to her, "What can I get for the lady?"

She eyed Rory's beer. "Really, Mr. Atlee. Drinking in the middle of the week? You'd get more detective work done if you stayed out of bars." Ray looked like he'd just swallowed a whale. Seneca didn't seem to notice. "Diet Coke, please." Then she focused her attention on Rory. "What a godsend I found you. I've been waiting on my report for the past month."

"You have?" He squirmed in his seat.

Ray returned, diverting Seneca's attention for a few moments as he plunked her drink down on the bar. While she thanked him and unwrapped her straw, Rory toyed with slipping out the back. But before both feet hit the floor, she spun on him.

"Going somewhere, Mr. Atlee?"

"Uh, no. Just standing. Helps the circulation in my legs."

"So about my case, what have you uncovered?"

He scratched his head. "Let's see. Your, um, case. Hmmm. It was a while back now, and I don't remember—"

She punched his bicep—*hard!*—then shot him a playful smile. "You're such a kidder."

He rubbed his arm. Screw this. As of tonight he was turning in his membership to the Bachelors Club of America and crawling back to DeeDee. "I have a confession to make."

She leaned forward. "It's bad news, isn't it?"

The door opened again, and Rory's eyes slid past Seneca to the familiar figure standing on the threshold.

Collie smiled at him. "Hey, Bro, what's up?"

"Seneca, can you excuse me a minute?" Rory slipped past her and zigzagged through a dozen tables to reach the door. He pushed his face close to Collie's and shot him a bug-eye warning.

Collie's smile melted away.

Rory spoke without moving his lips. "I'll explain later." Then hanging a friendly arm around Collie's shoulder, he guided him in Seneca's direction. "Rory," said Rory, "this is Seneca Simms." He tensed, prepared to defend himself against a flying fist if Collie recognized Seneca's name. He didn't. "Seneca, this is Rory Brouchard."

Seneca extended her hand. "It's might nice to meet you, Rory." Her southern lilt thickened to a drawl. "Are you and Mr. Atlee friends?"

Collie shook her hand. "I'd like to think so." Then he grabbed the barstool next to her and hailed the bartender. "Another beer down here, Ray."

Like every girl who'd ever laid eyes on Collie, Seneca's were glued to his face. "I didn't catch your last name, Rory. Is it Boo-chard as in 'boo-hoo I'm crying', or is it Brew-chard as in 'give me another brewski'?"

It was not funny but Collie rewarded her with a hearty laugh. Over her head, Collie met Rory's eyes. "Boo. As in boo-hoo I'm crying."

Rory jumped off his stool, upsetting his beer bottle. Foamy amber liquid spilled over the bar. "It's Brouchard. B-R-O-U-C-H-A-R-D."

Seneca stared at him as if he'd just lost his mind. Collie's mouth was quirked up into a little smile. Rory's head began to throb.

Seneca turned back to Collie. "I don't mean to be rude, Rory, but your friend is doing some work for me—"

Collie's eyes widened. "Really? What kind of work?"

Over Seneca's head, Rory drew his finger across his throat and shook his head at Collie. "Seneca, I insist we discuss the, ah, er, our business privately."

Seneca whirled her stool around and wagged a finger at Rory. "I've waited a whole month to find you. I'm not leaving until I get an update."

"Maybe we should step outside."

She patted his arm. "You're so sweet. But I don't mind if your friend hears." Behind her head, Collie winked at him.

Sweat rolled down the back of Rory's neck. "I don't have my report with me. I can't recall—"

"Take a few moments to gather your thoughts. I'll chat with Rory." She turned her attention back to Collie. "So tell me, what line of work are you in?"

"Well now." Collie drew out the words slowly. He met Rory's eyes over Seneca's head, all wide-eyed innocence. His gaze slid back to her face. "I sell cars. Maybe you've seen our ads on TV. Brouchard Carworks."

"I've never met a car salesman before." Seneca sounded like a gushing southern belle. A stab of jealousy pricked at him. Collie sure knew how to mesmerize a woman. Seneca scooted her stool closer to Collie. "I admire car dealers sooo much. They all seem so smart and so . . . . cute. Tell me all your little ol' secrets, Rory, darlin'. What do you say to the ladies who come to buy your pretty cars?"

No chick was that stupid. Rory frowned.

"The cars on my lot are lemons, but I tell the public what they want to hear. Fortunately for me, there's a sucker born every minute." Collie bestowed a radiant smile on Seneca.

"That's a crock of shit!" The half-dozen people in the bar turned their heads and stared at Rory. The only person who didn't look surprised was Collie. Rory's body tensed. "You punked me!"

"You tool! You scammed my client!"

Ray hurried down from the other end of the bar. "You boys take it outside, hear?"

Collie jumped off his stool. "Let's go."

"After you, asshole." Rory followed him out.

*

Guilt stung Seneca as she watched Collin and Rory stomp outside. It would be on her head if one of them got hurt. *Say your piece, Sen. It's the only way to clear the air.*

Outside the front window, Collin and Rory faced off, nose-to-nose. They roared at each other, shaking balled fists in the deepening gloom. Collin grabbed Rory by the lapels of his sport coat, Rory landed a punch on Collin's shoulder. Seneca gasped.

"Don't worry. They won't hurt each other."

Seneca swung her barstool around. Ray was mopping up the puddle of spilt beer as he watched the drama unfold. Deep lines criss-crossed the corners of his eyes and mouth and grooved his weather beaten cheeks. He reminded her of Poppy. "Have you known them long?"

"Rory's daddy grew up in this neighborhood. When he made big bucks in the car business he moved the family to Lake Forest. But he never forgets where he came from. He's been bringing those boys in here since they were shorter than the stool you're settin' on. We'd set booster seats at one of the tables and hoist them up. They'd order Buckaroo cocktails—" he winked at her, "—we never told 'em they were really Shirley Temples—and fries with extra ketchup."

"They get a little rough with each other sometimes, but don't let them fool you. Those boys are like brothers. Hearts of gold both of 'em. When Estelle, my mom, got sick, Collie visited her every chance he got. Rory lent me money to fix this place up a little after she died. 'You don't have to pay me back,' he said. Course I did anyway."

She turned back to the fight. Fists cocked, bodies hunched, they circled each other, throwing punches that didn't connect.

Ray spoke again. "Rory's doin' okay. Got his priorities mostly straight. But I worry about Collie. He hasn't been the same since he found his grandpa dead of a massive stroke. Blamed himself for not being home when it happened and went a little crazy. He was supposed to head off to college to be a baby doc just like his grandpa, but up and joined the army after the funeral. His dad tried to stop him, and they fought. Collie hasn't spoken to his dad or his mom in fourteen years." Seneca frowned at him. He held up his hands. "No exaggeration."

A name popped into her head. "Is his father's name Richard?"

"You've heard of him, huh?" Ray didn't wait for her answer. "He's a big shot lawyer. Tight with city hall. Collie could have the world on a platter—his old man is that rich and that powerful. He grew up in a big place in Lake Forest. A beauty. Right on the lake. I saw it once. But it's not worth crap when you consider what his folks lost. All the money in the world doesn't mean a thing without your only child."

"Fourteen years is a long time to hold a grudge."

Ray shook his head. "Collie's stubborn streak is a mile wide. Once he decided he was breaking with his folks, there was no changing his mind. Course, losing someone you worship the way Collie worshipped his grandpa can be tough on a kid, but you have to grow up and get on with things sometimes. All his friends have tried to talk to him. But, well, he's stubborn."

"It's a shame. If you listen to Rory, Collie broke his folks' hearts when he left. Course his was broke too." His gaze traveled to the window. "Looks like things are winding down out there. They'll be asking for cheeseburgers in a few minutes. What can I get you, ma'am?"

Seneca eyed the simple menu over the bar. Grilled cheese, cheeseburger, jumbo hot dog, chili. She was ravenous. "I'll have a cheeseburger, too." A serious violation of the *Action for Environmental Justice* manifesto. She'd volunteer at the rally as penance.

Ray nodded. "Three cheeseburgers coming right up." He disappeared into the kitchen.

She turned around and watched Collin and Rory do a double fist-bump and slap each other's back. Then they came inside.

With his shoulders sagging and his eyes downcast, Rory came to her. "I'm sorry, Seneca. I was way out of line."

He reminded her of Peabody Hill when she caught him munching on her slippers. "It's okay. Collin's on the case now." She touched his arm. "Sorry I punched you earlier."

"You're too nice," said Collin. He studied her over the bottom of his beer bottle. Seneca's eyes met his. She opened her mouth to blather off the old saw about forgiveness being divine, then she remembered Ray's story and swallowed her words.

Too late. He'd seen. His eyes narrowed. "Let's go."

Her stomach growled. "Ray's fixing cheeseburgers."

"We have a long drive ahead. We'll eat on the road."

Chapter 5

Collin didn't utter a word for a hundred miles.

Seneca fiddled with the radio, leaned into the Jeep's back seat to scratch Peabody Hill and played with her cell phone. She didn't glance in Collin's direction.

They were skirting Indianapolis when he stirred. "So what did Ray tell you?" The words shot out of his mouth like tight little fists punching at air.

"You know." She turned the radio up and played with the tuner until she found a country music station. Sugarland blared through the Jeep, filling the space between them. "I love Jennifer Nettles' voice, don't you?"

His hand swatted hers away from the radio and switched it off. "He had no right to talk about me."

"Why are you telling me? Tell Ray. Besides, wasn't that the point of going to Estelle's?"

"What are you talking about?"

"You were going to introduce me to people who could vouch for you." She turned the radio back on and began to hum along with Jennifer Nettles to *Baby Girl*.

He doused the tunes with a forceful punch. "For chrissake!"

Roused from his evening nap, Peabody Hill sat up. His dog tags tinkled together as he poked his nose into the front seat and sniffed at Seneca's ear. She ignored him. He drooled on her coat then pushed his snout against Collin's head.

Collin reached a long arm into the back and patted the hound's neck. "Sorry, boy. Go back to sleep." The dog lay down and shut his eyes. His heavy snores filled the Jeep. "It's not what you think."

"What's not?"

"I mean it has nothing to do with forgiveness."

"I'm your client, not your family. You don't owe me an explanation." She pressed her lips together and turned on the radio again. Dierks Bentley was singing *Free and Easy*. Silence settled over them again. She gazed out the window at the flat Indiana countryside and counted the mile-markers.

At the tenth marker, he spoke again. "Okay, maybe I'm a little stubborn—"

"Lord almighty, Collin, that's an understatement! Ray says you have a stubborn streak a mile wide."

"Bullshit."

"Whatever. As a paying customer, I think a little stubbornness on your part could prove useful in resolving my case."

"You're being ridiculous."

She shrugged. "If you say so."

He clamped his jaws tight and glared at the road. Thirty mile-markers later, he picked up where he left off. "Okay, here's what happened. I lived with my grandfather the summer after high school graduation—"

Chirp, chirp, chirp. A flock of startled birds erupted from her cell phone. The scowl on Collin's face deepened. The dog woke up and barked. "I'll just be a second." She pulled the phone from her purse but before she could press it to her ear, Collin's hands closed around the top.

"Give me the phone." His fingers were warm and surprisingly gentle as he waited for her to let go.

"Collin—"

"Please." She released the phone. He tossed it over his shoulder into the backseat. *Chirp, chirp, chirp.* Peabody Hill growled, and the birds quieted. He sniffed at the phone, then lay down and rested his jowls on it.

Collin took up his story again. "One night I tiptoed into my grandfather's townhouse at three in the morning and found him dead. While I was out with my friends, he'd had a stroke and died alone. I was destroyed. I admit it. I should have been taking care of him, not partying half the night. I was a naïve, eighteen-year-old kid who believed he could cure the sick and save people and stupid shit like that. I wanted to be a pediatrician like my grandfather. Did Ray tell you?"

She nodded. "Yes."

"My grandfather cared about people, especially children. I realized I wasn't selfless enough to follow in my grandfather's footsteps so I pulled out of pre-med at Stanford. When my dad discovered I wasn't going to college, he told me to get the hell out of his house or grow up. I did both. The second about three weeks into my basic training. Satisfied?"

She examined her hands so he wouldn't see he'd touched her. She was his client, his *engaged* client. "Sure."

"What?"

"Nothing."

"You're thinking something."

"Just wondering why the army? Ray says you had the world at your feet."

His hand flicked at the turn signal. He swung the Jeep into the left lane and roared past an eighteen-wheeler.

She could be stubborn too. "Why, Collin?"

A grim smile pulled at his mouth. "An adolescent desire to stick it to my dad. I wanted to die in battle, or—" He stopped and shook his head. "It doesn't matter."

"Or?"

He looked away. "Or do something to make him proud."

Sympathy welled up in her traitorous heart. "So thirteen years and forty-nine weeks ago, you got over the fight with your dad. Why do your friends still act like you're upset? Obviously you've put it behind you. Rory and Ray should too."

"Exactly."

She reached behind her and patted the dog. "Peabody Hill and I could sure go for a bathroom break. Can we pull off at the next exit?

Trucks and SUVs littered the McDonald's parking lot. Collin maneuvered the Jeep into an open spot beyond the lights and walked the dog on a grassy median while she ducked into the restaurant. When she emerged from the ladies' room, he was waiting for her inside.

"I need a rest. Let's sit down and eat."

They carried their trays to a quiet corner of the restaurant and slid into a booth. Collin unwrapped his hamburger and took a bite. He chewed it slowly as he watched her pry open the plastic lid on her salad.

"Have you ever killed a human being?"

"Likely be in jail if I had." Seneca squeezed a packet of dressing over her salad and speared a mouthful of wilted lettuce with a plastic fork.

"I have."

Her arm froze halfway to her mouth. She twisted her head around and scanned the dining room. No one paid any attention to them. "You shouldn't say things like that in a public place. People will misunderstand."

Collin pushed on anyway. "Besides my grandfather and my sergeant, Alex, two I know of." Collin set his hamburger down on the wrapper and picked up a French fry. He twirled it between his fingers. "I've probably killed more."

"You were a soldier doing your job, and any country fool can see you didn't kill your grandfather."

"The point is I have blood on my hands. My dad deserves a better son."

"Fine. Whatever. If you want to believe soldiering makes you unworthy of your father, that's your call. Why are you dragging me into this anyway? It's between you and your father."

"Exactly."

Her appetite had vanished. She set down her fork. "I need some fresh air. I'll meet you outside." She slipped from the booth and fled the restaurant.

Out in the night, a cold breeze stung her skin. Seneca buttoned her jacket, flipping the collar up to shield her neck from the wind, and stuffed her hands in her pockets. Beyond the parking lot, farm fields stretched west to the shadowy horizon. To the east, the lights of Indianapolis glowed and a stream of headlights transformed the bypass into a gold ribbon. One after the other, three trucks roared past, followed by the steady hum of cars speeding through the night. Her gaze lifted to the clear night sky, and she traced the Big Dipper with her eyes, following the handle to the North Star the way Poppy taught her. *Do you see it, Sen? If you're ever lost, find the North Star.*

Behind her the restaurant door opened, releasing a shadow into the square of incandescent light on the sidewalk, and she knew it was Collin. He stepped close and pressed his hand into the small of her back.

"I'm sorry."

"Why are you telling me these things?"

She waited, concentrating on the solid pressure of his hand at her waist. "I don't know. My demons are coming out tonight. I can't stop them."

Seneca turned to him. The wind lifted his blond hair. Wariness glittered in his deep blue eyes. He gripped a white paper bag in his hand. Two teenage boys pushed open the door and stepped outside. "Come on. We can't talk about this here."

He let her lead him across the parking lot. When they reached the Jeep, Seneca touched his arm. "Look, Collin, you were a soldier doing your job— "

"No!" He stepped back from her and set the bag on the Jeep's roof. "Just listen to me. Please."

The power of his voice glued her feet to the pavement. "Okay."

He stepped close to her. The toes of his boots press against her ballet flats. He stared down into her eyes and spoke softly. "When I broke with my family I was a kid. Just your average, spoiled

North Shore Chicago kid. I probably would have graduated from med school and ended up like Rory, playing golf at the club on weekends, driving flashy German convertibles and chasing tail to my heart's content."

Her eyes widened at the word "tail."

"Sorry."

Tail, indeed. His body was a breath away from hers, his mouth so close, the heat of his words warmed her face. *Please God, let them have a room for Collin at the Peabody Motel.* "Go on."

"I don't fit into my parent's life. My father made it clear almost fifteen years ago. He's a Chicago big shot. His friends are big shots. All the guys I grew up with are law firm partners or managing hedge funds. Do you really think my folks went around Lake Forest bragging about their son the lieutenant off shooting suspicious roadside objects when their friends' kids were at Harvard and Yale learning how to be millionaires? Don't you think they'd be embarrassed by Collin Atlee the gumshoe?" He paused. A tiny muscle over his eye twitched. "How would they feel about me if they knew I'd killed?"

"Come on, Collin. That's what soldiers do. They know you saw action in Iraq. They must understand the possibility exists."

"You don't get it. I've changed. I'm not the track star, A-student son they were so proud of anymore. Which is why it makes no sense for me to see them. They'll be disappointed, I'll be pissed, nothing changes."

"But Rory and Ray think your parents miss you."

"Rory and Ray are wrong. My parents don't miss *me*. They miss the other boy. The good one. The innocent one I was before my grandfather died."

Mr. and Mrs. Atlee might not agree, but mindful of Collin's pig-headed ways, she kept her opinion to herself. "You have to follow your own path. We all do."

"Exactly." His breath brushed her cheek. His eyes studied her through those killer lashes. His hands lifted, burning a trail as they slid over her shoulders and up her neck to her jaw. He tilted his head and brushed his lips against hers.

A virtuous woman is like a rare gem, Sen. She pushed him as hard as she could. He staggered backward.

"Chasing a little tail, Lieutenant?"

His eyes narrowed. A long second passed. Finally he answered. "No. Let's go."

Collin swung the Jeep back onto the highway, joining the stream of traffic headed south. "What's the deal with Michael?"

"Deal?" She tried to sound discouraging.

"What do you like about him?"

"Are you fantasizing about my relationship with Michael? That's gross."

In the back seat, the dog smacked his chops after wolfing down Collin's hamburger. She twisted around in her seat and scratched behind his ear. "How was your hamburger, boy?" He licked her hand, then yawned. "How can you be so sleepy all the time?" She gave him another ear-scratch. He sank down in the seat and rested his head on his front paws. Then he closed his eyes. So much for that diversion.

"I'm serious. When you met Michael, what was your first clue he was your soul mate?"

"You are really pushing the envelope."

"I shared my feelings."

"I didn't ask you to."

He plunged on anyway. "Is it idealism? Is it the hero you fell in love with? The man who's saving the environment for future generations?"

"You are obsessed!"

"That's ridiculous. Why would I be obsessed with Poindexter?"

"Good question. Is there something you haven't shared with the rest of us?"

Collin laughed. Then he cocked an eyebrow. "Well?"

"I don't want to talk about it." She folded her arms and stared through the windshield until the silence grew too heavy. "All right, fine! If you promise to stop bugging me, I'll share."

"Go on."

She gave her story a light, folksy tone. "Well, I'd never set foot outside West Virginia until I was twenty-three. One day I decided to pack my bags and head up north to Chicago. It was—"

"What made you decide to leave?"

She shrugged and tried to look casual. "Nothing in particular."

"I don't believe you. Something happened. Was it a broken heart?"

"Stop fantasizing about my love life."

"Come on. I want to know."

"You'll laugh."

"Bet I don't."

She'd never see him after tomorrow. "Okay. Well, I was working as a second grade teacher in Peabody. The kids were adorable, but my heart wasn't in teaching. Then one afternoon as I walked home from school, I heard the most incredible music. Someone was playing a violin. It sounded like Beethoven, and the music seemed to float off the north face of Peabody Ridge, which is impossible. No one lives up there, and even if they did, why would they be playing concert music? A folk tune, maybe. But Beethoven?"

"Anyway, I stood on the side of this old dirt road listening to this amazing music fill the air all around me, and I had this sudden flash."

"Flash?"

"I should move out of Peabody."

Barely the truth. She'd realized she couldn't live without music anymore and leaving Peabody—and Poppy—was the only solution. Seneca studied Collin's face. His expression was unreadable. "Am I addle-brained or what?"

"You are not addled-brained." He smiled at her. "Go on. How did you and Michael meet?"

"It's very boring. When I arrived in Chicago, I was homesick so I joined a birders group, and Michael was a member. He loves wild birds and birding, and so did Poppy. That's how it started."

It was a half-truth at best. The emptiness that opened up inside her the day the music swirled off Peabody Ridge grew during her first months in Chicago. She wandered the darkening streets after work, struggling to find her bearings amid the hustle of the big city. One evening a violin drew her eyes. It sat in the window of a half-lit pawn shop off Halsted Street. She spent the last of her savings to buy it, but she didn't have the guts to fling herself into the fires of hell, even for music. So it gathered dust on her closet shelf, and she joined a local birders club Poppy recommended.

"What's birding?"

"Sitting quietly in the woods, listening to the wild birds sing. You try to identify as many as you can by their calls. Poppy thought TV was a 'noisy contraption' so we didn't watch much. Birding was our entertainment. He took me up to Peabody Ridge whenever he could. We'd bring sandwiches and hot tea and make a day of it. I loved birding with Poppy. It's when he seemed happiest."

"Poppy and Michael were kindred spirits."

"Oh, my goodness, no! The one time they met, when Poppy and Peabody Hill came to Chicago to visit, they fought. You know how Peabody Hill feels about Michael. He started it, growling and baring his teeth until poor Michael was all flustered. Then Michael got off on the wrong foot with Poppy, lecturing him on the evils of hunting and eating meat and exploiting farm animals for food until Poppy nearly bust a gut. As soon as he could get a word in edgewise, Poppy reminisced about hog-calling contests and the best deer blinds and his famous venison chili until Michael's eyes bugged out of his head." Michael had been her first act of rebellion. When lighting didn't strike, she'd enrolled at the music conservatory. Then the lightning came, and it struck Poppy dead.

She expected Collin to laugh at her story, but he didn't. "So Poindexter had no redeeming qualities in Poppy's eyes?"

"Poppy was a soldier, like you."

"Nam?"

"No. The big war."

"The Second World War?"

Seneca nodded. "In the Philippines."

He frowned.

"I know what you're thinking, but it's impossible."

"What and why?"

"Because almost fifteen thousand people live in Peabody. Wouldn't someone have let the truth slip if Poppy had a son and Poppy's son was my father?"

"Don't know much about small towns, but they say they're good places for secrets."

Seneca yawned. "Look Collin, I'm beat. Do you mind if I close my eyes for a bit?"

"No problem."

*

As Seneca drifted off, Collin drove through the night sifting through the events of the evening. He hadn't meant to spill his guts, but he wanted this girl's respect. Had she understood him?

Chirp, chirp, chi . . . His hands tightened on the wheel. Damn tree-hugger. *Crunch.*

Collin raised his eyes to the rearview mirror. Dangling from Peabody Hill's mouth was half of Seneca's phone. "Good dog."

Chapter 6

Tom Simms bent his head and studied his reflection in the silvery surface of the mountain stream. Red hair with a bit of frost on top—just like Pop—bewildered blue eyes, a grizzled beard, weathered cheeks and worn denim overalls hanging on a thin frame. He squeezed his eyes shut.

He'd waited all summer and most of the fall for the familiar crunch of Pop's boots on the pebbly mountain trail leading to his cabin. But as the days wore on an eerie silence descended on his remote, mountainside home, and his nerves got stretched tighter than a Stradivarius. The other morning he'd dropped a spoon while he stirred his last cupful of grits over the wood stove inside the cabin. Momma used to say a dropped spoon meant strangers were coming. After he picked up the spoon, Tom reloaded his old Remington and set it by the door. Then he went back to his grits.

He wasn't starving yet. He had his hunting rifle and Peabody Hill's sister, Aida, to help him track game. He'd wanted to name Peabody Hill Radames after Aida's lover, but Pop said no. He told Tom the name Peabody Hill would be a clue for Seneca if anything ever happened to him.

Game was plentiful in the north hollows of Peabody Ridge where he lived. But winter was upon him now, and Pop hadn't come with his supplies to ride out the lean months ahead—flour, sugar, grits, cooking oil, salt, and powdered milk; waterproof boots and a warm jacket, bullets, matches, batteries, lamp oil, soap, and a charged cell phone for emergencies. He'd cut and stacked wood in the lean-to behind the cabin. While the weather held, he climbed on the flat cabin roof to patch cracked shingles and re-caulk the joinings where the stove pipe emerged from the cabin. But it wouldn't be enough. He needed supplies from Peabody to make it through the winter.

As he knelt by the stream and thought of all these things, he struggled to tamp down his fear. He was supposed to stay on the mountain forever. He'd done a terrible thing, and Pop agreed to help him if he promised to stay here and never leave. So he promised.

He'd found music again on this mountain. When he wasn't hunting or doing chores, he made music. His violin and his guitar were his only passions left over from the L.A. years. When he felt lonely, he liked to close his eyes and draw the bow across the strings of his violin in long strokes and let his hands summon the music like a genie rubbing a lamp. He could see the music curl up from his violin like smoke and dance around the little cabin like a harem girl without ever opening his eyes. Sometimes the romantic call of Schubert curled out of his instrument, sometimes Mozart laughed, and other times Beethoven roared from his hands like an angry lion. On the days he felt restless, he would pull out his guitar and play unplugged versions of classic Rolling Stones or the Instant Revolution—his own band— to Aida, his last and most faithful groupie.

Tom loved music more than anything else in the world now. But when he was young, he loved other things more. His love became an obsession that destroyed everything—and everyone— in its path. If he could go back . . . He couldn't go back. No one could.

He opened his eyes and stared down at his reflection again. He was scared. What if something happened to Pop? What was he supposed to do? How would he survive the long mountain winter? What if someone tried to take him away? The face reflected in the stream grew flinty. He had enough bullets to last a few more months if he was careful. No one was going to take him away. Not after all these years of living free.

What if Pop sent Seneca to help him? He and Pop talked about this once. Tom was to tell her he was a distant cousin. Then he would hand her his list of supplies and explain what he needed and when. Pop said Seneca was a good girl, a caring girl. She would help him.

He'd only seen Seneca a few dozen times after he came to the mountain, peering at his little girl through a screen of mountain laurel and dogwood on those rare occasions when Pop agreed to bring her up the north side of the mountain to bird watch. He was afraid to ask Pop if Seneca had music in her soul like Pop and Tom did, and they never talked about Seneca unless Tom asked a question. So he hoped she'd been spared that burden at least.

Chapter 7

Collin woke to bright morning sunshine. His feet hung off the end of Poppy's mattress and the tired old springs groaned under his weight. He'd never slept better. Poindexter was temporarily out of the picture, and an entire day with Seneca lay ahead. He stretched his arms and yawned.

Last night he'd been bleary-eyed and exhausted. He barely remembered driving through Peabody or pulling into the driveway beside Seneca's small clapboard house on Sleepy Hollow Road. But a few hours of deep sleep had energized him. He pulled on clean briefs and a pair of jeans, then cracked open his door and peered across the hall. Seneca's door was shut tight. He cocked his head to one side and listened. No sounds issued from her room. Grabbing a clean T-shirt out of his duffle bag, along with his shoes and a toothbrush, he tread delicately over the planked floor, down the narrow second-story corridor, and a creaky staircase. A quick wash-up in the downstairs bathroom, soldier-style—face, neck, armpits, teeth—and he was ready to go for coffee.

His battalion sat at attention on a blue-and-white rag rug by the front door. When he saw Collin his tail wagged. Collin hunkered down and rubbed the dog's neck, then he slipped his jacket off a wooden peg by the door.

"Move out," he whispered. The hound rose and followed him.

They stood in the Simms' front yard gulping deep lungfuls of sweet mountain air. Collin twisted his head up the street where the road disappeared over a rise, then down to where the hollow bottomed out, looking for a landmark to point him in the direction he'd driven in from last night. He gave up. "Hope you're up for some reconnaissance, boy."

The dog panted eagerly.

With the sun angled low behind its southeastern hip, Peabody Ridge cast a cool, dark shadow over the neighborhood. Collin zipped his jacket against the chill wind blowing off the mountain and stared up at the mass of jutting rocks and deep forest. Thick mist circling the top like a dull cap drew his eyes. He shivered.

"Let's go find that coffee shop, boy." They marched down the front path in double-time.

"Hey there!" An elderly man in the next yard leaned over the white picket fence and waved his arms frantically at Collin. The dog yipped cheerfully and trotted over.

"Good to see you, Mr. Hill. Takin' care of your mistress?" He stooped and rubbed the hound's ear through the fence slats. Collin sighed and followed. Seneca was not going to be happy about this. The Peabody Motel was dark and quiet by the time they'd reached the outskirts of Peabody, and he assured her no one in town would ever know they'd slept under the same roof. He'd also been forced to swear there'd be no "funny business" as Seneca delicately put it, unless he wanted to end up sleeping on the backseat of his Jeep. Despite giving his solemn oath, the lock on her bedroom door clicked sharply as he undressed last night.

The old man straightened up. He was nearly as tall as Collin with the barrel chest of man headed for a quadruple bypass. Dressed for a day in the shadow of Peabody Ridge, he wore a thick flannel shirt, tan corduroys and heavy work boots. His eyes were warm and brown. He offered Collin his hand.

"Name's Henry Stiles. You must be Seneca's fiancé." He frowned. "Michael, isn't it?"

So Poindexter had never bothered to visit his fiancée's hometown. "It's Collin." He shook the older man's hand. "Lived next door to the Simms long?"

Henry nodded. "Over fifty years. Watched your Seneca grow up."

Collin winked at Henry. "She's quite a girl."

Henry grinned. "Are you two still gettin' hitched at the zoo? Gotta tell you, Woody was fit to be tied when he heard. Around here, that's what churches are for."

The zoo? Collin rubbed his chin to hide the amusement curling the corners of his mouth. "We're still talking about it." He knew he should stop there, but he couldn't. "Call me old-fashioned but I'm still hoping for a church wedding." He shook his head. "You know Seneca—once she gets a notion in her head, there's no talking her out of it."

Henry nodded. "Didn't realize it was her idea. The way Woody went on about it, sounded like it was the other way around." His eyes lost their focus for a moment. "That girl hasn't been right since Woody tossed her fiddle in the trash heap and packed her off to the Teacher's College over in Jotham."

Collin's eyes widened with interest. "Say Henry, Peabody Hill and I were on our way downtown for coffee. Thought I saw a little diner across from the county building when we came through last night. We'd sure like it if you joined us."

Henry waved him away. "You put those cars keys away and git on over here. I got coffee brewing and bacon frying inside. You can't start the day with a cup of that dishwater they call coffee down at the Mountain Mist. You need real coffee and a decent breakfast, too. I'll have you fixed up in no time."

Collin glanced up at Seneca's bedroom window. The shade was drawn tight.

Henry followed the direction of Collin's gaze. "The gals need their beauty sleep. Leave her be, son."

Henry Stiles' house was a woodsy-crafty wonderland. Someone—probably Henry—had paneled the square living room with dark pressboard. Framed cross-stitch samplers of a squirrel, hedgehog, chipmunk, and porcupine, each with big, childlike eyes, added a bright note to the dimness. The *pièce de résistance* was the stuffed raccoon crouched on the mantle. Its beady glass eyes glared at Collin.

"Got a raccoon, I see."

"Rocky, I call him. When my Em was still with me—" Henry

brushed a tear from his eye, "—poor Rocky had to stay in the basement. But it's just him and me now, and of course, old Katy." Henry patted Collin's shoulder. "Well come on in and make yourself at home. How about a cup of coffee?"

The delicious smells of fresh coffee and sizzling bacon wafted through the house. "Sounds good, Henry. Lead the way."

The kitchen had most definitely been the domain of the deceased Mrs. Stiles. Pink counters, pink cabinets, pink dishtowels, and a pink tablecloth. Even the floor was checkered in pink and white tiles.

"Redid the kitchen for Em on our twenty-fifth anniversary." Henry pulled out two Holly Hobbie mugs with freckle-faced children painted on the sides. He filled the cups with steaming coffee. "Yessir. My little lady loved pink." He sniffed back another tear.

On a frayed remnant of gold carpet near the stove, an Irish Setter with white whiskers on her chin snored loudly. She didn't stir as Collin and Henry settled into the kitchen, but when Peabody Hill poked his snout into the room, the Irish Setter lifted her head, and Peabody Hill, with a lazy shake of his tail, ambled over to the stove to say hello.

"Peabody Hill's always been a little sweet on our Katy." They watched the dogs circle each other in a little dance. "Hope the bloom don't fade from the rose now that he's moving in for good.

So Peabody Hill had a sweetheart. The dogs settled down together on the gold carpeting. Collin gazed down at them and wondered if Seneca was awake.

"How do you like your eggs?"

"Doesn't matter."

"Sunny-side up okay?"

"Sure." He pulled out a chair and sat down at the kitchen table. Henry deftly cracked three eggs and slid them into the frying pan, then popped slices of bread into the toaster. "What happened to Woody's son?"

The gnarled hand holding the spatula froze in midair. For long seconds the sound of eggs crackling in bacon fat filled the kitchen like distant gunfire. Peabody Hill raised his head and sniffed. Then the toaster popped, and Henry jumped. He put the toast on a bright pink plate, slathered it with butter, scooped the eggs out of the pan and added three strips of bacon that were draining on paper towels beside the stove. He carried the plate to the table and set it in front of Collin.

"I'm a little surprised to hear you mention Tommy. Woody wouldn't let anyone talk about him, especially around Seneca. Guess the cat's out of the bag now."

"Sort of. She has some questions."

Henry fetched his coffee from the stove and sat down across from Collin.

"Don't want to eat your breakfast, Henry."

"Go ahead. I'm supposed to be on one of those low cholesterol diets so you've probably tacked a few extra days onto my life. The doctor will thank you."

Collin took a bite of bacon. "Outstanding breakfast." He wiped his hands on his napkin and leaned forward. "What happened to Tommy?"

Henry shook his head. "Woody wouldn't like it if he knew I was telling you about him. But me and my Em, we always thought he was wrong to hide the truth from Seneca. That gal had a right to know where she come from, I always said. Em thought so, too."

"Makes sense." He thought about his own father and mother. A right, not necessarily a blessing.

"Don't know a whole bunch about Tommy, but I'll give you what I got. You'll be gentle with Seneca when you tell her, won't you?" Henry waved a hand at him. "Eat up, son. I'll talk whilst you eat." He watched Collin shovel a forkful of eggs into his mouth and take a bite of toast. Then he dove in.

"Well, you must know the Simms are a musical clan." Henry shook his head. "They got the gift all right. Lord almighty."

"My, ah, fiancée hasn't talked much about music."

"Woody was one of the best fiddlers in West Virginia. Rather famous in these parts. So no one was surprised when Tommy turned out to be a chip off the ol' block. But times being more modern and all, they put a violin in Tommy's hands and taught him to play classical music. That boy was surely gifted. He'd play all that fancy Mozart and Bach stuff, then turn around and fiddle 'Barbara Allen' to make you cry." Henry's eyes misted. "Yes sir, that boy was surely gifted." He returned to the present and peered down at his empty coffee cup. He rose and brought the carafe to the table.

"More coffee, son?"

"Please." Collin set his pink paper napkin down beside his empty plate and leaned back in his chair. "So what happened next?"

Henry sat down and took up his story again. "This is where things get confusing. After high school, Tommy went off to New York City—got a scholarship to study music. At first Woody and Lori were proud as punch. But those were tough times for young people. Temptations were everywhere, and Tommy traded his violin for one of those electric guitars. At first Woody and Lori were fit to be tied, but they got used to Tommy dressed in farmer's dungarees and playing 'noise' as we called it. That's what my generation thought about rock and roll in those days."

"Tommy married a Spanish gal, I gather. She never came to Peabody so I didn't meet her. About a year after the wedding, the Simms stopped talking about Tommy. They got all glum and kinda huffy when folks asked after him. Then one day Woody flew to California where Tommy lived and when he came back, he brought Seneca with him and told everyone Tommy and his wife died and he never wanted to hear his son's name spoken again. Said Seneca was his daughter. Course we knew better, but Woody wasn't afraid to put his dukes up if he was crossed. People kept their mouths shut."

Henry shrugged. "That's about all I know except Woody stopped playing the fiddle and took a job at the post office." Henry shook his head. "Damn shame. Seneca got the gift too, but Woody wouldn't allow any music around him after Tommy died. Probably afraid that Tommy's daughter got the devil inside her like her daddy. Reverend McAllister had to put the fear of God into old Woody just so that poor gal could play the organ in church on Sunday mornings and sing in the choir. Had the voice of an angel, she did. Of course when Woody caught her playing the violin with the high school orchestra, that was the end of it."

. . . I heard something, well actually, violin music. Beethoven, I believe . . . Collin's eyes narrowed. Seneca left out the best part of the story last night. "I hope she had some friends to lean on."

Henry shook his head. "There was one gal who kept coming around. Lived on the other side of the ridge. But Woody was a suspicious son-of-a-gun. Most of the kids didn't pass muster with him." He glanced over at Peabody Hill and Katy. "And when it came to boys . . ."

Collin straightened up. "When it came to boys, what?"

"Woody chased one off with a gun. Caught him kissing her. Most boys don't want that kind of trouble. Tried to tell him she was old enough to make her own decisions, but he wouldn't listen until she up and moved to Chicago. Course, by then it was too late." Henry sighed and drained his coffee cup. "Are you going to tell Seneca about her daddy?"

"Of course." And he would. But not just yet. "Where's Tommy buried?"

"California, I guess. All I know is Woody and Lori never brought him home. Broke his momma's heart. Did you know she died just a few years after Tommy?"

"Seneca told me she died awhile back." Collin pushed his chair away from the table and stood. He picked up his empty plate and carried it to the sink. "Well, I better get back. Seneca will worry." More likely have a meltdown if she saw him coming out of Henry's house. "Can I help you with the dishes first?"

"Nah. Katy and I can handle it. She gives the dishes a good rinse, then right into the dishwasher they go." He grabbed Collin's dirty dish from his hands and set it on the floor next to the Irish Setter. She managed to lick it clean without moving her body. "There. See?"

Collin shrugged into his jacket.

"See you got a tattoo there. You Green Beret?"

"Been out about a year."

"Enlisted?"

"First time. Re-upped after college."

"See action?"

"A little." *A lot.*

Henry looked sad. "Got two grandsons in Afghanistan. Regular army. Glad to see you come home safe and sound, son. You stay that way now, hear?"

Collin gave him a hearty slap on the back. "Sure thing. Thanks for the chow."

Seneca was sitting on the Simms' front porch steps gazing at the little clouds gathering over Peabody Ridge. She wore blue jeans and a white T-shirt, and her feet were bare. Collin's breath caught in his throat. When she spotted Collin, Henry, and Peabody Hill, she rose to her feet, pulling an oversized green sweater over her shoulders. Green sparks shot from her eyes. Even spittin' mad, she was beautiful.

Henry apparently shared his taste. "You're a lucky man."

When they reached the fence, Henry stopped. "I'll leave you to her, son, but I just gotta say Woody was sure wrong about you. You're no puddin' head." Then he waved to Seneca. "Hey there, Seneca. Nice to finally meet your fiancé."

Seneca was in a lather by the time Collin reached her. "How could you?"

"I was going for coffee. He waved me over and assumed I was your fiancé. I was just trying to protect your reputation."

"What happens if my real fiancé visits?"

"Oh come on, Seneca. If Poindexter hasn't made it down yet, he's never coming."

"Stop calling him that! His name is Michael."

He glanced back at the Stiles' house. Henry was watching them. He waved. Henry waved back. "Let's go inside." He pressed a hand to Seneca's waist and pushed her up the porch steps. She let him guide her into the house, but before they closed the door, he dropped his mouth to her ear and whispered, "Are we really getting hitched at the zoo?"

She squealed and pushed his arm away. "It's the nature center and none of your business!"

Chapter 8

Waves of cold mist rippled around Tom's cabin. A sure sign winter was coming to the mountain. Tom peered through the swirls of gray vapor, straining to catch a glimpse of Aida. He could hear her rapid pants as she pushed through the underbrush in the woods, hunting for prey only she could scent.

"Aida! Come here, girl." She barked once, sharply, before plunging deeper into the woods surrounding the cabin.

She'd started acting crazy last night. While he'd slept in his narrow bed beside the potbelly stove, she pressed her wet nose against his forehead. Her rank dog breath blew into his mouth, and he nearly gagged. Annoyed, he pushed her away. "Go on, girl. It's the middle of the night. Can't you hold it till morning?"

Aida snapped at his hand and barked until he rose from his cot and padded over to the cabin door to let her out. He'd barely slipped the wood latch from its cradle when she pushed past him. Galloping into the small clearing in front of the cabin, she lifted her muzzle skyward and howled at the quarter-moon as if it were a UFO attacking Mother Earth.

"Hush now. You'll get us both in trouble." But Aida continued to bray until he plunged into the night and dragged her back inside the cabin. She stood by the door sniffing at the thin gap where cool air leaked in. When he bellowed at her to lie down, she barked at him.

"Have it your way." He gave up and went back to sleep.

While Aida kept watch at the door, Tom's dreams became nightmares, and he wished he'd stayed up with Aida. In his sleep Sonny called to him. "Tom, Tom," in her soft Latina voice. When she said his name, it came out as "Tome." It used to turn him on. Then Sonny's face and slender, dancer's body appeared, and she twirled across the cabin clearing to him. "Why Tome?" He tried to say, "I'm sorry," but his mouth wouldn't work.

He woke up before daybreak, groggy and upset, and he remembered his dream. He didn't think about his wife very often anymore, but he did now. He was playing the cool rock star, hanging out at a dark, smoky party in a smoky nightclub on the strip when she caught his eye. She wore a short leather skirt and tall boots, and her long hair, black as midnight, swept past her waist. She glided through the room like the ballerina she was. Hands down, Sonny was the most beautiful girl at the party.

When he introduced himself, she smiled at him and said, "Call me Sonny, Tome." Her Argentinean tongue made English sound sexy. By the end of the night, they were both a little high. She let him take her home from the party. A few months later, she moved into his apartment, and a year after that they married after an Instant Revolution concert in Paris. Both still a little high.

Sonny left the Ballet so she could travel with the band. Tom loved his beautiful, exotic party girl. Wherever he played, he'd look down at the row right below the stage to find his Sonny, glittering like a diamond among the screaming groupies. But from the perspective of nearly thirty years, he accepted that he had a mistress he loved more than his young wife.

His true love was fame. He bowed and scraped and worshipped at her feet, forsaking Sonny and Seneca to bask in the flattery of strangers and fall into the warm beds of adoring girls whenever Sonny's back was turned. He thought he was nearly a god himself until his life began to unravel—as it was bound to do.

Chapter 9

"This is my hometown! What happens if Mr. Stiles asks to see my wedding pictures or Mrs. Matthews across the street? What if my best friend sees you? She's coming to the wedding. What's she going to think when she meets the real Michael?" Seneca took a breath and looked up at Collin's face. A pair of sapphire eyes stared blindly at the dark clouds floating across the top of Peabody Ridge.

"Collin! Did you hear what I said?"

"You're mad at me."

They stood outside the Mountain Mist Coffee Shop in downtown Peabody sipping coffee from paper cups. It was a few minutes before nine, and the city of Peabody was awake and opening for business. Traffic was heavy on Mountain Mile Road, Peabody's main drag. Mud-caked pick-ups, SUVs, and mommy vans streamed from traffic light to traffic light. Along the sidewalks people who overslept or lingered too long over their coffee scurried to make it to work before the clock struck nine.

She watched Collin inhale the steam rising from his coffee and study the Peabody county building across the street as if he were planning to storm its walls. Then he took a loud slurp from his cup and grimaced. "Man, Henry's right. This stuff tastes like dishwater."

"Henry's an old curmudgeon." Since Collin and Henry emerged from the Stiles' house this morning, a sour mood had gripped Seneca. How long was Collin over there? What did they talk about? She'd bet her last dollar that they discussed her situation, and probably Poppy too. The entire incident steamed her.

But Collin was being cagey about his *tête à tête* with Henry, and her attempts to pry information out of him—and when that didn't work, to scold it out of him—were fruitless. Impersonating her fiancé didn't improve her mood—even if he was right about the probability of Michael ever coming to Peabody.

She tilted her head and traced Collin's perfect profile with her eyes. Maybe not so perfect. He had a stubborn chin. *Honey works better than vinegar, Sen.* She took a long, slow sip from her coffee cup. "Mmm, I love Mountain Mist coffee. Like snuggling under the covers on an icy cold West Virginia morning."

He tore his eyes from the county building and gazed down at her.

She shot him her best attempt at round-eyed innocence. "Well, Lieutenant, what's next? You said you couldn't conduct your investigation in Peabody without me. So here I am, reporting for duty. What's my first assignment?" She lifted her hand to her brow and gave him a mock salute.

Collin's smile was knowing and his eyes wise. "Let's go across the street and talk to the county clerk about the birth certificates." He lifted a dark brow. "Who knows? Perhaps there's a simple explanation for everything."

The way his voice lightened as he said "simple explanation" made her think he already knew what that simple explanation was. Her cranky mood crept back. "It won't do any good. I've already talked to the clerk, and you know what happened."

"Consider me warned. Come on."

He turned away and tossed his coffee cup into a nearby trash bin. Seneca stepped into the street. *She* was not waiting on him anymore. A horn blared. Brakes screeched. Her eyes flew up to the cab of the truck racing toward her and met the horrified eyes of the driver. Then, a pair of strong arms slid around her ribs and lifted her up. The dump truck rumbled by.

Collin held her tight against his chest. His fingers pressed against her breasts. His chest rose and fell against her spine. Her shock gave way to embarrassment. She kicked at the air beneath her feet. "I'm okay. You can put me down." The soles of her ballet flats touched solid ground. Pressing a hand against her pounding heart, she spun around. "Thank you."

Collin's normally tanned face was pale, his eyes wide and unblinking. As she watched, the color seeped into the skin covering his cheekbones. His eyelids flickered. "Don't ever do that again." He slipped her arm through his, drawing her close to his side. Her shoulder fit into the curve of his arm, his hip was warm and solid against her waist.

"What are you doing?"

"Making sure you don't get run over." She tried to pull away but he held her tight. "I like the way you fit under my shoulder, like we were made for each other."

She jabbed his side with her elbow. "Your actions are entirely inappropriate for an employer and employee."

"I promise not to sue you."

Employee reminded her of some critical business she needed to clear up. "Uh, Collin?"

As a van barreled toward them, he pulled her across the last lane of traffic to the safety of the sidewalk. "What?"

"How much do you think your bill will be?" Her face grew hot. "I brought this up with Rory, but I forgot when I hired you."

He released her. "How much did you budget?"

"I don't want charity."

"Did I say anything about charity? How much?"

"Five hundred dollars. That's what Poppy had in his bank account when he died."

"Won't Michael miss the money?"

"I didn't exactly tell him about it."

Collin folded his arms across his chest. "Why not?" He frowned at her as he waited for an answer.

"Sen! Sen!"

A slender blonde in a navy blue pantsuit and blue-and-white stadium pumps half-ran, half-stumbled toward them. She balanced a chubby baby on her hip. An enormous diaper bag hung from her shoulder. A whining toddler pulled at her free hand. She teetered up to them and smiled. "Sen! Why didn't you tell me you were back?"

Janie Highsmith released the toddler's hand and hugged Seneca. "Oh sweetie pie, how are you?"

Seneca hugged her close. "It's so good to see you, Janie. I've barely heard from you since Poppy's funeral."

"My life is utter chaos" Janie hugged her again. "But Jim and I are excited for the wedding. Momma's taking the boys so it's going to be a second honeymoon for us." Janie's baby squealed and squirmed in her arms. She bounced him gently as she turned to Collin. "You must be Michael."

He graced Janie with a sexy half-smile. "Collin."

She frowned. "Sorry, Collin. I don't know why I thought your name was Michael. I'm so addle-brained these days. That's what happens when you have two terrors running around the house and the county cuts your budget and doubles your workload."

The toddler, a chubby three-year-old with curly blond hair and pink cheeks, tugged on Janie's jacket. "Mommy, I tired." He stared up at his mother with teary eyes and raised his arms to be picked up. "Peez."

"Oh, honey lamb, Mommy's arms are full."

The little boy raised his arms higher. "Peez, Mommy."

Collin bent down and scooped up the toddler. "Hey there, sport, come on up here." He settled the boy in his arms. "What your name, son?"

The little boy blinked, and Seneca waited for him to burst into tears, but Collin rubbed the boy's nose with his finger and winked at him. "No crying in front of the ladies. Next thing you know, they'll be plucking our eyebrows and forcing us to wear loafers with tassels on 'em." The boy studied Collin for a long moment, then his face broke out in a sunny smile. He pounded his chest. "Jake-O."

"His name is Jacob," said Janie.

"Well now, Jake, it's a pleasure to meet you."

Jake smiled again. Then he put his chubby little arms around Collin's neck and laid his head on his shoulder. Collin settled him into the crook of his neck. "You're a good boy."

Seneca's eyes narrowed. How did he manage to charm others so effortlessly? First Peabody Hill, then Henry Stiles, now Jake Highsmith. If Michael tried to pick up Jake—not that he would— the little boy would be screaming and Michael would be hurt and she would be apologizing to Janie for upsetting Jake. Instead, Jake smiled from his perch in Collin's arms and from the look on Janie's face, she was charmed too.

Janie smiled up at Collin. "You never told me your fiancé was so handsome, Sen."

"He's not—"

Collin cut Seneca off. "Thank you, Janie. Can I call you Janie? My fiancée didn't formally introduce us, but I feel I know you already. Fine boy you have here."

Seneca's eyes widened with horror. She was going to kill him! How would she ever explain this *lie* to Janie?

"God, Sen," Janie drawled, her eyes still glued to him. "If I'd known Chicago was growing men like Collin, I'd have packed a bag and moved up north with you."

Seneca blinked. Great. Her best friend had just joined Collin's fan club. "As I recall you were engaged at the time to your husband Jim. Jim Highsmith. Remember him?"

The giant clock atop the county building hit nine o'clock and in the distance, a church bell began to peal. The deep gongs broke whatever spell Collin cast on Janie.

"God, I'm late again." Janie tore her eyes from Collin's face and looked at Seneca. "Are you here long? We haven't talked at all! I know! Dinner. Come tonight. Jim and Collin—" Janie's eyes slid back to him for a moment, "—will get along great. We'll make them barbecue so we can have a quiet chat over a glass of wine."

Her eyes widened. "Gosh, I'm so sorry. You're a vegan, right?"

"I eat a little me—"

Seneca jumped in before Collin could do more damage. "We're just here on a little business, Janie. Collin and I have to drive back tonight." *If he was still breathing.*

Janie shook her finger at Seneca. "Don't you leave without saying goodbye." She turned to Collin. "And don't you let her."

Collin grinned. "I promise." He disentangled Jake from his neck. "Time to move out, son. Be a big boy and help your mother."

Janie took Jake's hand, and they climbed the steps of the county building where Janie dropped off her boys each day at a small daycare center for the children of county employees. Poor Janie. The daycare was great but her job as a low-paid, over-worked attorney for the Peabody County Public Defender's Office sucked. In Peabody jobs for lawyers were not many, and Jim loved his role as the high school athletic director.

As soon as the Highsmiths disappeared inside the county building, Seneca punched Collin's arm as hard as she could. "I am going to kill you!"

He looked down at her through his long lashes. "Before you put on your boxing gloves, tell me why you kept the five hundred dollars a secret."

"I have a better idea. Let's go talk to the clerk before I commit a capital crime right here on Mountain Mile Road in broad daylight."

His face fell. "I'm sorry, Seneca."

"Why are you telling people we're engaged?"

He studied her, his intelligent eyes assessing her face, his mouth drawn tight. He drew a deep breath and looked away. "I don't know."

She tilted her head. *What was bothering him?* "As I said, the five hundred dollars was Poppy's life savings."

The smile lines around his mouth deepened. "And?"

"I don't have to tell you money is tight." Some days she couldn't think about anything else but how she was going to manage her rent and buy dog food for Peabody Hill, plus pay Michael her share of the mortgage on the new house. "It's just that I had to sell Poppy's sacred Ford pickup to pay for his funeral, and the house is next. The property taxes are coming due." She couldn't go on so she shrugged.

Collin finished the story for her. "The five hundred dollars is all that's left of Poppy."

"Something like that."

*

Behind the grimy front window of the Peabody Appliance Store and Repair Shop, catty-corner to the county building, a pair of light brown eyes watched Seneca Simms and the tall, blond-haired man cross Mountain Mile Road. There was something familiar about the way the blond-haired man walked and held his shoulders back. The watcher's eyes narrowed as the man wound his arm around Seneca's small body and tip his head down to whisper in her ear. Where had he seen that profile before? The straight aristocratic nose, the high forehead, the dark brows. One corner of the watcher's lips drew up thoughtfully when the man's face turned in his direction. He knew that face better than he knew his own. He'd seen it a thousand times. Atlee.

Of all the people in the world to turn up in Peabody, he would never have expected to see Atlee.

Chapter 10

The cramped office on the third floor of the county building reeked of burnt coffee and perspiration. Seneca wrinkled her nose then turned her attention back to Mr. B. A. Steele, Peabody County clerk, who sat at his 1950s-era metal desk staring at Collin from behind steepled fingers.

"What exactly can I do for you?" Mr. Steele was still annoyed with Collin for making a ruckus when they were informed B. A. Steele couldn't see them until next week.

Collin appeared unperturbed by the clerk's displeasure. He lifted a hip off his slippery plastic chair and pulled a sheet of folded paper out of the back pocket of his jeans. "I appreciate your flexibility, Mr. Steele." Seneca hoped the clerk didn't hear the irony in his voice. "We are only in town for the day so it's important we clear this up now."

He unfolded the paper and revealed a second sheet of paper nestled inside the first. "Seneca wants to know why she has two birth certificates. Certainly you can understand her confusion, and I'm sure you want to help her clear this matter up." He set the copies of the birth certificates on Mr. Steele's desk and ironed them out with his hand so they lay flat against the metal surface.

She watched the clerk wrinkled his already wrinkled forehead. His caterpillar-shaped eyebrows touched just above the bridge of his nose. "It's not possible to have two birth certificates."

"And yet, Seneca has two birth certificates with official state seals, and stranger still, one of them has your signature on it." Collin pushed the copies closer to him.

The clerk regarded Collin through the thick lenses of his steel-rimmed glasses. "What are you insinuating?"

Collin's mouth curved into a lazy smile. "Mr. Steele, do you want to waste time picking a fight with me that you won't win or do you want to clear this matter up? We are not going away until you tell us why Seneca has two birth certificates."

The clerk's eyes slid down to the pages Collin pushed toward him, then up to Seneca. The smell of sweat grew strong. "Your—father—would be ashamed of you. Coming back to Peabody to stir up trouble after he's gone is reprehensible. He told you everything you need to know, and if he decided to keep certain facts from you, it was for your own good. You're a disgrace to his memory."

Collin leaned forward in his chair until his face was a few inches from the clerk's. "Seneca is not a child, and you have no right to treat her like one. Please answer the question."

Mr. Steele unsteepled his fingers and pulled off his glasses. From his top desk drawer he pulled out a handkerchief and wiped the lenses. Then he folded the cloth and placed it back in the drawer before he slipped his glasses back on. He studied Collin. "You're a government agent, aren't you?"

"I am a private citizen with a very simple question. Why does Seneca have two birth certificates?"

"You sound like an FBI agent."

"I did some law enforcement work when I served in Iraq, but I am not here in any official capacity." Collin inched the papers closer to him.

Mr. Steele turned to Seneca. "Okay, young lady, you win. I'll tell you what I know, although I think you'll regret you didn't let sleeping dogs lie. Your *friend*," he glared at Collin, "will have to wait outside in the hall. Family matters mayn't be discussed in front of nonfamily. County policy."

A cold chill crept up Seneca's spine. Maybe Mr. Steele was right about sleeping dogs. Did it really matter where she was born and who her birth parents were? Poppy loved her. He *was* her father. She bit at her lower lip. Mr. Steele didn't think Poppy wanted her to know the truth, but Poppy left the second birth certificate behind on purpose.

"Seneca?" Collin's brow knitted with concern. "Are you okay?"

She didn't know what Mr. Steele was going to say, but it wasn't going to be good news. "Collin is, ah, um, my fiancé." She nearly choked on the last word. "So he's more or less family. I want him to stay."

Collin lifted his fingers from the birth certificates and took her icy hands. "It's okay, baby." The warmth in her fake fiancé's voice felt genuine. She looked at him. His eyes were kind, his sudden smile encouraging. He turned back to Mr. Steele. "So about the certificates."

"There's not much to tell. I'd never seen this—" He poked a finger at Seneca's California birth certificate, "—until Seneca brought it to me last month. Woody told me it was lost in Tommy's junk."

"Tommy?" Seneca shivered.

"Your natural father."

"And—and Woody?"

He dropped his head and stared at the birth certificates. "He was your grandfather."

"This is preposterous, Mr. Steele. Why would my-my-my grandfather do this?" Her voice bounced off the metal desk and reverberated around the cramped office.

He rose from behind his desk. "I don't know, Seneca. Woody asked me for a favor. At the time, he was a good man in a lot of pain. He'd just lost his son and daughter-in-law. So I didn't ask any questions."

"How did they die?" It was Collin.

Mr. Steele studied Seneca's pale face. "Woody told me it was an accident. I didn't ask him for details. He didn't offer any." He stepped around his desk. "I'll give you a few minutes alone."

When the office door clicked behind the clerk, Collin slid an arm around her shoulder. "Are you okay?"

She considered his question. "Yes. Actually, I am. I don't mean to sound callous, but it's hard to miss parents I didn't know existed until five minutes ago." She shook her head. "I guess it all makes sense. Poppy lost my first birth certificate so he asked Mr. Steele to help him."

"It makes sense? People lose their birth certificates all the time. They don't forge a new one. They send in for a new one. Probably costs twenty bucks."

She pulled away from him. "Maybe Poppy wanted to spare me the pain of losing my mom and dad."

"But you just said it didn't hurt because you never knew them. Besides, it's much simpler to raise you as a granddaughter than to try to hide the truth in this small town. Don't you think?"

How had Poppy kept it a secret all these years? Surely if Mr. Steele knew about Tommy, other people—Seneca stiffened.

"Are you all right?"

She turned and punched his arm as hard as she could.

"Ouch! Do you know you've hit me in the same place twice today?"

"You deserve it!"

"For what?"

"You found out Poppy was really my grandfather this morning. Henry told you." She shook a finger at him. "Don't bother denying it. I can see it on your face." He looked guilty as hell.

"Come on, Seneca. If I told you this morning, you wouldn't have believed me. You'd have marched over to that poor man's house and started squawking at him."

The nerve of him! Blaming her for his bad behavior! She tried to punch Collin's arm again, but he grabbed her wrist before she could do any more damage. She yanked her arm away from him.

"First of all, I do not squawk. Second, I am the client, as I have reminded you more than once, and withholding information is not part of the deal."

A mischievous gleam lit his eyes, and she suspected he was about to hit her with one of his wise-ass comments. Then his expression sobered, and he turned his gaze from Seneca to the small window behind the desk where the mist-hung top of Peabody Ridge rose up.

"What are you thinking, Collin? Did Henry tell you something else?"

"Just that your father was a musician. He played the—" Collin broke off.

A neglected corner of her heart stirred. "Played the what?"

He stood. "I've gotta go."

"Where?"

"I have a few calls to make. Why don't you go find Janie. Maybe you can grab some coffee together and catch up."

"Collin, wait!"

But he was already out the door and a few seconds later when she stuck her head out of the office, corridor was empty.

Chapter 11

Cell phone pressed against his ear, Collin paced back and forth in front of the county building as he tracked down an old college friend who was now an L.A. detective.

When Joe Ianni's voice finally barked at him on the other end of the line—"Ianni here"—Collin held niceties to a minimum.

"It's Atlee."

"What's up, Coll?"

"I need a little favor. Can you do a search on two people who died in the early eighties in L.A.?"

"Names?"

"Thomas Simms and Sonja Albers Simms. Two ems in Simms. I need cause and date of death for each of them, plus any warrants that were outstanding, investigations, police records, whatever you can find with their names on it. Also, see if there's any record of a baby. Her name was Seneca Simms. Can you call me back at this number A-Sap?"

"Are you investigating a crime?"

"No crime. My client wants to fill in some holes in her family's history." He tried to dampen his friend's curiosity. "You know how it is. Everyone has to discover their roots these days."

"I'll run the names through our system. See if I get any hits."

"Thanks."

Collin paced the sidewalk in front of the Courthouse, impatiently waiting for Joe to call back. At the corner of the block, he halted and peered up at the sky. Dark clouds gathered over his head, eclipsing the morning's bright sunshine. He sniffed the air. Rain was coming.

"Come on," he muttered under his breath to his silent phone. Seneca thought the case was solved. She was going to march out of the courthouse in a few minutes ready to pack her bag and drive back to Chicago. He could stall her for a few hours, but if it rained before Joe called him back, he would have to wait until tomorrow to tie up the case. Seneca would fight any attempt to stay over in Peabody one more night. He rubbed his bicep where her sharp knuckles had already connected twice and smiled. He'd had it coming both times.

Something hard and sharp crashed into the back of his legs. His knees buckled, and he nearly fell. His cell phone flew from his hands and clattered against the concrete.

"Shit!" That phone was his lifeline. He bent to snatch it up. A long arm reached out and grabbed it first.

"Lose something?"

He spun around. "Mush!"

Matt Peterson, his buddy since basic training, grinned up at him from a wheelchair. "Hey there, Hollywood."

Collin's nickname came from his good looks. When he started basic training, his fellow recruits spoke the name derisively with a Mr. in front of it and never to his face.

Mush, short for Mushroom, had a late adolescence, post-enlistment growth spurt to thank for his handle. When the sarge noticed his boot tops peeking out below the cuffs of his pants, he said, "You're growing like a mushroom, boy. Must be the good army chow we're feeding you." The guys teased Mush about it, and the nickname stuck. It didn't hurt that Matt (Mush) Peterson of Peabody, West Virginia, reminded his fellow recruits of a mushroom. His mop of light brown hair sat atop a wide face with a wide nose and a wide mouth prone to grinning. Below his chin, his body used to drop in a long vertical line to the ground like a mushroom.

The mushroom cap part of Matt was just as Collin remembered from basic training, but a suicide bomber broke his stem in a bazaar in Baghdad. Collin was on patrol near Tikrit when he heard. By the time his unit returned to base in Baghdad, Mush had been evaced stateside.

Collin hunkered down in front of Mush and swallowed the lump stuck in his throat. Another broken soldier, making the best of it. It made him sad and proud all at once.

"Hey Hollywood, what's new?"

"Nothin' much." Collin picked a thread off the knee of his jeans.

"Bagged the little Simms girl, huh?"

He shrugged and changed the subject. "So what are you up to these days, buddy?"

Mush tried to smile, but a drop of bitterness clung to the corners of his mouth. "Livin' the dream, Hollywood. Working part time down the street at the repair shop. Staying at a sort of assisted-living house they have here in Peabody for wounded vets, but one of these days . . ." He trailed off.

"Someone said you were doing something with computers." Collin's tone was controlled, but it upset him to see his old friend abandoned and on his own after he gave so much to his country.

"They tell me I need a degree to get into the game. The nearest school is over in Jotham, about twenty miles up the road from here." He gave Collin a little shrug. "Got no wheels 'cept these." He rubbed the wheel rims on his wheelchair with the heels of his hands. "It's no big deal. I'm doin' better than lots of the guys."

They grew quiet as they remembered the men who'd not come back from the war and those who'd lost even more than Mush. Mush sighed. "May God bless and keep them all."

"Amen."

Mush reached across his lifeless knees and slapped Collin's thigh. "What'd you do to Seneca's old man? I heard some guys at the shop talking about you. Old Man Simms didn't like you much."

The truth was out of the question, but so was a lie. Not to his old friend who deserved so much more than he had now. So Collin just shrugged and picked another thread off his jeans.

Finally Mush said, "Well her daddy never let her out much. He probably couldn't tell the good guys from the jerks. Rumor was he chased away every boy who cast an eye in her direction. Never figured out why she put up with it for so many years."

"Maybe she loved him," said Collin, but he wondered what Woody Simms was afraid of. According to Henry, Seneca was a serious teenager whose one act of rebellion was playing the violin behind her grandfather's back. Not exactly a juvenile-delinquent-in-training.

*

"Do you two know each other?" Seneca emerged from the county building. At the bottom of the steps, her old schoolmate Matt Peterson and Collin chatted like old friends.

"You remember me?" asked Matt.

"You were one of the cool older boys who used to smoke behind the gym at lunchtime when the teachers weren't around. I remember." She gave him a warm smile.

"And you were the cute little freshman girl who spent every afternoon after school playing the violin in the music room. I remember you were quite good."

Her smile faded. "I gave up music. I-I'm focused on the environment—"

Collin's phone began to blare reveille.

Matt lifted Collin's cell phone from his lap and twisted his head so he could read the display. "Hey Hollywood, your agent is calling from New—"

Collin snatched the phone from Matt's hand. "Got to get this. Excuse me." He jumped to his feet and pressed the phone to his ear. "Atlee, here." He strode away.

Deep regret seeped through Seneca as she gazed down at Matt. "I gotta get off my feet." She took a few steps backward and plunked down on the county building steps. Matt followed her in his wheelchair. He wore a desert camo jacket with 'Peterson' stamped on the breast pocket, a pair of baggy khakis to hide his lifeless legs, and a green T-shirt. She remembered the first time she laid eyes on Collin. He was wearing desert camo too. "How did you meet Collin?"

"Basic training down in Fort Benning."

"Did you serve in Iraq together?"

"Nah. Collin punched his ticket after two years. I stayed with the unit."

"I don't understand. Collin fought in Iraq, didn't he?"

Matt eyed her curiously. "Don't know much about your fiancé, do you?"

She blushed. "We-we don't, ah, talk about the war much."

He held up a hand. "I know, I know. Most of the guys don't like to talk about what happened over there. I never say much to people. Either they think I'm asking for sympathy or I'm just one rung down from a serial killer." He paused, then shrugged. "Collin left the regular army for the reserves after two years. He wanted to go to college and be a doc. Would have been a great medic if he followed through. He was always the first one on the scene when one of the guys got hurt. He knew how to keep everyone calm and figure out if the guy was really hurt or just banged up a little. When the war started in '03, he re-upped with Special Forces. I ran into him in Baghdad. He was recruiting civilians for the new police force, so he was doing community relations stuff."

"That seems tame."

Matt shook his head. "Not in Iraq, especially right after the invasion. You never knew who was your friend and who was about to blow himself up in your face. After I was evaced stateside, I heard Atlee trusted the wrong guy and got his buddy killed. I guess it hit old Hollywood hard. He blamed himself, of course."

She turned away from Matt and gazed across the street at Collin.

His phone was pressed against his ear, and his free hand rubbed the back of his head in sharp strokes. Determined to fight the world just to help her with her little problem, even if he only ended up with five hundred bucks in his pocket. She suspected five hundred dollars didn't even cover his costs for the past two days.

"Hey, Seneca." A sympathetic smile curled Matt's wide mouth. "Don't worry about Hollywood. He's a solid guy. I shouldn't have said anything."

"I'm glad you told me." She clapped her hands together. "Enough gloom. Tell me why you call him Hollywood."

He laughed. "You'll like this story, and I bet you'll never hear it from him."

She glanced across the street again. Collin was still deep in conversation. She turned back to Matt and leaned forward. "I'm all ears."

"Well, Atlee looked like he walked straight out of *Sports Illustrated* or *GQ* when he joined up. Not so much as a pimple on his pretty face." He winked at Seneca. "Most of us guys were from small-town America. We wanted to see the world and earn some dough so we could go to college or get some technical training. That was during peace time so guys with other options didn't really consider the military. Now it's patriotic. Do your duty and all that. Then it was a way out of the corn fields or the backwoods," he shrugged. "Or the inner city. Lots of guys joined to get away from the drugs and gangs too."

"Collin must have seemed pretty exotic to you guys."

"Yeah, 'pretty exotic' just about says it all. As I said, most of us were there for a shot at the good life. We were grateful for the privilege. But not Atlee. He stepped off the bus at Fort Benning with major attitude. Capital A on attitude."

"What do you mean?"

"He acted like he was smarter than all of us and smarter than the sarge, too. He kept to himself and walked around with his perfect nose in the air like he was the victim of some terrible tragedy the rest of us were too ordinary to ever understand. Plus he didn't know how to look after himself. He'd never made a bed or washed his own skivvies or peeled a potato. But mostly he wasn't used to taking orders, especially by someone as unrefined as the sarge.

"It really got to the sarge, too. He was always screaming at Hollywood, 'Get the silver spoon out of your ass, Atlee.' Sometimes the sarge rode Hollywood so hard I felt a little sorry for him."

"But not that much."

"Nah, not that much. He was big and fast. I found out later he was a track star in high school. He could hike for hours and the ropes course was nothin' to him. He'd leave the rest of us behind to eat his dust. But whenever the sarge would get on Hollywood for the housekeeping stuff, Hollywood would get this look on his face like the sarge was being petty and a neat footlocker was a waste of his precious time."

"But he changed."

"Yeah, he changed. After about three weeks the sarge got pissed and decided to teach Hollywood a lesson. So one night, just before lights out, he pulled a surprise inspection of our barracks. We were all dead on our feet. Even Hollywood. It was a brutal day—twenty-mile hike through the swamp, climbing those frickin' walls. And you know how Georgia can get sometimes, so hot and sticky you want to take your skin off. It was one of those days.

"So the sarge arrives, and we all know the drill. We drag ourselves to our feet and stand at attention next to our bunks and wait for him. Now Hollywood's bunk was the last one, and the sarge started his inspection with the first bunk and worked his way down to the end of the barracks where Hollywood was standing at attention. It took forever. He stopped at every bunk and checked and double-checked everything. He bounced a quarter off beds, went through the footlockers, checked belts and shoes. When he found an infraction, he was nice, which wasn't like him. One of my shirts wasn't folded right, and he said, 'Next time be more careful, Peterson.' Then he moved on. The tension in the barracks got heavier and heavier as he went along, and everyone sort of knew what was about to happen."

Seneca's heart seized up. "He was gunning for Collin, wasn't he?"

"Yup. When he got to Hollywood's bunk—the very last one—the sarge tossed his quarter on the bed and it landed like lead. Of course everyone could see Hollywood didn't even tried to smooth out the blanket or tuck the sheets in. Forget hospital corners. So the sarge says to him in a deadly calm voice, 'Get your gear and come with me.' Then he marched Hollywood out to the dirt yard in front of the barracks.

"It was dark by then and drizzling, but there was enough light from our barracks that we could see what was happening to Hollywood just fine from the window. In the middle of the yard Hollywood was standing at attention with all his gear on his back and the sarge was screaming at him that he was a candy-ass and pretty boy and he didn't belong in the army. 'Go home to your mommy and rich daddy,' he hollered at Hollywood.

"Then it began to rain and the ground got muddy and the sarge picked up a big slug of soupy mud and slung it at Hollywood's face. 'Now you look like we do after a hard day's work,' he said."

"What did Collin do?" She felt sick.

"Just stood at attention while mud dripped down his face. An order is an order. The sarge says stand at attention, you stand at attention. The rain was really coming down by then, and the sarge was getting wet, which he didn't like. So he called us guys outside and said, 'You all see Atlee?' And we said, 'Yessir.' And he says, 'It's gonna be a long night for him unless one of you volunteer to help him. Here's the deal. If one of you agrees to get your gear on and stand out here with him 'til midnight, when the time is up, you're both dismissed. You can go back inside and bunk down for the night. Otherwise, Atlee's here 'til reveille.'"

"No one volunteered, did they?"

"No one. And every hour the sarge would wake up to check on him and sling some more of that red Georgia dirt. By reveille, Hollywood's uniform was soaked through with rain and mud. After the rest of us washed and dressed, he lined us up outside facing Hollywood. Then he said to Hollywood, 'If this was a war and I was the enemy, you'd be dead because not one of the guys in your outfit has your back. Hell, you're the kinda soldier that got shot from behind by your own side in Nam. That's 'cause those candy-ass soldiers were a liability and so are you.'"

"Did Collin say anything?"

"Not then. I don't know what he thought about while he stood in the rain all night, but he was a changed man. The sarge made us hike again that day right after chow. I was so tired I had to concentrate just to put one foot in front of the other, and I'd gotten some sleep. Hollywood did it on no sleep. He stumbled a lot, but he always managed to pick himself back up and keep walking. Didn't say a word to anyone all day. Later, he apologized to each of us in private and the sarge, too. He started giving the slower guys a hand on the ropes course and the climbing walls. Held him back a little, but he didn't mind if he didn't get the top score. When we got some R&R, Hollywood insisted on coming into town with us, and we ended up hanging out with the prettiest girls. They couldn't get enough of him." Matt smiled. "We were the envy of every guy on the base after that. Anyway, by the end of basic it was as if the little asshole rich kid never existed. Hollywood went on to Special Forces and got a bronze star, and he owes it all to the sarge."

Seneca's heart ached. It hurt her to think of that angry, frightened teenager standing out in the rain without a friend to help him. But the sarge did a good job making a man out of him so maybe that's all that mattered.

Collin plopped down on the steps beside her. "Must be one fascinating story Matt was telling you."

"He told me about your night standing alone in the rain during basic training." She half-expected him to get huffy like he did when Ray told her about his family. But he didn't seem to mind.

"Yeah, that was the longest night of my life. At first I was so pissed at the sarge a tornado couldn't have made me break formation. But he got up every hour and came outside in the rain to call me a momma's boy and throw dirt balls at me. Around three in the morning, when he appeared for the fifth time, I realized he was trying to help me, and I'd been too stubborn and too spoiled to appreciate it. Got my head on straight after that." Collin bowed his head. "He could have just stayed in bed and let me fail. I owe him a lot."

Matt sighed. "Yeah, the sarge is a good man. We all owe him. Well, I better get back to the shop. There's a broken toaster oven on the workbench in the back calling my name."

Collin and Seneca stood, and Seneca held out her hand to Matt. "Take care of yourself."

He took Seneca's hand in both of his. "I'm glad to see you happy. Do an old friend a favor and take special care of Hollywood. He deserves to have a good woman in his life." He winked at her. "But if things don't work out with him, come back home to Peabody. I'll wait for you."

She tried to smile. The lie just kept growing.

Matt studied her. "Did I say the wrong thing?"

"No. I'm feeling a little emotional, I guess."

Collin pulled his cell phone out of his jeans and stepped between them. "What's your number, Mush?" Matt recited the numbers as Collin punched each one into his phone. Matt's phone rang from his jacket pocket. "Okay. I got your number and you've got mine." He slapped Matt's shoulder. "You call me if you need anything. I don't care what it is."

"How about a pair of legs that work?" Then Matt pursed his lips and shook his head. "I didn't mean that. Just feeling sorry for myself."

"Hey, buddy. You know I would if it were possible."

"I know." He looked past Collin and Seneca. "I *really* gotta go. My boss is staring me down over there." He pointed at the repair shop across the street.

Collin and Seneca turned and saw a middle-aged man with the creased face of a heavy smoker. The man cupped his hands around his mouth and shouted, "Hey Matt! You join the Peabody Welcome Wagon or are you still working for me?"

Matt rolled his eyes. "Thinks he's a comedian." Then he shouted back. "Still working for you, Boss." He released the brake on his chair. "Later," he said and rolled himself back to the repair shop.

Chapter 12

As they drove back to the Simms house, Collin was lost in thought. A deep frown creased his forehead. His eyes had a faraway look.

"You look like a hound dog that's just scented a fox."

He blinked and a half-smile curved his mouth. "Nice of you to say so."

"Will you tell me what's going on?"

"Nothing is going on." His voice rose an octave. To her ears, it sounded more like a protest than reassurance.

She raised an eyebrow. "Well that's certainly a definitive answer. Then there's nothing to keep us in Peabody, is there?" She didn't wait for his answer. "When we get back to Poppy's house, I'll throw my things in a bag, take Peabody Hill over to Mr. Stiles' house and we can leave for Chicago. By tomorrow evening I'll be in my beautiful new home with my real fiancé, Michael."

"I need a few more hours."

"But you solved the case!" She frowned. What had he caught scent of? He dashed out of Mr. Steele's office like the building was on fire, then he ran off on Matt to answer a *very important* phone call, now he was evading her questions. "The case is solved, isn't it?"

"Of course." His voice hit that tell-tale high octave again. "Hey." He reached over and squeezed her shoulder. "Show me around Peabody a little. Where did you teach school? And, oh, show me where you heard the violin music."

"I didn't *hear* it, I *imagined* it."

"Okay, show me that place then."

"There's nothing to see. It's just a bunch of trees."

"I can't leave until I've seen it for myself."

"You're being ridiculous."

He shrugged. "Maybe."

He was stubborn. "Fine, I'll show you and then we go straight home." She pointed through the windshield. "Take a left at the stop sign."

Collin turned into a narrow dirt road that curled around the foot of Peabody Ridge. The woods crept close to the road on both sides, and the only sign of human habitation on the quiet stretch was the occasional glimpse through the trees of an unpainted shack leaning into the mountain. She lifted her arm and pointed beyond a small house teetering forward on wood stilts. "Here."

He shifted the Jeep into Park and stared up at the mountain behind the lean-to. "It came from up there?"

"It seemed like it at the time. Why are you asking me all these questions? What's going on?"

"Nothing."

"*Something* is going on."

He twisted around to face her. "I don't know what's going on. I just have a feeling there's something more to the story, that's all. Give me a few hours. If I don't find anything, we can leave." His long-lashed killer blue eyes pleaded with her.

Seneca lowered her gaze and studied her hands. His face should be registered as a lethal weapon. "Okay."

Collin murmured "thank you" and made a sharp u-turn. He eased his foot off the gas and cruised by the tilted house one last time. "I'll drop you off at the house, then I'm—"

His foot hit the brake so hard, the Jeep's tires screeched, and Seneca was thrown forward with force enough to lock the shoulder strap on her seatbelt. He whipped his head around and stared at her. He looked as though he'd just seen a ghost. His eyes were round, his face pale and for the first time since she met him, his jaw was slack. His Adam's apple bobbed as he swallowed hard.

"Did you lock Peabody Hill in the house before we left?"

She rubbed the back of her neck. "What is wrong with you? You almost put me in the hospital."

His voice was low and serious. "Answer me, Seneca. What did you do with Peabody Hill before we left the house?"

"You-you saw me. I locked the front door. The dog was inside."

Her heart began to pound. "What's going—"

Collin flung open the car door and leapt out. He sprinted across the road and through the underbrush at the base of Peabody Ridge, then disappeared into the woods.

"What the hell?" Seneca rubbed her shoulder where the seatbelt had dug in and stared dumbfounded at the spot where he crashed through the woods until she realized the Jeep was still moving. "For chrissake, Collin! Do you want to kill me?" She fumbled for the latch on her seatbelt and dove into the driver's seat. She slammed on the brake. The car stopped just short of a ditch on the side of the road. Once she'd parked the Jeep along the side of the road, her attention returned to the mountainside. She scanned the woods, straining to catch a glimpse of Collin through the underbrush. Not a leaf moved.

Heavy, black clouds from the west were pulling in a chill wind. Seneca wrapped Poppy's old green sweater tightly around her as she reached out and shut the car door Collin flung open. Really! He was too much. Off chasing ghosts through the woods while she struggled with a runaway Jeep. She could have been injured! Seneca peered up at the mountain again. What was he doing up there anyway? Should she follow him? She looked down at her flimsy ballet flats. She wouldn't get far in the rocky terrain wearing those.

A gunshot rang out. "God Bless America! What are you doing, Collin?" She pushed open the car door and jumped out. "Collin? Where are you? Are you okay?" Ignoring the bite of gravel against the soles of her thin shoes, she ran toward the woods, propelled by curiosity and concern. Collin didn't know how things worked in Peabody. A hunter might mistake him for a deer and shoot him. He was supposed to wear an orange vest or jacket when he wandered through the woods, especially at this time of year.

She didn't even make it to the other side of the road before Collin suddenly reappeared near the same spot he entered the woods. He was hunkered down as he half-walked, half-ran, and he looked behind him twice. When he saw Seneca in the middle of the road, his eyes widened.

"Why aren't you in the Jeep?" He sounded downright pissed as he picked up his pace and ran toward her.

"I thought I heard a gun."

"So you decided to stand out in the open?" He took her arm and escorted her around the Jeep to the passenger's side and helped her inside.

"I was worried."

"I can take care of myself."

"Really?" A hint of sarcasm crept into her voice. "Then why are you traipsing around in the woods dressed like a tree?" She let her eyes sweep over his olive T-shirt and brown leather bomber jacket. "These mountains are crawling with hunters. You're supposed to wear something orange."

He looked at her as if she was crazy. "Maybe I should just pin a target on my back."

"Whoever shot at you probably thought you were a deer! Jeez, Collin, for a Green Beret you sure don't know much about hunting."

"Do you get a lot of deer around in these parts hollering, 'Don't shoot'?" He didn't wait for her to answer. "Time to get you home." He shut her door.

Sleepy Hollow Road and the Simms house were just a few blocks away. He made the trip in just under two minutes, squealing into the driveway before jumping out of the car. The keys dangled in the ignition, but at least he put the Jeep in park and turned off the engine. She watched from the passenger seat as he took the front steps two at a time and tried to pull open the door. It was locked, as she told him, and she had the only key.

When he turned back and scowled at her, she sighed and let herself out of the Jeep. She dug around in the pocket of her jeans for the key as she climbed the steps. Before she even inserted the key into the lock, the dog's claws scratched at the door.

"Where did Peabody Hill come from?"

"Why are you—" The eager bloodhound barreled through the door and into Seneca. He began to butt at her thighs with his nose until she finally stooped down to scratch behind his ears and let him cover her face with dog slobber.

"Stop it, you." She giggled as his long tongue tickled her face. She tried to push him away. But the dog's tail continued to whipsaw back and forth.

"That's enough." Collin's tone brooked no disobedience. He stared at the dog. Peabody Hill stopped dead in the midst of a joyous lick. He looked at Collin. "At ease, soldier." Her bloodhound sat at attention.

Still kneeling, she tipped up her head. "You do realize he's a dog, don't you?"

Collin gave her a melting look from beneath his lashes and held out his hand. "Let me help you up."

Her eyes slid over his square palm and long fingers. She laid her hand on his and let him pull her. His grip was gentle, his skin warm. Her hand lingered for a moment, then she pulled away. She'd spent years in this house waiting for a handsome hero to ride up and take her away. Just her luck, he arrives two weeks before her wedding to someone else.

"Seneca? Where did Peabody Hill come from?"

She forced herself to look up at him and feel nothing. "Why?"

"Please, just answer me. Where did he come from?"

She sighed. "There's no big story to tell. He came from Bluefield. A few years before I left for Chicago, Poppy went to visit a friend of his in Bluefield—just over in the next county—and when he came back, he brought the dog with him."

"Who named him Peabody Hill?"

"Poppy did. He said something a little crazy when he told me the name. He said he named the dog Peabody Hill so I would 'know where my responsibilities were.' I suppose Poppy meant my responsibilities to the dog if anything happened, but it was weird the way he said it. And nobody calls the ridge Peabody Hill expect Poppy and a few old-timers."

"Not sure I understand."

"Just their way of saying the Ridge wasn't all that big. They could climb it like it was just a little hill."

Collin's attention returned to the dog. Peabody Hill's panting quickened and his tail slid from side-to-side across the porch's wood planks. Collin considered the dog thoughtfully. "What secrets are locked away inside you, boy?" Chocolate eyes met Collin's and the hound barked. "I wish I knew what you were saying." Then he opened the front door and went into the house. The dog followed him.

Seneca stood on the edge of the porch as Collin's head and broad shoulders disappear up the stairs, followed by his narrow waist and low-slung hips, and last, but not least, his long legs. *She'd bet her last dollar he looked sexy as hell with his clothes off.*

When she could no longer see the heels of his shoes, she frowned. He was up to *something*. It was time she did a little detecting of her own.

Chapter 13

Joe Ianni didn't find much on Thomas and Sonja Simms, but what he did uncover gave Collin plenty to chew over. There was a death certificate on file for Sonja Albers Simms, but the cause of death box on the document was blank. Joe also reported that no death certificate was filed in L.A. for Thomas Simms, but there was an outstanding warrant for his arrest.

When Collin heard that news, his blood ran cold. "For what?"

"He was subpoenaed and never showed up. Looks like it involved his wife's death."

"How did she die?"

"Fell five stories from an open window in the Simms' apartment. It was headline news at the time. Tommy Simms was a rising star on the rock and roll scene. After his wife's death he disappeared into thin air."

"Do they suspect him of murder?"

"It's hard to read some of these old notes, Atlee. The handwriting sucks. But obviously the circumstances surrounding Mrs. Simms' death were suspicious and the investigating officer suspected Simms witnessed his wife's last moments. Simms was certainly in the apartment when the incident occurred."

"When you say the circumstances surrounding Mrs. Simms' death were suspicious, what exactly are we looking at?"

"The officer didn't have enough evidence to determine if Mrs. Simms' death was accidental or suicide or, well, murder. That's all it says in the officer's notes, but the subpoena was issued because he wanted to question Mr. Simms about what happened before she fell."

"Anyone still looking for Thomas Simms?"

"If you come across the guy, we need an official statement so we can close the case. I don't think prosecution is likely. It's a twenty-seven-year-old unnatural death with no witnesses except

Simms and no evidence. Of course, depending on what Simms says, that could always change."

When he glimpsed a dun-colored hound that looked exactly like Peabody Hill watching him from the spot in the woods where Seneca heard violin music, Collin suspected *who* he would find when he hiked to the top of the mountain, which is what he planned to do. After the phone call, Collin knew Tommy Simms was alive and living on Peabody Ridge. He wasn't sure *what* he would find or *why*, but the warning gun shots fired over his head at close range said he wasn't going to stroll into Tommy's front yard and start asking questions. He'd be forced to disarm Tommy first. Once he knew Tommy didn't pose a threat to Seneca, he would bring her into the situation.

In Poppy's old room, he threw his bomber jacket across the bed and pulled on his desert camo field jacket—not exactly appropriate for North American forests but it was all he packed. He dug around in his duffel bag for his combat boots and put them on, lacing them up over the legs of his jeans. In the pockets of his jacket he stuffed gauze and sterile tape, two power bars, a bottle of water, his old black watch cap, a pebble of charcoal, and a small flashlight.

He was still missing a critical piece of gear—his Glock semi-automatic, which he kept locked in a concealed compartment in the Jeep. Unfortunately, he was going to have to leave the Jeep at the house since Tommy might still be hiding nearby. He noticed the woods came down to the edge of the street that crossed the dirt road. On foot, he could enter the trees behind the place Tommy had been hiding and surprise him. Piece of cake, except for one small problem. Between him and the Jeep was Seneca. If she caught him pulling a gun out of the truck, she'd insist on an explanation, and probably demand to come with him.

Collin studied the window in Poppy's room. He'd have to climb out, hang off the sill and drop to the ground below without landing in the rose bushes. Lifting the sash, he poked his head out to make sure Henry wasn't out in his yard, then he lifted one leg over the sill. Beyond his locked bedroom door, Seneca's light footsteps pattered up the stairs. She emitted a loud yawn. Then her door click shut across the hall.

That girl had perfect timing. He abandoned the window and left Poppy's room swiftly and silently, edging along the wall to avoid the creaky center of the upper hallway. Peabody Hill was asleep in the kitchen. When he saw Collin, he sat up at attention. The dog hadn't eaten since last night's hamburger, and they had a long march ahead of them. He opened up cabinets until he found a container of dog treats. It would have to do. He shook some onto the floor and filled a bowl with water. "Gas up, boy. We got a mountain to climb." The dog lowered his head and began to munch a bone-shaped treat.

While the hound ate, Collin open the front door just enough to slip out. He soft-footed it out to the Jeep for his Glock. His gaze flicked up at Seneca's window. The shade was tightly drawn. He went back inside for Peabody Hill. While he waited for the dog to slurp the last drop of water from his bowl, he checked the safety on the Glock.

"Off to roust a few squirrels, lieutenant?"

Seneca leaned against the curved frame of the alcove between the kitchen and hall. Her arms were folded, her feet bare, and a smart-ass smile curled her mouth. His gaze dropped to her white T-shirt and the lacey outline of her bra. *Damn, he liked her.* Orange spice. The words wafted through his head like perfume. The mission could wait a few more minutes.

He slid the Glock into a small leather holster under his field jacket, then breached the space between them in one long stride.

"I like the way you say 'lieutenant.'"

He cupped her shoulders and looked into her eyes. They glittered like pieces of bottle-green glass. He pressed his mouth against hers and gave her a tentative kiss. Her lips were warm and yielding. He kissed her again with more confidence, moving his mouth against hers in a slow, sensuous rhythm. Her eyes closed.

He tilted his head and kissed the corners of her mouth, trailing little kisses across the hollow of her cheek to her ear. He nibbled her ear lobe until her breath came in short gasps. She pressed against him. He covered her lips with his mouth and they parted for him. He bit her lower lip gently with his teeth and the tip of her tongue traced his mouth. His tongue pushed into her sweet mouth, sweeping along her teeth and twisting around her tongue.

He slid his hands between their bodies. His fingers found her breasts. They were firm and fit his hand perfectly. With his thumbs, he rubbed the tips through her bra until her nipples tightened. He groaned and pulled his mouth away.

"You know where this is headed?"

She pulled away from him and exhaled the words, "Oh Collin, what am I going to do with you?" The question brushed warmly against his jaw.

Combing his fingers through her fiery hair, he inhaled the sweet, lemony scent of her skin. His lips pressed against her smooth temple. He whispered back. "What would you like to do with me?"

When she raised her eyes to him, they looked sad. "I'm engaged to be married in two weeks."

"Do you love him?"

She turned away. "I waited all my life for Michael. He's sacrificed everything to protect the earth. I get to share that with him."

His heart lifted. "You didn't answer my question."

"Of course I do. He's my fiancé."

That sounded like something people say about their pet. *Of course I love Fido. He's my dog.* Where was the passion? The heat? Collin tilted his head. "You let me kiss you because he doesn't turn you on. That's it, isn't it? You like the noble, tree-hugger side of him, but he can't turn you on."

Her cheeks flamed. "Don't be ridiculous. Michael and I have a very active sex life." She met his gaze. Her eyes narrowed. "Not that it's any of your business."

"Active is not the same as hot."

"Okay, we have a hot sex life. Are you happy now?"

"Hardly. And I don't believe you." He studied her. "I know the timing sucks, but I like you."

Her eyes grew round, but he couldn't quite read her. What she afraid? Surprised? He hoped the latter.

The sound of thunder rumbled in the distance. He remembered his mission. "My friends call me Collie. I'd like it if you did too."

She tilted her head and looked into his eyes. "Poppy called me Sen."

He smiled. "Sen."

"Collie." She smiled back at him.

More thunder rumbled. It sounded closer. He pulled her close and bussed her lips. "If you ever get tired of hugging trees and find yourself in the mood for a little war game, let me know."

"War game?" She looked confused.

He winked at her. "I'll be the marauding soldier, and you can be the village maiden."

She laughed. "Or I can be the marauding soldier, and you can be the village idiot."

"Works for me." His nostrils widened as he caught the scent of rain in the air. Time was running out. "Well, the squirrels are waiting. I better go."

Her smile faded. "Where are you going? What's going on—"

He cut her off before she could finish her question. "We're just taking a little walk. I want one last look around. See if I missed anything. You stay here and get packed. We'll leave as soon as I return." Then he looked down at Peabody Hill who sat at attention by the door. "Move out," he commanded. The bloodhound rose and the little Peabody Battalion of two was on the march.

Chapter 14

Collin hoofed it down Sleepy Hollow Road as quickly as he dared with Seneca's dark green eyes burning a hole in his back. As soon as he disappeared over the hill, he breathed a deep sigh of relief and stopped for a few moments to make sure she wasn't following him. Then he and the dog jogged the last few blocks to the dirt road.

Slipping behind a tall clump of arrowwood by the side of the road, he hunkered down. "Here, boy." The dog trotted up to him and sat. He patted the hound's head and scratched one of his soft ears. "I'm depending on you to help me find Tommy." The dog licked his hand eagerly, his dog tags tinkling with each bob of his head. "You're going to give our position away before we ever get close." Collin's hands slid to the dog's neck. He unbuckled his braided leather collar and thrust it beneath the branches of the arrowwood for safekeeping. Then he pulled the black watch cap out of the waist pocket of his field jacket and yanked it down over his honey-colored hair.

He fished around in the inside pocket of his jacket for the remnant of charcoal and studied Peabody Hill. Collarless, the bloodhound was a silent companion, but now he was indistinguishable from Tommy's hound, and two identical hounds on the mountain, one friend and one possibly foe, was dangerous. He slashed a thick X across Peabody Hill's back using the charcoal. With a deft hand, he darkened his own features in a few quick strokes before reaching under his jacket and pulling the Glock from its holster.

With a half-dozen long strides he ducked into the cover of the woods at the side of the mountain. The dog stayed close behind him. The brittle fall leaves on the forest floor crunched under his boots. He slowed, walking gingerly as he moved from tree to tree to stay out of the open. The dog followed his lead, bringing up the rear with soft steps and an economy of movement. The air cooled on his skin, and daylight dimmed to twilight gloom as they moved deeper into the forest. He hoped Tommy was close by, keeping watch on the road. They'd ambush him from behind and neutralize him.

The bloodhound's teeth tugged on the leg of his jeans. When he turned around, the dog pawed at the ground. His tail wagged rapidly from side to side. Collin hunkered down to see what excited his interest. Two brass shell casings lay hidden among the wind-blown leaves. He scooped them up and examined them. No dirt clung to the oiled shafts, evidence they were dropped very recently. He rolled the brass shells around in his palm and studied the small clearing. This was where Tommy stood earlier and sighted him through the scope of his rifle. Collin would have to be very careful. Tommy knew these woods, and his rifle gave him a long-range advantage over Collin. Besides, you never knew what a man would do if you cornered him.

In the canopy above them, raindrops hit the leaves with heavy plops, but the cover of leaves kept Collin and the dog dry. He inched down through the trees, looking out for movement or the other dog. A squirrel suddenly dove into a pile of leaves, and he jumped. Peabody Hill grumbled but didn't bark. They crept onward. A sliver of the faded lean-to beside the road flashed through the trees. He was yards from the dirt road. Tommy wouldn't venture any further from the cover of the trees and risk detection.

Collin turned his head away and gazed up toward the top of the mountain. The faint odor of wood smoke hung in the air. Beyond two ancient yellow buckeyes, the ground began to rise steeply. He sighed. There was no place for them to go but up.

From habit and a superstitious belief it brought him luck, he dropped to one knee, bent his head, and closed his eyes to pray. But instead of his standard "Save me from mine enemies" invocation, thoughts of Seneca came to him. She'd let him kiss her. A good sign. But women like her didn't stick around him for long. He remembered all the women he'd been with. Too many to count. But smart women, classy women, women who wanted more than a good time, didn't stick around when they understood his feelings were locked deep inside, and he'd lost the key a long time ago. Hell, the longest he ever dated the same girl was six months, and that happened back in college.

He bent his head and began to pray. Really pray. Not the usual invocation for aid in his mission and keeping him and his men—dog—safe. "Please help me." He thought about Seneca who waited for him a few blocks away. "Help us," he amended, and murmured an "Amen."

He rose from knees and unlocked his Glock. "Let's go, boy."

The hound trotted ahead of him, not bothering to scent the air or sniff at the ground. He led Collin straight to an overgrown trail hidden by heavy underbrush. The dog grew excited as he climbed ahead of Collin, wagging his tail, panting eagerly, slobbering in happy anticipation.

Poppy must have brought Peabody Hill with him when he visited his son. Seneca's words replayed in his head—*He said he named him Peabody Hill so I would know where my responsibilities were.* The old man must have planned for Peabody Hill to lead Seneca to her father if anything happened. By why? Why hide his son in the mountains? And why hide him from Seneca?

Chapter 15

From the front porch, Seneca narrowed her eyes as she watched Collin and Peabody Hill meander up the street. Collin was too clever by half. Dressed for World War Three and armed to the teeth, he tiptoes down the stairs and dashes out of the house to take the dog for a walk? How stupid did he think she was? He probably broke into a run the second he disappeared over the hill.

"What are you up to, lieutenant?" He must have seen something out of the ordinary behind the lean-to. Something he mistook for a bloodhound. Probably just a fawn or an overgrown raccoon. But the look on his face! As if he'd seen a ghost!

"*Something* is going on!" Her words hung in the humid air. But what? The mystery of the two birth certificates was solved. Poppy was her grandpoppy, and a man and woman she'd never met gave her life, then died. She'd already conjured up a narrative for Michael. *Parents died tragically, infant left behind, grandfather adopts and shields child from the terrible truth.* She could handle it. Michael's political future could handle it.

"And yet, you smell something rotten." That did it. Collin was deranged if he expected her to sit around the house and wait for him to trot home and drop whatever it was at her feet like Peabody Hill offering up a snake he just killed.

The black clouds overhead drew her eyes. They swirled angrily over the top of Peabody Ridge. The air around her was thick with the anticipation of rain. She'd have to hurry.

*

Seneca parked the Jeep in front of the lean-to and got out. She slowly pressed the door closed to dampen the sound. The latch clicked, and she thrust the keys into the pocket of Poppy's orange hunting vest. Unlike Collin, *she* had no intention of being mistaken for a deer by a half-drunk hunter. She'd tucked her jeans into a pair of old rubber rainboots with green and purple umbrellas printed on a white background, and she'd stuck a waterproof hunting cap—also neon orange—on her head. She felt a little self-conscious, but for a rainy day on the mountain, it was a good choice. As if on cue, a drop of rain plopped on the brim of her hat and rolled down her nose.

"Great."

She swiped at the raindrop and scurried to the shelter of the woods behind the lean-to. At the edge of the trees she froze, straining to hear the tinkle of dog tags. But the only sounds in the forest were the distant rumble of traffic out on the highway north of Peabody and the patter of rain against the canopy of leaves above her head. She peered through the shadowy light beneath the trees, straining to catch a glimpse of desert camouflage or honey-gold hair. The woods were deathly quiet. Not even a bird stirred.

This was the forbidden side of Peabody Ridge. The loose rocks and sharp, brush-covered rises and washes of the northern face were difficult and dangerous. No decent paths flowed through the landscape, so getting lost was nearly a certainty—unless you had a hunting dog with you like Collin did. The southern side of Peabody Ridge was riddled with trails looping up scenic ridges. A hunting lodge, dozens of cabins, and a handful of camping grounds dotted the gentle hollows. Peabodyites avoided the rugged northern side of Peabody Ridge.

Except for Poppy. When he wanted to be alone, he'd climb the 'hill.' Sometimes he brought Seneca, and they'd perch high on the ridge to bird watch. He knew an old gravel-strewn path, nearly overgrown with saplings and brush but still passable. It twisted around the steep drops and loose rocks so they could climb safely. *Where was that darn trail?* She veered left, walking in the direction she remembered Poppy taking to reach the path, batting back branches of low shrubs as she searched for a thin stream of gravel.

She passed under the limbs of a gnarled oak. A lone ovenbird warbled on the branch above her. She shivered. Second thoughts popped into her head. Maybe Collin and the dog *were* walking around Peabody. Maybe they hadn't come this way at all. If she ended up lost on this isolated part of the mountain, no one would find her until spring. Besides, hadn't Poppy always told her never to climb the mountain alone? She had nearly talked herself out of continuing her search for Collin, when the intermittent drips of rain on the forest canopy grew into a roar.

She twisted around. Raindrops bounced off the hard dirt road and fast-running rivulets poured from the roof of the Jeep. Deep in the woods, under the canopy of trees, it merely misted. She'd wait out the heavy rain. If she didn't find Collin by then, she'd leave.

She scrounged through the underbrush for the old trail, kicking at the scrub and studying the trees for familiar landmarks. She also glanced over her shoulder every few minutes to make sure she didn't lose sight of the road. As she reached for the trunk of a young oak to pull her up a steep wash, her boots slipped on loose stones. Her heart pumped a little faster. The trail must be close by. She pushed aside a thick screen of mulberry branches just a few feet further on. Beneath them lay the old path.

Her eyes traced the ribbon of gray pebbles as it rose and was swallowed by the trees pushing against it on either side. Above her head, a branch rustled. Had Collin's bloodhound apparition been real? What if there was a wild creature in the woods? She glanced around. This was a bad idea.

Skidding on a patch of mud, she made a hasty retreat down the slope. As she grabbed at a tree to steady herself, her eyes fell on a fresh clump of dirt beside the trail. She stooped down and traced a large boot print. Her knees hit the ground as she pushed aside the branches of a mountain laurel and found another print. A set of paws had imprinted the damp earth beside it. Her head snapped up, and she gazed at the rising path. Collin *had* passed this way. Her mouth tightened. He had no right to come up here without her.

She pulled the hunting cap down low on her head to shield her face from the rain and set out. As she climbed, the knees and thighs of her jeans grew damp and water soaked through the sleeves of the old wool sweater that she wore under her vest. She listened to the raspy crunch of her boots on the path amplify in the deathly silence of the woods. Her march slowed. She hesitated. Her better judgment kicked in again. She was crazy! Collin and the dog were probably home, sitting in the warm, dry kitchen, wondering where the hell she was. But a little voice inside her said they weren't at home and she shouldn't turn around and that *was* Collin's footprint in the dirt. She crept forward, setting one rainboot in front of the other, each tiny step accompanied by the thump of her heart.

She began to hum Miranda Lambert's *White Liar* under her breath to keep herself calm. She wanted to call out for Collin but he'd know right away that she was scared if he heard her. And if someone or *something* else heard her, they'd know it too. She walked on with just the tune to *White Liar* for company.

The path ahead took a jagged turn and disappeared between a dead oak and a yellow hickory. The refrain of *White Liar* died on her lips. When he took her birding up here, Poppy always stopped before this point in the trail. *Plenty of birds right here, Sen. No point winding ourselves.* Then he'd take her hand and lead her to a comfortable spot under the trees where they listened for their favorite birds.

She stuck her nose in the air and sniffed. Smoke from a wood fire hit her nostrils. It came from further up the trail. Poppy never mentioned anything about a cabin on this side of the mountain. Maybe someone was camping up here. Stray hunters, probably. She forced her feet to keep moving, but the threat of people nearby pushed her to the edge of the path where her boots didn't crunch on the gravel.

Seneca cleared the oak and the yellow hickory. Up ahead, the trail zigzagged again. As she rounded the second curve, a thick clod of mud got stuck on the heel of her boot and she was trying to scrape it off as she walked so she didn't see Collin sprawled on the ground across the path until she nearly tripped over his legs.

"What are you—"

Collin flopped over on his side. His eyes were wide and the whites of his eyes blinding in the black mask of his face. "Get down!" He grabbed her legs, pulled her to the ground, and rolled on top of her. She struggled to catch a breath with a one-hundred-and-eighty-pound male lying on her back like dead weight. She wiggled and pushed up with her arms, fighting to free herself from him.

"Do not move," a very angry male voice whispered into her ear.

She twisted her head around and spit out a mouthful of dirt. "What is going on? Why are you here?" From a short distance away, she saw Peabody Hill, a giant black "X" scrawled on his back, watching her through sad brown eyes. He didn't look pleased to see her either.

"Quiet!" Collin rolled away from her, but kept a hand pressed into the small of her back. His eyes were narrow slits, the blue gleaming like daggers. His mouth was thin and hard. "I told you to stay put."

Frightened and confused, she came out swinging. "I am *not* one of your men, lieutenant. I do not take orders."

"If you were one of my men, I'd have you court-martialed! You are jeopardizing this entire mission." His eyes narrowed as he took in her orange vest and her boots with the purple and green umbrellas. "Did it ever occur to you that you are dressed in the most inappropriate uniform for reconnaissance?"

"Me? You're lying on a mountainside in West Virginia dressed for World War Three. You look like Rambo, for chrissake." From a grove of trees about fifty feet away, a shot rang out and a bullet sailed over their heads.

"Shit!" Collin turned his blackened face toward her. His expression was grim. It began to dawn on her that this was not some sort of imaginary "mission" he conjured up so he could play soldier. It also dawned on her that they might get killed up here.

"Sen," Collin whispered, "Listen to me. Here's what you're going to do." As he spoke, he scooped up a handful of mud and began to rub it over the back of Poppy's orange hunting vest.

"What are you doing?"

"Listen to me, dammit!" He'd gone beyond angry. He was furious. "I want *you* to crawl backward. Now. Keep your knees and elbows on the ground and your ass down. Do not stand up until you are around the bend and out of sight. Am I clear? Then run like hell."

"No." It didn't take a genius to figure out his "mission" involved her. "I want to know why that man—or that person—is shooting at us. I am not going anywhere until you tell me. And I want the truth, all of it."

His face smoothed and his eyes softened. "Please, Sen. Go back down and wait for me. I swear I'll tell you everything as soon as I get back to the house."

"No. Tell me now."

He reached out and cupped her chin in his palm. His eyes glittered bright blue in the coal dust smeared across his face. "Please. Go back."

"In case you haven't noticed, my life in turning into a freaking made-for-TV movie, Collin. I am not going to crawl away on my belly and go home like a good little girl. Tell me what is going on now. If this involves me, I have a right to know."

He nodded. He leaned into her and brushed a soft kiss across her lips. "Sen, baby, I'm sorry." Then he pulled back and let it rip. "I'm ninety-percent sure the person shooting at us is Thomas Simms."

"No!" She tried to scramble to her feet, but Collin pressed his hand against her bottom and held her down.

"I'm sorry."

Seneca closed her eyes and shook her head. "You're wrong. It's impossible."

Another bullet whistled over their heads. "Whoever you are, you're trespassing on private property." The man's voice sounded like Poppy's.

"Sen?" Collin whispered. "You have to get away from here. Can you crawl backwards down the trail?"

But she was too numb to do something so complicated now. She shook her head.

He studied her. "I've made a mess of this." Then his mouth tightened. "You will stay right where you are. If you so much as twitch before I give you a signal to move, I will have you flogged."

That registered with her. "By whom, lieutenant? Your battalion consists of one dog."

"Just stay down, baby. I don't want a stray bullet grazing that hot little body of yours."

She opened her mouth to remind him that he was her employee, but he'd already crawled away. Just before he disappeared, he turned back to her and pressed a finger to his lips. Then he headed deep into the underbrush and Peabody Hill, nose to the ground, fell into line behind him.

One side of Seneca's face lay on a nest of wet leaves as she watched Collin until the heels of his boots disappeared from sight. Despite cover from the branches of a tall hemlock that stretched over Seneca's head, rain ran off her hunting cap and dribbled down her neck. Her jeans were soaked and mud-caked, and her palms throbbed where she'd scrapped them when Collin tackled her, but she didn't dare lift her head to adjust her position or examine her hands.

Her father was alive! She knew it was true the moment the strained voice that sounded exactly like Poppy's shouted through the trees. Seneca frowned. What about her mother? Then the enormity of discovering parents she never knew existed hit her, and it took her breath away. She wished she could turn the clock back one week because if she could, she would have never returned to Collin Atlee's office and then none of this would be happening to her.

Chapter 16

After he narrowly eluded the tall, blond man down on the old dirt road, Tom Simms hiked up the mountain. His progress was slow since he was forced to drag an unwilling bloodhound by the scruff of her neck with one hand and hold a rifle with his other hand. When he reached his cabin, he cracked open the door, shoved the dog inside and slipped in behind her. Then he sank against the rough-hewn planks of the cabin wall and closed his eyes. He was so tired. Tired of running from the law, tired of hiding on this mountain, tired of his tiny, one-room cabin and these empty woods. Most of all, tired of worrying about Pop.

He'd made up his mind to venture down the trail on the next moonless night and slip through backyards to the house. It was the only way he was going to find out what happened to Pop. But he was afraid that after three decades Peabody would be changed. If he stumbled around in the unfamiliar yards or turned the wrong way at a street corner, someone might see him and call the cops who would transport him back to California in handcuffs. But as the days grew shorter and cooler and death on the mountain from exposure and starvation grew more certain, he accepted that he would have to go to Pop's house directly after the harvest moon waned.

The October moon was still in its last quarter phase when Aida got it into her head to leave the mountain in broad daylight! Twice this morning he chased her nearly to the edge of the forest and dragged her back to the cabin. When she escaped this afternoon, his worst nightmare came true. A blond-haired stranger spotted her and chased her into the woods. Cornered and panicked, Tom fired over the man's head to give himself some cover for escape. As Tom scurried up the mountain with a whimpering dog in tow, the man's car pulled away, and he breathed a deep sigh of relief.

He rose from the cabin floor. He needed to be ready if the blond man followed him. He stamped out the warm embers in the stove and pulled his chair up close to the window beside the front door. He sat tense and alert in the cold, dark cabin and watched the trail. But after nearly an hour of hyper-vigilance, he grew weary. He took a deep breath, stretched his back and thought about relighting the fire in the stove, when the dog, sprawled on the rough wood floor beside his chair snoring softly, raised her head and sniffed vigorously.

She jumped to her feet and barked at him. Then she trotted over to the cabin door to scratch at the floor beneath it with her paws. He leaned forward in his chair and peered out the window, but nothing moved. He turned back to the dog.

"What is wrong with you, girl?"

Her barks turned to low, aggressive growls, and from the corner of his eyes, he saw a flash of hunter's orange in the thicket of hemlocks near the trail. In a blink, it was gone. He froze. Could someone be out there? Did the blond man follow him after all?

He surged out of his chair and grabbed the door knob. Cracking open the door, he slung his leg across the gap so the dog couldn't slip through and listened, but it was impossible to hear anything through the rain. Then he saw it again! Another flash of bright orange! He thrust his arm back into the cabin and his hand closed around his rifle. It rested against the wall by the door, still slightly warm from his run-in with the blond man. He settled it into the crook of his shooting arm and squinted into the gun sight. Then aiming high above the place where he saw the orange, he fired a shot. He counted to five and fired again at the same spot. If the orange belonged to a hunter who'd strayed onto the north side of Peabody Ridge, the shots should be enough to warn the hunter off. If it was someone who knew he was up here and had come for him, he'd have to make a run for the cover of the woods.

Through the crack in the door, Aida pawed away at the back of his ankles and finally managed to thrust her head between his legs. He pushed her into the cabin with his foot before turning back to the clearing. He concentrated on the spot where he'd seen the orange. Nothing moved. The circle of hemlocks appeared to be empty. Then his eyes widened as the sound of human voices drifted toward the cabin door. Impossible! He shook his head and listened hard but it was difficult for him to hear in the rain. Just in case, he fired one last shot into the hemlocks and called out, "Whoever you are, you're trespassing on private property."

By now Aida was throwing herself against the cabin door, which in turn was hitting the same spot on his left shoulder and calf over and over again. "Ouch! Stop it you damn dog!" He pushed the frantic dog backwards into the cabin again and shut the door. From deep in her throat a low growl began, and she bared her teeth at him.

"Aida! Down!"

He spoke sharply to the hound as he pointed at the floor in front of him. But she refused to obey his command. She barked sharply at him. He pointed to the floor again. "Down, Aida." She whined, then hunched down on the floor and watched him through resentful brown eyes.

He sat again in the chair by the window, alert for any movements in the stand of hemlocks. But all was quiet. He allowed himself a deep breath. Maybe it was just a piece of paper tossed about by the wind. Maybe he was too hyper, what with his worries about Pop, then the blond man chasing Aida up Peabody Ridge. Maybe he'd let his imagination run away with him. He propped his rifle against the wall and leaned back in his chair.

Aida's head popped up again. Her head tilted, her dark eyes widened. She barked at him.

"What is it, girl?"

His heart began to pound. The little one-room cabin had a single window and door. Both faced the clearing. If someone crept up on the cabin's blind sides, he wouldn't know until it was too late to escape. For the first time since Aida woke him last night, he was frightened. He lurched from his chair and knocked it backward.

It clattered to the floor, but he didn't notice. He grabbed his gun and pulled his rain slicker from the peg by the door. Aida tried to push in front of him as he twisted the door handle, but he shoved her back with his foot and slipped out the door, switching his rifle from hand to hand as he shrugged the slicker on and pulled the hood over his eyes to keep out the rain.

His finger hard against the rifle trigger, Tom pressed himself against the cabin and scanned the woods past the clearing. Rain dripped off his hood and into his eyes, but he didn't dare take his hands off the rifle to wipe his face or pull the hood more securely over his head. If he could make a run for the bushes opposite the east edge where he'd seen the orange flash, he could guard the approach to the cabin on all four sides. He'd be vulnerable for the few seconds he'd be in the clearing, but he was desperate and cornered and fresh out of options.

He was about sprint for the woods when a heavy shadow darted into the clearing from his right side. His trigger finger pulled back before a single thought traveled through his head. The crack of the rifle split his ear followed by a sharp wail of pain. As smoke curled from his rifle, he wiped the rain out of his eyes and peered down at the muddy ground at his feet. Peabody Hill lay in the mud. Blood streamed from a gaping wound in his shoulder. A gun clicked behind him and a deep voice said, "Keep very still unless you want to join Peabody Hill." He froze.

"Mr. Simms, my name is Collin Atlee, and I am here to help you. But we both need to be safe so I want you to listen carefully to me and do exactly what I tell you. Put your left hand behind your head."

He was too stunned to comprehend what Atlee—*was that his name?*—said to him. He'd just shot Peabody Hill! And who was Atlee and why was he here? "Did my father send you?"

"Please, sir, put your left hand behind your head. We'll talk in a minute." Atlee's voice was calm but insistent.

Tom lifted his left hand and placed it behind his head. What else could he do? This man's gun was aimed at him, and Peabody Hill needed help.

"Now lean down—slowly—and lay your rifle on the ground. Gently, sir."

He did exactly as Atlee instructed him.

"Now you're going to take your foot and push the rifle toward me, then you're going to put your right hand behind your head."

He kicked the gun backward and raised his other hand to his head.

"I'm going to check you for weapons. Just relax, sir."

An indignant protest rose in his throat. Then Peabody Hill whimpered weakly and the words died on his lips. An invisible hand patted his shoulders, arm pits and waist from behind him. The solid touch of Atlee's hand brought the reality of his situation home to Tom. He'd been captured! After nearly thirty years in hiding, he was no longer free.

"Am I under arrest? Are you a cop?"

The man's left hand patted his thighs and legs, then his ankles. "You can put your hands down."

He dropped his hands and turned. Despite the black cap and darkened face, he recognized the man who'd chased Aida into the woods earlier in the day. The man was dressed up like a Viet Cong guerilla, and he looked deadly serious.

"I hoped for a more civilized introduction, but we have wounded. I was hired by your daughter. I am not a police officer."

Tom's jaw dropped. "Does she know about me? Pop said—"

Atlee cut him off. "Mr. Simms, no more questions right now. We'll talk later. Right now I need to move my wounded out of the rain. Can you control the dog inside if I open the cabin door?"

Tom remembered Aida. No wonder she was frantic all day. She must have smelled or sensed Peabody Hill's presence. But he wasn't sure what she'd do if a stranger walked into the cabin. As far as he knew, she hadn't seen another human being—except for Pop—in years.

"I don't know for sure. Let me open the door first. I'll try to calm her."

Atlee's mouth tightened but he nodded. "I know I can trust you, sir," he said, and to Tom's ears his words sounded like a threat.

But Atlee didn't need to worry about Tom. He was done fighting. He'd already shot Peabody Hill. He was lucky he didn't shoot Atlee! The mountain would be crawling with cops if a man were shot up here. Besides, his only other weapon was his hunting knife. And what good was a knife against a man half his age and twice his size?

Tom pushed the cabin door open just far enough to slip his hand inside and grab Aida by the scruff of her neck. She panted eagerly as her body strained against his hand.

"Shhh, girl. Slow down." He spoke as gently as he knew how. She whimpered and eased up a little bit. He swung the door open and stooped down in front of her to hold her in place. "She wants to come out to you and Peabody Hill."

Atlee hunkered down a few feet behind Tom. "Let her go." He held out his free hand to Aida. "Here girl." She stood, wagged her tail and went to him. "What's her name?"

"Aida."

"Aida," Atlee repeated as he scratched one of her ears. Over her head, he called to Tom. "Spread a blanket out near the stove. I'll carry him in."

Atlee stuck his pistol into a holster under his jacket. Then he gently slid his arms under Peabody Hill and lifted him up. He pressed the wounded dog against his chest, whispering, "There now, boy," over and over. He carried the dog into the cabin and laid him on the floor in front of the potbelly stove where Tom stirred the ashes to get the fire started again.

Atlee knelt on the floor beside the dog and looked up at Tom. "Do you have any hooch, Mr. Simms?"

He was confused. "Hooch?"

"Liquor. Do you have any?"

This man wanted a drink now? But he was in no position to argue with anyone—much less a man with a gun. "Got a little bourbon."

"Bring it."

Peabody Hill whimpered, and Atlee laid one of his wide hands on the dog's head. "There now, soldier, you rest. We're going to get through this." His voice rumbled softly, gliding soothingly over the dog, and even Tom felt reassured. The dog relaxed and closed his eyes.

Tom fetched the bourbon from his nearly empty cupboard. "Do you want a glass?"

"Put some in a bowl for Peabody Hill."

He filled a tin pie plate with a few fingers of bourbon and carried it to Atlee, who pulled a bottle of water from an inner pocket deep inside his jacket and poured a measure into the tin. He slid it under the dog's nose.

"Come on, soldier. I need you to drink up for me. This will make you feel better." Again, one of his wide, capable hands spread itself against the dog's head. Peabody Hill's eyes opened. "Here boy." He helped the dog lap up the potion. When he finished and laid his head back on the blanket, Atlee petted the hound in long, gentle strokes until he closed his eyes.

Atlee turned to Tom and began to bark orders."I have to see where the bullet went so I can assess the damage. You will hold him as steady as you can and keep him calm. Can you do that?"

Tom nodded. He knelt down on the edge of the blanket and placed his hands beside Atlee's on the dog's head and back. The dog whimpered as Tom's hands replaced Atlee's, but his eyes remained shut.

Atlee picked up the bottle of bourbon and splashed the amber liquid over his hands. "Okay," he said, and bent over the hound's shoulder where blood still seeped from the bullet hole. The dog jumped when Atlee touched the wound. "Hold him!" Tom applied gently pressure to dog's back and head and managed to keep him still except for an occasional whimper. The seconds ticked by slowly as Tom watched Atlee probe the wound. His body, still wrapped in the thin, rubbery rain slicker, clutched and began to shiver from the damp, chilly air curling into the cabin through the open door, but he couldn't let Atlee and Peabody Hill down so he stilled himself by playing the music to *Who Will Stop the Rain* in his head. Finally Atlee straightened and lifted his hand from the blood-stained shoulder.

The music in Tom's head stopped, and he tensed as he waited for the prognosis.

"He's lucky. The bullet missed the bone. It's lodged in his muscle. I don't think it's life threatening but the bullet is too deep for me to remove without instruments. We'll have to get him to the doc's before infection sets in."

Tom's heart was lodged in his throat. He didn't dare leave the mountain to help Peabody Hill. Pop said the cops were still looking for him. And he needed supplies. Would Atlee take a message to Seneca? Agitated and nervous all over again, he rose from the blanket to stretch his legs and ponder how much to tell Atlee, when he saw a flash of orange pass in front of the open cabin door. Atlee saw it too.

"What was that?"

"It's your daughter, sir."

"She's here? I-I-I shot at my daughter?" He'd nearly killed his own daughter! First Sonny, then Seneca. He wouldn't be able to go on if the blood of his daughter was on his hands, too.

Atlee rose and went outside. He stood in the frame of the door and held out his hand to Seneca who stood behind the door where Tom couldn't see her.

"Come on, Sen. I'm right here. It'll be fine."

A woman's voice mumbled something that sounded like *I can't*, then Atlee shouted "No! Shit!" Tom listened as light footsteps splashed and slurped through the mud and leaves rattled and branches cracked as a body threw itself through the thicket at the edge of the clearing.

Atlee turned and looked at him. Their eyes met. Tom read fear in his eyes and something inside him, something he'd managed to keep closed and hidden by never thinking about it cracked open. It felt like it was sucking the life out of him. He saw his empty, useless life stretched out behind him and yawn before him, and he was sick. His stomach heaved, and the bit of stew he'd managed to choke down the second time he brought Aida back to the cabin roiled.

He hated that Atlee watched him, but he couldn't control his nausea. He staggered outside and fell to his knees and vomited in the blood-spattered mud beside the cabin door. When the nausea passed, he coughed a few times and swiped the back of his hand across his mouth. The gentle hand that had soothed Peabody Hill pressed his shoulder. "Are you okay?"

He nodded. It was a half-truth but at least physically he was okay. Atlee must have understood. "I know you're feeling overwhelmed, sir, but you and your daughter will work through this." He hunkered down beside Tom. "Your daughter is out in the woods so I'm going to go find her before she gets hurt. Give me your word you'll stay put and watch over Peabody Hill."

The last time Tom lived in the world beyond the mountain, people did their "own thing" and inconvenient promises were thoughtlessly broken. How could this man rely on the promise of a selfish, heartless man like him?

"Sir, your daughter."

Tom nodded, and he knew he'd rather spend the rest of his life in prison than let this man down. "Take Aida. She can track anything."

Atlee jumped to his feet and grabbed Tom's rifle, where it lay forgotten in the mud. Tom realized that if it weren't for his problematic presence, Atlee would have bolted after his daughter the second she ran for the woods.

"Come on, girl," Atlee said.

Aida barked, and man and dog raced for the woods, crashing into the underbrush while Tom crouched in the foul mud outside his cabin, worrying about Pop and steeling himself to face his upcoming ordeal.

Chapter 17

Collin sprang over a boulder and crashed through the tangled limbs of a mountain laurel at the spot where Seneca disappeared. A rubbery branch from a nearby yellow hickory careened off his hand and whipped against his cheekbone. But he barely noticed the sharp sting or the sudden wet ooze from the gash. Pushing through the thick brush with Tom's clumsy rifle clutched in his hand for safekeeping made for slow-going. As he leapt across a shallow drop in the forest floor and past a wide clutch of arrowwood, he threw the rifle as far away from him as he could, pausing for just a second to watch it spin through the air and disappear. Then he began to run again.

"Sen, Sen, where are you?"

He was desperate to hear her voice. But she didn't call back to him. He crashed through a tall hedge of dogwood and nearly ran headlong into a tree. He pulled up short, and Aida fell into his legs from behind.

The rain had let up, and the eternal forest twilight began to deepen as the day waned. He estimated it was late afternoon. He needed to find her before nightfall. She was out there in the woods somewhere, lost, frightened, confused. And it was *his* fault. He managed the ambush badly and got his troops shot. He should have knocked Tommy to the ground and hog-tied him after he shot Peabody Hill. Then attended to the dog and Seneca.

Collin slowed to skirt another tree and began to sprint again. Instead, respectful of Tommy as Seneca's father, he tried to keep him calm and control the situation as he'd been trained to do. The slow minutes it took to disarm Tommy were torture. He longed to drop to the ground and help Peabody Hill, and to call for Seneca to come to him. But he wasn't sure if Tommy sincerely surrendered or if he was playing along until he could overpower Collin or disappear into the woods. His assignments in Iraq had taught Collin he must keep civilians—Seneca—away from the action until he had a chance to assess the suspect's state of mind and check the area for weapons. He should have known she would never stay put. Hell, she'd followed him up the mountain, didn't she? Dressed in white boots and a bright orange hunter's vest! She might as well have brought a spotlight with her. *Where was she?*

"Seneca, where are you?"

He listened to his words bounce against the endless tree-covered hollows of Peabody Ridge, growing fainter and fainter until they disappeared. But Seneca didn't answer. As the darkness deepened, he struggled to keep his balance over the rough ground beneath his feet without slowing his pace. But it was impossible. The toe of his boot caught in the gnarled root of an ancient oak, and he fell flat on his face. Cold, hard despair washed over him. Half-serious, he swore to himself that if anything happened to Seneca, he would kill her father with his bare hands.

He studied the foliage on either side of him. A never-changing vista of oak trees and mountain laurel greet him. How was he supposed to remember which direction he came from or which way he was headed without decent landmarks? And if by some extraordinary stroke of luck he managed to stumble onto Seneca, he'd never find his way back to the cabin until morning—if then! How would Peabody Hill make it through the night? Would Tommy stay with him?

He rose to his knees. His cheek was bloody and his palms bruised, but he didn't care. He just needed to find Seneca, then get the dog evaced to the doc's. They were his responsibility, dependent on *him*. His mouth tightened. Nothing would happen to them! Nothing! He would not allow it.

Aida's warm, soft tongue licked his face. He raised his head and looked into her eager brown eyes.

"Help me, girl. Please. Find Seneca for me, and get us back to Peabody Hill."

She yipped at him and, wagging her tail, dropped her nose to the ground and trotted into the bushes. He stood and brushed the dirt off his hands. Then he followed her. After passing endless groves of bushes and trees, she stopped and barked at him excitedly.

"What is it, girl?"

He hunkered down to examine whatever it was she'd run to ground. She pushed an orange cap toward him with her nose. He picked it up and inspected it. Inside the cap, "W. Simms" was neatly lettered in indelible ink. He pressed his nose against the crown and smelled Seneca's hair. She passed through this grove, and he was relieved.

He stuffed the cap in his back pocket. "Good girl."

Aida yipped again and took off, weaving between trees. She doubled back, turned sideways, moved forward again, snaking back and forth through the woods. What if Seneca came to her senses and tried to get back to the cabin? He hated to think of her frightened and lost in the forest.

Collin tripped again and fell to his knees. The dog's eager pants and occasional barks moved further and further away from him. "Aida! Wait!" he called, and a moment later her head reappeared between two bushes. When she saw him kneeling on the ground, she barked at him. "Come on!" she seemed to say. He remembered the mini-flashlight he'd stuck in his field jacket and dug it out. He rose to his feet, turned on the flashlight and trotted after the dog. He kept the flashlight aimed at the forest floor and managed to stay on his feet as he chased after her, roaring "Seneca!" until his throat hurt.

A little more sure-footed with the flashlight beam slicing through the darkness, he picked up his pace. But the beam missed a knotted root jutting up from the forest floor by his left foot, and he tripped a third time. A sharp stone impaled his knee as he landed. He stumbled to his feet, battling a searing pain just below his kneecap and growing despair—Seneca lost, Peabody Hill wounded—it was like Iraq all over again. He was still a screw-up like he'd always been. Whenever he was in charge, the ones he cared about got hurt . . . or worse. He shuddered.

Aida's yips turned into loud, triumphant barks. He half-limped, half-ran toward her. He pushed aside a wall of dogwoods and stumbled into a small glade. Aida butted her nose against something beside a tree, then sensing his presence, she pulled back. There was Seneca. Huddled against the trunk of a thick-rooted tree, she was curled into a ball, knees tight against her chest, head buried in arms folded over her knees. His heart lifted.

He staggered over to her and dropped to his good knee beside her. His arms closed around her shaking body, and he pulled her onto his lap. His lips pressed against her damp cheeks. He began to kiss her over and over again—cheeks, chin, forehead, ears, whatever his mouth touched. Her body relaxed against him and her arms slip around his neck. She was so cold! He unbuttoned his field jacket, opened it, and folded it around her so he could share his warmth with her.

He held her as tightly as he dared. He pressed his mouth and nose against the side of Seneca's face, inhaling her woman scent and palpable misery. Then he closed his eyes and a warm tide of contentment washed over him.

She twisted her head and her lips locked onto his. Her sweet mouth opened. He tilted his head and devoured her like a starving dog who finds a bone, kissing her roughly, burning her soft face with his beard stubble, and she tightened her arms around his neck and met his intensity with her own passion, crushing his mouth with hers until his teeth ached.

She broke away first. "Oh Collie."

A strange emotion filled him. *I love you*. He pulled away from her so he could look into her eyes.

She searched his face and gave him a brave smile. "Do you know what I wished after you and Peabody Hill snuck off through the bushes?"

He brushed his fingers against her hair. "What?"

"I wished I had never come back to your office last week. That none of this ever happened, and I could keep my memory of Poppy as my father instead of that man who shot Peabody Hill."

You would never have met me either.

"It's my fault, Sen. I didn't realize he was so jumpy. I sent Peabody Hill out to distract him so I could come up from behind and disarm him. I underestimated the danger."

He shook his head in disgust. *I underestimated the danger.* Wasn't that always the problem with him?

"I still wish he'd died when I was a baby."

"Sen." He pulled her close and cradled her in his arms. "You'll get through this. I'll be here for you as long as you need—want—me."

"Thanks, lieutenant. You are an honest-to-goodness hero," she whispered, then leaned against him.

Lieutenant. That's how she thought of him. In her eyes, he was her soldier, her detective, her employee, her hero, but not her man. The loneliness living inside him since Grandpa Collins died was as cold and hard as a block of ice. It's what a fuck-up like Collin Atlee deserved. He slumped back against the tree and closed his eyes and wondered what it was going to feel like to love someone who didn't love him back.

Chapter 18

Collin wanted to kiss the ground by the time he reached the cabin with Aida trotting proudly ahead and Seneca dragging her feet behind him. His knee throbbed, and each step of the rugged terrain was its own victory over roaring pain and Seneca's fear. At least a half-dozen times as they followed the dog through the endless woods, Seneca stopped and dug the heels of her rubber boots into the ground and folded her arms across her chest. He was forced to limp back and retrieve her, taking her hand so he could drag her forward until she moved on her own.

"Come on, Sen," he said when she drew up short at the edge of the cabin clearing. They could smell the fragrant wood smoke and see a light glowing from the open door. Aida barked cheerfully and loped through the hemlock-ringed forest glade and into the clearing. She sniffed at the door, then disappeared around the side of the cabin.

"I don't know what to say to him. I don't even know what to *call* him!"

"Look, as far as what to say, he doesn't know about your Poppy. He asked if his Pop sent me. So that's got to be first." He turned her toward him and tipped her chin up with his finger so she looked at him. "There's more."

Seneca's eyes nearly popped out of her head. "Lord help us, he's a criminal, isn't he?"

Her guess was so close to the truth, he was taken aback. "Why would you say that?"

She put her hands on her hips. "Well, he's been up here for going on three decades, plus you have that tragic expression on your face that people get when they're about impart unwelcome news like 'you have three weeks to live' or 'your father is a cold-blooded killer.' A wild guess, but I've decided to go with the killer option."

Despite the pain in his knees and the seriousness of their situation, he laughed. "It's more complicated than that."

"He's a murderer with three weeks to live."

He suppressed a grin. "Come on, Sen, be serious."

Her eyes narrowed. Then she pulled back and punched his arm. "How do you know so much, Collin? Why am I just finding out about my father now? Henry told you this morning, didn't he?"

"No, Henry didn't tell me. When you were talking to Mush, I called a friend who's on the LAPD. He gave me some background on your family. Your father is not a murderer, and he doesn't have three weeks to live. But your mom is dead, and your father was the only witness to whatever happened just before she died. The police don't necessarily believe he killed her, but they have some questions for him."

"What happened?"

"That's what the LAPD wants to know."

He took her shoulders and turned her in the direction of the cabin. "Stop stalling. You have to talk to your father sometime. Might as well be right now." She allowed him to push her into the clearing.

The cabin door was open and on a small crudely-fashioned table near the stove, an oil lantern illuminated the cabin and clearing. He studied the room where Seneca's father spent three decades of his life, and it reminded him of a prison. In one corner of the room stood a roughhewn cupboard with slightly crooked shelves. A metal mug, a tin plate, a saucepan and a cast-iron skillet sat on the top shelf. Beneath it a clear jar with a small measure of flour, a gallon can of vegetable oil and a nearly empty bottle of bourbon huddled in the center of an otherwise empty shelf. The next shelf held a violin and a neatly folded stack of clothing. The last two shelves were bare. Behind the stove, pushed against the wall was an old cot with a thin mattress of blue ticking. A guitar leaned against the wall beside the cot. On the floor in front of the stove, Peabody Hill lay on his side, eyes closed, breathing harshly.

"Oh, Peabody Hill," cried Seneca when she saw him. She took a few unconscious steps toward the open cabin door, then froze. "Where is he?"

Not in the cabin. *Shit!* If Collin had to chase another Simms through the woods, he would not make it down the mountain hauling a one-hundred-pound, wounded canine tonight. He was dead tired. It felt like years since he woke up this morning in Poppy's old bed. His knee was killing him, and his cheekbone burned where the hickory branch ricocheted off his face. Plus Peabody Hill needed help, A-Sap!

Collin closed his eyes and sighed. How did a simple reconnaissance mission get so complicated? The civilian factor. They tended to be unpredictable because they thought with their hearts instead of soldier-style—with their heads. All those damn feelings tended to get in the way during a crisis. *He knew that.* He spun around and scanned the edge of the clearing for signs of Tommy. "Mr. Simms? Sir? Where are you?" Collin shouted up at the overcast sky. His impatient voice was carried off by the gusty, cold wind blowing in behind the rain.

From close by Aida barked. Then Tommy called out, "I'm down by the stream."

At the sound of her father's voice, Seneca's eyes grew round. "I-I-I can't tell him about Poppy. Please Collin. You go."

"You have to talk to him eventually."

"I know. But I don't want the first thing I say to him to be about Poppy dying. What if he goes crazy or something?"

He sighed. He didn't think Tommy would go crazy, but he didn't want to waste time arguing the point with her. Maybe if he left her alone for a few minutes while he talked to Tommy, she'd pull herself together. Besides, at this point he would do almost anything to move this mission along and *get off this godforsaken mountain!*

"You," he barked at Seneca, "will go into the cabin, shut the door and stay there while I talk with your father. Are we clear?"

Seneca gave him a jerky salute. "Yes, Lieutenant Atlee, sir."

"I'm not kidding, Seneca," he continued, dropping the military bark for sincerity. "If I have to chase you again, I won't have the energy to carry the dog back to the house."

She patted the pocket of her hunting vest. "I drove the Jeep over. It's parked at the bottom of the mountain."

Despite his weariness and a body that ached everywhere, he grinned. "Of course you did. Why am I even a little surprised?"

Her hand stretched up to him, and she cupped the uninjured side of his face. "Thanks, Collie. I promise you I will go in and sit next to Peabody Hill and not move a muscle until you come back."

Through the soft glow of the lantern, her green eyes sparkled. He pulled her against him and hugged her fiercely. Then he pointed to the cabin door. "March. And close the door behind you." She did.

He flicked on his flashlight and scanned the woods behind the cabin where Tommy's voice called from. "Mr. Simms?"

"Down here. There's a trail. Look under the big evergreen."

His flashlight beam illuminated a narrow footpath that climbed up the rim of the hollow where the cabin was nestled. He tread the footpath cautiously, mistrust and uncertainty about what he would find slowed his steps. When he finally stood atop the rim of the hollow, he peered down and caught his breath as he gazed across a broad valley twinkling with the lights of Peabody. He looked around and took stock of his terrain, swinging his flashlight from side-to-side until he illuminated a burbling mountain stream, swollen with rain, rushing past him on the left. It curved sharply along the high northern edge of Peabody Ridge. His flashlight picked out two dark figures—Tom and Aida—sitting together by the stream as they stared out at the lights of the town spread below them.

Collin skittered down the side of the hollow, his feet displacing bits of gravel and dirt as he half-walked, half-ran down the steep slope. As he closed in on the stream, he dug in the heels of his boots and managed to come to a halt just behind Tommy. He hunkered down, grimacing as the skin on his wounded knee stretched and the deep cut split and began to bleed again.

Tommy didn't turn around. His eyes remained focused on the lights of Peabody. "You found my daughter."

It wasn't a question so he didn't answer. He took a deep breath. Time to deliver the bad news. "Mr. Simms—"

"Tom. Please call me Tom."

"Tom." How did one deliver crushing news to a stranger? Especially one as vulnerable as Tom Simms. Poppy was the only human being he'd seen or talked to in decades. And now Poppy was gone, and Tom was all alone. *Get on with it, Atlee.* "Your father died of a heart attack last spring. I'm sorry." He said the words softly as if it would lessen the pain of the news.

"Oh, Pop." Then Tom curled his body into a tight bundle and sobbed while Collin kept watch. A thought stumbled across his mind. One he could not bear to ponder—What would he do when *his* father died?

As Tom's sobs died away, words began to bubble up inside him. He raised his head and stared out at the chalky night sky. "I knew something was amiss when Pop didn't come. I waited all summer for him, and he was dead."

Aida turned and licked the side of his face. Tom lifted his arm and laid it across her shoulders. It was one of the loneliest sights Collin had ever seen, and he thought when his father's time came, he would want someone he loved—Seneca—to hold on to, although he wasn't sure why he'd mourn a man he no longer cared about.

Peabody Hill needed help now, and he was going to hit a wall himself if he didn't move out soon. But he couldn't leave Tom alone on the mountain. "Tom, you have to pack up your gear, man, and come down to Peabody with us."

Tom shook his head. "I can't. If my daughter can bring up supplies a few times a year, I'll be fine. I have a shopping list in my cabin. It's not much."

From the woods above, an owl hooted. Tom's loneliness was so close to the surface, Collin could almost taste it. "I can't leave you up here, sir."

"Why not?" The question sounded like a wail.

"Your daughter needs you down there."

Tom's head jerked around, and he looked at Collin. "Why? What can I do for her?"

"You're all she has left. You can be her father," Collin urged, and tried not to think of that other father—the one sitting in a cozy mansion in Lake Forest.

The trees behind Collin rustled, and Seneca's voice called out. "Collin? Where are you?"

Collin rolled his eyes. Did that woman ever follow a direct order? Stay put meant stay put! Then he smiled. He loved that about her. She would keep him on his toes . . . if he could separate her from the noble Poindexter before the Halloween wedding.

He directed the beam of the flashlight up toward the rim of the hollow. "Down here." A moment later a white boot with green and purple umbrellas appeared, then a mud-caked, jean-clad leg, then the rest of her materialized. She slid down the slope and landed on her bottom beside him.

Tom's arm slid off Aida's shoulder. He twisted around and faced Seneca, and Collin gave him at least a few points for that. He studied Seneca for a few moments in the pale glow of the flashlight, which Collin directed at the ground between them. Then he said, "Daughter." He sounded sad.

Seneca nodded as she slipped her hand under Collin's arm and touched his hand. He laced his fingers through hers and squeezed tight. Silence grew into long minutes. The trio listened to the rush of the stream and the rustle of leaves as gusts of wind blew through the tree tops. The owl hooted again, this time closer. He stirred himself.

"We need to get Peabody Hill to the doc's. Let's help Tom get his gear packed and move out." He shivered as a cold blast of wind went through his field jacket. "The trail down to Peabody will get slippery with the cold front blowing in."

"I told you," said Tom. "I can't ever leave here."

"Are you wanted by the police?" Seneca's voice was small.

He nodded. "I killed Sonny. Your mother."

"I don't believe it, Tom," said Collin.

"The cops think I did, and though I didn't lay a hand on her, it's my fault she's dead. I could have saved her, but I didn't."

"Tom, be reasonable." He was losing patience. It was time to go.

Seneca cut him off. "I think I need to hear his story, Collie."

He sighed as the vision of a hot meal and a soft bed flitted briefly across his mind, then disappeared.

*

Barely two years after their marriage, Seneca was born, and Sonny stopped washing and dressing, and she refused to leave the apartment. In the early afternoons as he prepared to leave for his studio, she'd grow sullen and weepy. By the time he stuffed his wallet into his back pocket, she was begging him not to leave her alone with the baby—one time she begged him on her knees with her forehead touching the tops of his boots—but he could not bear to forsake his true love.

So in the long, lonely afternoon hours after he was gone, Sonny began to drink, usually gin without the pretense of lime or tonic. By the time he got home in the early morning hours—after clubbing and whoring all night—she was passed out. He usually discovered her sprawled on the sofa in front of the TV, still in her bathrobe from the morning, although a few times he nearly tripped over her half-naked body passed out on the bathroom floor. One night when he came home Seneca had cried herself to exhaustion, and he had to change and feed her before he crawled into bed. After that he hired a nanny to watch over his daughter and his wife, then he told his agent to arrange a tour so he could get out of L.A. for awhile.

At the time Tom couldn't see his own culpability in Sonny's "problem." He managed his life, why couldn't she manage hers? It wasn't his job to babysit her. *Get a hold of yourself,* he shouted at her during their frequent battles over her craziness and his carousing. *I'm your wife, Tome. Please love me,* she'd scream back at him. From where he was now, it no longer sounded like a scream. It sounded like a cry for help. But gods like Tom weren't born to serve the needs of mere mortals like Sonny. So he turned his back on his wife and daughter until the gods he worshipped forced him to face his own mortality.

As in most tragedies, the central character—Tom—never saw his fatal flaw until it was too late. With a smug attitude he would soon deeply regret, he congratulated himself for finally getting everyone and everything in the Simms household under control. The nanny had the apartment cleaned, organized, and running like a top, and it dawned on Tom that maybe there was actually something wrong with Sonny so he dragged her to a doctor who diagnosed postpartum depression. Now she saw a shrink a few times a week, and Tom's agent managed to book Instant Revolution on a thirty-city, international tour with the deliciously evil title, "Wrecked and Dangerous—A Summer of Naked Rock." It was the perfect solution for Tom who desperately needed to get out of the apartment until Sonny was herself again. Once she had her head together, he planned to have a serious discussion with her about a divorce. It was time he got on with his life.

As the day he was scheduled to leave on the tour drew near, Sonny was frustratingly still "not herself." The pills from the shrink were taking their own sweet time to kick in and every afternoon when Tom left the apartment to go off to his studio, she still raised a stink and every dawn when he tiptoed into the apartment, she was passed out drunk somewhere in the apartment, although almost never in their bed.

The love he once felt for her was gone. At the time he didn't wonder whether his own partying and bed-hopping took its toll on his marriage—although in the long years on Peabody Ridge, he pondered that question many times. At the very least he wanted to feel sympathy for Sonny as a fellow traveler on the road of life who'd hit a rough patch. But all he felt was anger. Sonny was supposed to be his muse! But as he studied his once-beautiful wife, what he now saw was a pale, gaunt face, haunted eyes, cracked lips and snarled hair that reminded him of barbed wire. And instead of love or sympathy, anger grew inside him.

The launch of "Wrecked and Dangerous" was five days away and counting, and he couldn't wait any longer to tell Sonny about his departure from L.A. In their bright, spacious living room, he found her huddled in her Arne Jacobsen egg chair, still wrapped in a stained bathrobe from the night before. The sun streamed through their tall front windows overlooking the Ocean, and Sonny stared out at the bright tops of trees and blue spring sky.

He sat down opposite her on the custom white-leather sofa that cost more than his boyhood home and cleared his throat. "Sonny?"

She blinked and turned a dull gaze on him.

"I-I've got some fantastic news! Instant Revolution has a great gig for the summer. You-you might have read about it in *Rolling Stone*." He forced a smile to his lips. "We're traveling with the "Wrecked and Dangerous" tour. This is the big break we've—"

"How long?" She licked her dry lips as she waited.

He prepared to jump up and run for the door as he said, "Only about two months. We play in thirty—"

"I mean how long before you leave."

He had the grace to bow his head. "We leave Saturday."

She slid out of the egg and stood. Her attention returned to the scene beyond the front window. "I see, Tome." Then she turned and strode from the room.

He expected nonstop drama and hysteria from Sonny in the final days before the tour, but what he got instead was a miracle. When he slunk into the apartment that night, he found her asleep in their bed, and when he dragged himself out of bed just before noon the next day—fuzzy-headed and dry-mouthed—he found her in Seneca's room rocking the baby as she crooned a Spanish lullaby. Sonny's dark hair was washed and combed and she'd applied rosy blush to her cheekbones and pink lipstick to her mouth. She wore a clean pair of dark slacks and a gauzy, embroidered peasant top, and he was reminded of the girl he once desired above all others.

She held the baby, bundled in a pink blanket, up to him. "I think she looks like you, Tome."

He tried to smile but his head ached too much. He grunted, then dragged himself to the bathroom, stuck his head under the faucet and turned on the cold water.

Day three and day two of the countdown to "Wrecked and Dangerous" passed in the same manner as day four. He woke around lunch to find Sonny smiling and serene, performing her duties as wife and mother impeccably. She bid him a cheerful goodbye when he left for his studio—and the nightlife that followed studio time—and was asleep when he returned in the wee hours of the morning. Her transformation was nothing short of amazing, and he began to hope she'd turned a corner.

Day one promised the same domestic bliss of the previous three days until he walked out of the kitchen with a cup of coffee and found her perched on the ledge of an open window in the living room. It was a warm afternoon, and she wore a pale green blouse and a pair of professionally frayed jean shorts that hugged her trim brown legs. Her eyes rose to meet his as he entered the room.

"Sonny! Get off the windowsill. What if you fall?"

Her smile was sad. "What happened to us, Tome?"

He took a step closer and set his coffee cup down on a Haslev rosewood end table next to the egg chair. "Sonny, please get away from the window."

"I miss you, Tome."

"I-I-I'm right here, Sonny."

She shook her head. "No, Tome. You are out there." She tossed her head backwards, lost her balance, then righted herself before she fell.

His breath caught in his throat.

"Do you still love me, Tome?" Her body tensed as she waited for him to answer.

"Sure I do! Of course." Even to Tom his affirmation of love sounded flat.

She shook her head. "I don't believe you."

"I do! Honest, Sonny." He couldn't bring himself to say the word 'love.'

She leaned back and stared down at the street, five stories below.

"Sonny, please. Get away from the window. Let's talk."

"I don't want to talk."

"What then?" Anger rose in his throat, and he choked it back.

"Choose, Tome."

He was confused. "Choose?"

"Yes. Do you want me or do you want what's out there?" She leaned backward again before grabbing the window frame, and the coffee roiled in his stomach.

"Sonny, I—"

"No, Tome. No more talk. Stay here, be with me and the baby, or go on your tour, sleep with your whores, get wrecked, savor the cheers of all those fans who don't know the price you paid to sing to them."

His body turned to granite. His feet were glued to the floor. He was just a few steps away from Sonny, but he couldn't move. A shred of a song from his childhood played in his head. *All around the cobbler's bench, the monkey chased the weasel, the monkey thought 'twas all in fun, Pop! Goes the weasel.* "Please, Sonny—"

She smiled triumphantly. "That's what I thought." Then she leaned back, lifted her ballerina arms as if to fly, and fell five stories to her death.

His body came alive. His feet propelled him forward. His arm stretched toward the window. But there was no longer anyone perched there to save. The next day, "Wrecked and Dangerous" left California minus Tommy Simms. He was at home—just as Sonny had wished—polishing off his third bottle of bourbon. He thought he remembered talking to two cops, but he wasn't sure if it was real or imaginary, and he had no recollection of what he'd said, but if alcohol was a truth serum, he'd told them he killed her.

He stayed drunk for three weeks, and the apartment was plunged into a permanent state of filth and chaos. The nanny was holed up in the baby's room most of the day and night and only ventured out of her sanctuary to warm bottles, answer calls of nature and, when the weather permitted, walk the baby near the ocean. Tom drifted in and out of an alcoholic stupor, rising from the living room sofa or the rumpled bed he'd shared with Sonny only when the delivery boy from the liquor store around the corner rang the bell or the nanny and the baby returned from a walk, bringing him a bag of hamburgers or a pizza.

Then the other shoe dropped. A detective and two cops appeared at the apartment to take Tom in for questioning. He was passed out in his bedroom, and the nanny, frightened, lied and told them he was not home. After a very brief deliberation, she gave up hope that he would pull himself together. She phoned his father and told him about Sonny and the police visit as she gulped back tears of remorse, as well as fear for Tom and Seneca's future.

What Woody found the next day when he arrived in L.A. was hell on earth. Empty booze bottles littered the tony apartment, ashtrays overflowed and half-eaten sandwiches and pizza wedges rotted on greasy paper plates. From his prone position on the white leather sofa, Tom opened one swollen eyelid and looked at his father. "Help me, Pop. Don't let them lock me up." Woody bundled up Seneca and packed Tom's things and got them both the hell out of California.

There are many kinds of prisons. Woody never spoke about what he saw or felt in California—at least not to his son. But the joy and pride that was his essence died after L.A. Tom, living in a shack on Peabody Ridge and sealed off from the world, knew his father took little pleasure in a life empty of music, his son, and finally, his wife.

*

Tom peered through the darkness at Seneca and Collin. "If I leave here, they'll send me to prison for at least manslaughter. I don't have much freedom up here, but at least I have my music and this little patch of God's earth.

"Tom, you didn't kill your wife," said Collin.

"But the cops—"

"I talked to the LAPD this morning. They aren't planning to charge you with anything. They never were. But you were an eye witness. They want to interview you for the official record. Your wife deserves that, doesn't she?"

He nodded. "But it was my fault. If I'd tried harder." He closed his eyes. "I was such a mean little shit to her. She was my wife! The mother of my child, and I just let her fall out the window, and I didn't even care."

"I think you did care. That's how you ended up here," said Collin. "Fortunately for most of us, being a shit is not against the law. You need to come with us. You will have to talk to the authorities, but if you cooperate you will not be arrested." He winced as he stood and straightened his injured knee. "Okay?"

Seneca rose and stood next to him. She studied this scarecrow of a man for a moment before she dropped her eyes to her boots. "You were callous and terrible, but you've paid with twenty-seven years of your life. Come with us."

All the fight seemed to drain out of Tom, and he didn't protest anymore. The solemn little party of three humans and one dog clambered up the embankment and returned to the cabin. Less than ten minutes later, Tom closed the cabin door for the last time. With his guitar slung over his shoulder, he led the way down the mountain, lantern held high in his hand so Collin and Seneca could pick their way along the rugged trail. Collin followed behind Tom with Peabody Hill's injured body in his arms. Seneca and Aida brought up the rear. In her right arm, Seneca cradled Tom's violin like it was a precious child, and in her left hand she grasped his rifle—easily retrieved by Aida—and the leather strap tied to the handle of his hunting knife.

Chapter 19

Collin pulled the Jeep into the driveway at the Simms house and glanced over his shoulder. Seneca sat in the back with Peabody Hill's head cradled in her lap. Their eyes caught and held.

"Tom, why don't you get Aida and your instruments out of the back. We'll go in the house and get you settled while Collin takes the dog to the vet's."

He nodded and jumped out of the Jeep. She bowed her head to punch in Doc Metcalf's phone number and warn him Peabody Hill was seriously injured and on his way. Then she raised her eyes to Collin's again and gave him directions. Her voice sounded breathless even to her, but she couldn't help it.

Tom pulled his guitar and violin from the wayback and coaxed Aida out of the Jeep to inspect her new home. The back slammed shut.

"Hurry back. I don't know what to say to him."

Collin's hand groped for hers in the darkness and squeezed it. "You'll be fine."

His touch was warm, and she turned away from him reluctantly, slipping her hand out of his grasp and stepping from the safety of the Jeep. Collin peeled down the driveway and into the night.

Tom hadn't uttered a word since he'd padlocked the cabin door. As she walked behind him on the trail down Peabody Ridge, Seneca couldn't see his face. But as soon as they emerged from the woods and stepped onto the old dirt road, she saw the most unexpected expression in his bright blue eyes—childlike wonder.

By the time they reached the house, his initial pleasure had disintegrated into uncertainty. He waited, shoulders hunched, eyes downcast, while she fumbled nervously to insert the key in the front door. When the lock finally clicked, she reached inside the door to flip on the porch light and the table lamp in the entryway. She pushed the front door wide open before turning to

Tom. His eyes were somber, his feet planted firmly on the porch's sun-bleached floorboards.

"How do you feel about coming back home?"

He raised his head and studied the frosted globe fixture above his head. "Sad."

He hitched his guitar higher on his shoulder and pressed the violin close to his body then crossed the threshold. As he stepped into the hall, his eyes darted from side to side and his feet shuffled forward, as if he expected the bogeyman to jump out and surprise him any second. He stopped and watched her expectantly. She slipped into the role of hostess.

"Well, make yourself at home. You can set your instruments down anywhere."

She waved her arms, taking in the living room butting up to the hall on the right, the dining room hidden behind pocket doors on the left, the alcove opposite the front door, and the kitchen beyond. She noticed he still wore his rain slicker.

"Can I hang up your coat?"

But he didn't answer. Instead he turned away from her and wandered into the living room. He ran his hand over the worn plush of Poppy's old easy chair. "I remember when this was new." The tarnished brass floor lamp across the room caught his attention. He shuffled over to it, ran his fingers up the brass pole and pulled on the beaded cord that dangled below the yellow shade. Light filled the room, and he turned from the lamp to gaze at each object—the lumpy plaid sofa, the pine end tables with framed school portraits of Seneca, the braided rug in the center of the room, the painting of a primeval forest on the wall over the sofa. Seneca and Aida watched him from the hall.

Seneca—still playing the chirpy hostess—interrupted his exploration. "Tom? It's okay if I call you that, isn't it?"

"Dad would be better." He headed for one of the end tables covered with her photos, picking up a particularly vile one—in her opinion, at least—of Seneca at an awkward, preteen age. It was the year she'd poodle-permed her hair and gotten braces put on her teeth.

"It's a terrible picture of me. I don't know why Poppy insisted on keeping it out."

He studied the photo carefully. "I like it."

A man of few words. Her growling stomach reminded her she hadn't eaten anything since Collin insisted on buying her a pumpkin muffin for breakfast at the Mountain Mist. Unfortunately, there wasn't much food in the house. She cleaned out the fridge in the spring and sent the perishables in the kitchen cupboards to the local food pantry, but she'd left behind a few things that would keep just in case. "Are you hungry?"

He set her seventh-grade portrait back among the others. "If it wouldn't be too much trouble."

"Let's go see what we can find." He set his guitar on the easy chair and laid his violin on the end table beside her portrait gallery. In the semi-darkness of the living room, the guitar looked like a headless visitor. Seneca turned and led the way into the kitchen, and he followed her.

The cupboards held a meager collection of jarred spaghetti sauce, a few boxes of dried pasta, canned corn and green beans, and soup. They stood side-by-side, and stared into the barren cupboards.

"You pick," she said.

He took a step forward, pulled out the can of Campbell's Chicken Noodle Soup. "This."

There were a few cans of hearty, non-condensed soup in the cupboard. "Are you sure? Some of these other soups might be more filling."

He shook his head. "This is the one Momma made. Are there crackers?"

Seneca pulled out a saucepan, dug out the can opener from the utility drawer and put the soup on the stovetop to warm. When she turned around to ask Tom to pull two mugs and spoons out of the cupboard, he'd disappeared. His soft footsteps creaked on the stairs above her.

"We'll let him wander around a little," she said to Aida, who had curled up on Peabody Hill's mat by the stove. "He needs to get his bearings."

The dog's tail wagged twice. Then she laid her head on her paws and closed her eyes.

It was strange enough for her to discover her real father was living in a cabin just a few miles from her childhood home. She couldn't imagine how much stranger it was for him to be back in the house he thought he'd never see again among all the things he'd thought were lost to him. Ordinary things like cars and canned soup and photographs and real beds and sofas and showers and iPods and computers and . . . She was overwhelmed just thinking about all the things Tom would need to learn or relearn.

He would need her with him until he was acclimated. The realization took her breath away. What was she going to do? She couldn't take him back to Chicago with her. Michael would be appalled at the semi-mute mountain man newly discovered to be her "real" father. She couldn't secretly install him in her little apartment since it was already sublet starting on Halloween. Would she have to quit her job and move back to Peabody? What about the wedding in less than a week-and-a-half? She stood at the stove pondering this dilemma when Tom's voice made her jump.

"Look. It's Old Maggie."

She spun around. "What?"

Framed in the doorway, he held up a country fiddle and a horsehair bow. He'd taken off his slicker and underneath he wore a pair of denim overalls and a plaid flannel shirt so faded it was impossible to determine its original color. He looked like an iconic dustbowl farmer about to entertain buyers at a foreclosure sale.

"Old Maggie." Then he saw her confusion and his eyes grew sad again. "It's Pop's. He always called it Old Maggie."

A lump caught in Seneca's throat. She'd heard rumors as a child that Poppy played the fiddle, but he'd always refused to talk about it. She took a step toward him and held out her hands. "May I see?"

He handed her the fiddle and bow, and watched as she settled the fiddle under her chin. "You have the gift, don't you?"

"The gift?" She straightened up and thrust the fiddle back at him.

"Music. Like Pop and me."

"Poppy said music was Satan's work."

"No, Seneca."

The words shot out of her like an accusation. "Poppy wouldn't let me play. Then one day as I passed by Peabody Ridge I heard violin music. Beethoven. It must have been you. That's when I left Peabody. After awhile, I bought a violin but the same day I worked up the nerve to play it, Poppy died. Now whenever I look at a violin, I remember that I killed him."

He laid the fiddle and bow down on the kitchen table. "Pop's heart had been broke since Sonny died. It was nothing to do with you."

Seneca closed her eyes. Poppy had missed music as much as she did. "In all the time I knew him, he never laughed."

"I'm sorry, daughter."

The lid on the saucepan began to rattle, and soup boiled over the top of the pan onto the stovetop with a sharp hiss. She turned away from Tom to rescue their supper. A few minutes later she set two earthenware mugs filled with chicken noodle soup on the linoleum-topped kitchen table. One mug in front of Tom— who chose her place at the table as if it were once his own—and one mug at the place where Momma sat. She couldn't bear to take Poppy's place. Then she dug two cellophane packs of oyster crackers she'd picked up at Estelle's from her backpack and set one beside each mug. They bowed their heads and gave thanks before attacking their supper.

Seneca slurped up a stray noodle at the bottom of her mug and popped her last oyster cracker into her mouth, then looked across the table at Tom. He'd finished his soup and was leaned back in his chair studying her.

"That blond man—"

"Collin. Collin Atlee."

"Collin. He told me he worked for you. Is it true?"

Why try to explain what even she didn't understand. "Basically."

"Felt like there was more between you."

"It's complicated."

"I don't mind listening." He looked down at his hands. "I won't judge. Not after everything I've done."

The whole Collin-Michael story was bound to come out eventually. Why not get it out in the open now, before Collin came back.

"I'm engaged to someone else."

She cringed, tensing her muscles and curling her back against her chair as she waited for Tom to scold her about virtuous women and falls from grace like Poppy would have done. But Tom seemed to take the news in stride. His eyes slid to her hand.

"No ring. Michael is an environmentalist and sort of a humanitarian. Most diamonds come from Africa, and there've been wars fought over the mines. Michael believes diamonds have blood on them."

"Do you?"

"I don't know. If no one buys the diamonds, the people who work in the mines won't have any money to eat or buy clothes or build houses."

"Did you say so to Michael?"

"He says you have to take a stand. Deal with the consequences as they arise."

"I see. Do you love him?"

"I thought I did." She rolled the empty cellophane bag between her fingers. "I'm not sure anymore. I have a powerful attraction to Collin. But is that love?"

"I don't know. Love's a tough one to figure out. It seems to me that you need to find out before you marry your environmentalist."

"Yeah." *Would less than two weeks be enough time?* "Thanks for listening, Tom." Pushing her chair away from the table, she stood. "Do you want to help me with the dishes?"

Seneca washed and Tom dried the mugs and spoons and put them in the cupboard. He knew exactly where they went.

"Last dish," she said as she set the scrubbed saucepan on the drying rack.

Tom's fingers twisted the towel. "The bedroom upstairs . . ." He trailed off.

"Poppy's room?"

He shook his head. "The other one. My, uh, y-y-your room."

"Is that where you want to sleep tonight?"

"I'd feel better. It was mine." He tilted his head up and looked at her. "But where will you sleep?"

"Don't worry. The living room sofa is fine for me."

He frowned. "No."

"If I ask him, Collin will give me Poppy's room and take the sofa."

He nodded. "Okay then. I'm a little out of my depth with all these changes."

He dried the saucepan and disappeared into the living room. She watched him retrieve his violin, then led him up the stairs where she fetched a pair of Poppy's pajamas, clean underwear, and a toothbrush for him before she carried her things into Poppy's room.

Once Tom was in bed, she could take them downstairs to the living room. Collin deserved a good night's sleep after single-handedly rescuing every member of the Simms family in one afternoon. Besides, he would have to fold himself up like a pretzel to fit on the sofa.

The floorboards creaked under Tom's feet as he came down

the hall from the bathroom. He called out to her from his room. "Good night, daughter."

"Good night."

The bedroom door clicked shut, and Seneca breathed a sigh of relief. She pulled her pajamas out of her case to change before heading downstairs to the sofa. As she closed Poppy's door, an unfamiliar sound filtered out of her old bedroom. She frowned. Was Tom tuning his violin? A long moment of absolute stillness followed. Then Poppy's house was filled with the most beautiful music she'd ever heard. Mesmerized, she sank down onto the side of the bed. She was certain he was playing a Bach violin concerto—a sad one—though she was not familiar with the particular score.

She closed her eyes and let the music enfold her. Her bones melted away and her body swayed with each new wave of sound. All sense of time and place disappeared. Chords and movements and emotions swirled through her body like life's blood. The music touched a well of sadness inside her, and her heart ached to know Bach—and Tom, her father—felt it in exactly the same way. Her left hand lifted and her fingers pressed invisible chords on an invisible violin. Her right arm pulled a ghostly bow back and forth to the music. She played along with him and knew he'd chosen this movement on purpose. With his violin, he could share with her his sorrow and regrets more eloquently than uttering a thousand words.

When the movement ended, and her father stopped playing, Seneca's sweat-dampened body slumped against the pillows in exhaustion. In her old room, the bedside light clicked off. The house grew silent and still again. She padded down the hall to the bathroom. She needed a shower.

Chapter 20

An icy wind rattled at the living room windows and crept under the front door. Seneca wrapped Momma's old crazy quilt more tightly around her shoulders and punched up her pillow. But sleep was elusive on the scratchy living room sofa.

She opened her eyes and stared at the shadows of wind-tossed branches writhing against the faded wallpaper. She tried to close her eyes again. The glow of the porch light seemed to penetrate her eyelids and they popped open. Reaching over her head, she grabbed her wristwatch from the end table. Eleven-fifteen. Why wasn't Collin back yet? Had something terrible happened to Peabody Hill?

A headlight sliced through the front window and flashed briefly across the living room wall. Then the Jeep pulled into the driveway. A door slammed. She rose from the sofa, pulling the crazy quilt with her as the front door opened.

He was surprised to see her. "What are you doing up?" He flung his field jacket on a hook by the door. Then he answered his own question. "Peabody Hill is fine. Doc just wants to keep him for a few days so he doesn't put too much pressure on his shoulder."

"Good. I'm glad."

He limped across the room to her, and she realized for the first time the left knee on his jeans was shredded and bloody. "Where's your father?"

"He went to bed. He's sleeping in my room. It used to be his, and he wanted to sleep there tonight."

He frowned. "You can't sleep down here. You take the bedroom. I'll get my gear and bunk on the sofa."

"Don't be impossible. It's barely long enough for me. Besides, I'll be fine down here. You go on up to bed."

He limped closer until he was standing over her. Dark stubble covered his face, and weariness creased the corners of his eyes. Three butterfly bandages held an angry-looking gash together on his cheek. The scent of his perspiration stung her nostrils. He studied her until she was breathless.

She had to say something. "I mean it, Collin. Don't try to be noble because I'm not going to let you."

A corner of his mouth quirked up. His hands cupped her jaw. He lowered his head and kissed her hungrily, devouring her lips, her mouth, her tongue, her teeth. The crazy quilt slid off her shoulders when she let go to press her hands against his solid chest and kiss him back.

His hands slid down her throat and slipped the straps of her pajama top off her shoulders. She shivered as chilly air hit her breasts. His head dropped. He planted a soft, wet kiss in the hollow of her throat. Her legs wobbled, and her knees buckled. Her bottom hit the sofa.

He sank with her, hunkering in front of her, a soldier even in intimacy. He kissed the valley between her breasts, his beard brushing roughly against the sides of her tender skin. He traced a path up one mound to her nipple, wetting it as he sucked. Exquisite pleasure rose from below her belly.

He lifted his head. "Do you want me to stop, Sen?"

She released a long sigh. "No."

His warm hands pressed against her spine and his wide, generous mouth moved across the top of her other breast to slip the nipple into his mouth. He sucked and played and teased with his tongue and teeth. She buried her nose in his soft hair and curled her body around his head and shoulders. He took her breasts in his hands. "Perfect," he whispered into her neck.

She smiled and slid down his body until she knelt in front of him. She rubbed at his gorgeous chest and his male nipples hardened under his shirt. She groped for the hem of his shirt. "Can I—can you . . ."

He pulled the T-shirt over his head and tossed it aside. She stared at him. Dark hair covered a broad, tanned chest, the muscles were well-defined and powerful. The darkness tapered to a vee below his pecs, trailing over a flat abdomen to disappear into the waistband of his jeans. He waited until she drank her fill. He was a treat after Michael's thin, hairless chest. She laid her palms against his nipples and tipped her head up. "You're beautiful."

He planted a kiss on top of her head. "Come here." He pulled her legs out from under her and laid her on the living room carpet. He pushed his wadded-up tee shirt under her head. She rolled her head away from him to breath in his male scent clinging to the dark fabric. When she turned back he was stretched out on the floor beside her.

She closed her eyes as his mouth descended on hers and his hand slid into her pajama bottoms. Warmth coiled through her body as long fingers teased a trail down her belly and across her inner thighs. Then his finger moved between her legs, and he probed her wetness and softness. His fingers shifted, and he found the center of her warmth.

Her breath caught at the new sensation as gentle fingers turned the fire into an inferno. *Why didn't she feel this way when Michael touched her?*

Seneca's breaths turned to short gasps. Her spine arched up as she sought something just out of her reach. He rose to his knees and pulled off her pajama bottoms. A veil began to lift. She wanted something from him. Something . . . If she could just see her way to the other side. Then he tore the veil in half, as he curled his long body and bent his head and kissed each inner thigh, reducing her conscious world to the places on her body touched by his mouth. His tongue probed, licked, and caressed until she cried out and her body was rising up to him, responding in a way she never experienced. When she came it was in shudders that shook every part of her body. The words spilled out before she could stop them. "I didn't know."

He lifted his head and looked at her. His mouth curved into a wicked grin. "I was right. Nature boy doesn't turn you on."

Bare-chested, rumpled blond hair reflected in the glow of the porch light, a heart-stopping bulge in the front of his jeans, he looked deliciously sexy. She raised her arms. "Come here."

"Answer me."

Not happening. "He's special in his own way."

His eyes widened. "I get it. He was your first."

"Jeez, Collie! Do you want to talk about sex or have it?"

"First I want to talk about it."

Her warm after-sex glow was fading, replaced by irritation. "Fine. I was a twenty-four-year-old virgin when I left Peabody. I've been with exactly one man in my life. Michael. Go ahead and laugh if you want."

He pulled her up and hugged her close to his chest. "I want you upstairs with me tonight."

*

Seneca sat on the edge of Poppy's bed and watched Collin toss his black T-shirt on the floor. There was a streak of mud across his forehead, charcoal dust peppered his cheeks, and the backs of his hands were mud-splattered. He examined his hands and the blown-out knee of his jeans then looked at Seneca.

"Give me ten minutes to shower and clean up."

He pulled his Dopp kit from his duffel and left the room. The door closed behind him with a soft click.

She listened to the shower go on down the hall and tried not to think about what she was about to do, which was probably throw away her life. Okay, Collin had just proved that Michael couldn't turn her on. Was that important? And what was she going to do with Collin? Did she care about him? Or was he a catalyst, forcing to face her true feelings for Michael?

The door opened, and Collin slipped into the room. He smelled of shaving cream and deodorant soap. He'd wrapped a towel from the bathroom around his hips. She surveyed his freshly shaved face, his broad chest, his narrow waist and hips. Her eyes slid further down, and she noticed the thick gauze taped to his knee. The end of a black thread poked out the top of the white square. "Did you go to the hospital?"

"No."

"You have stitches on your knee."

"Yup."

"You let a veterinarian treat you? An animal doctor?"

With one hand holding the towel around his hips, he gazed at her through his eyelashes. Then he flicked off the lamp beside the bed, and the room was plunged in darkness. The towel dropped to the floor. "Get into bed, Sen."

Her heart began to thud, but she obeyed, and he slid in beside her. "You didn't answer my question. Did you or did you not—"

His finger pressed against her lips. "Stop talking."

Why was she suddenly so nervous? They'd nearly done this on the living room floor. Yes, but that was playful and accidental. This was love-making. His body shifted beside her in the bed, and he raised himself on his elbow and looked down in her face.

He lifted one of her hands and planted a kiss on the palm of her hand, then his mouth pressed against her inner wrist, the crook of her elbow, the soft skin where her arm met her shoulder, her neck where a tiny pulse throbbed. His kisses burned her skin then cooled as the wetness from his mouth lingered. She forgot about stitches and pajamas and most of all, Michael.

He bent over her body and kissed her other arm. She raised her just-kissed arms, looping them around his neck and felt his warm skin beneath her hands. He lifted his head, tilted his mouth over hers and brushed his lips against hers. The kiss was so gentle and fragile it felt like a he was worshipping a goddess. His kiss deepened then into a luscious ballet of tongues and teeth, but she tucked away the memory of his goddess kiss.

Seneca's skin came alive under his palms as they glided down her shoulders, pushed the straps of her thin top down her arms and exposed her breasts to him. Downstairs he gave her instant gratification, but now that she was in his bed, he played. He swept his fingers around her breasts, touching every inch of her skin as if to memorize it. She arched up at him, begging for him to hurry up and touch her nipples. *Please.* He pulled his mouth from hers and bent his head to her breasts. *Finally.* But he was in no hurry. His tongue tasted the skin his finger touched, licking wet circles across her aroused skin.

"Please, Collie." Her nails dug into his shoulder, her mouth sucked at the cords of his neck.

He lifted his head. "We're dancing, baby. I lead, you follow."

He pressed a light kiss on her lips before dropping his head again. His tongue flicked at one of her pebbled nipples and she gasped. His tongue flicked again, barely touching her breast. An exquisite sensation of warmth and wetness and expectation flowed through her. His tongue touched her other nipple in the same gentle licks, until it was moist.

Her thighs grew damp with desire. She brushed her hands down the smooth curve of his back and over his backside, pressing his hardness close to her thighs. He pushed away from her until her arms loosened from his back. He pulled her top down, stretching it over her waist and down her legs, along with her pajama bottoms. He threw them on the floor behind him. Freed from the thin shreds shielding his skin from hers, she threw her leg across his raised hip and pressed herself against his erection.

Collin raised his head, and she looked up at him. His eyes were dark with passion. He kissed her eyelids before slanting his mouth over hers again. With her leg slung wantonly over his hip, she was exposed to him, and he took full advantage. His hands slid over the curve of her back, lingering at her waist before brushing over her bottom and between her legs. His finger slid inside her and her body pulsed around it. His other hand pushed her legs higher on his waist. "You're already wet again." He kneaded her bottom with both hands, stretching her, preparing her body for him. She was hot with need, hungry for him to take her. She rubbed herself against his belly until he pushed her back on the bed and spread her thighs. His fingers played between her legs, caressing her desire. Her hips rose to meet each caress. *Hurry!* But he was still slow dancing.

Seneca released his neck. Her hands slid over his chest and across his belly until they closed around his penis. Hard, hot, silky smooth, it burned in her palm. She tightened her fist around him until he groaned. He rolled on top of her and settled between her legs.

Her hips lifted, and she pressed herself against him, inviting him to enter her, but he pushed himself up, his manhood rubbing leisurely against her wetness. She opened her eyes and looked up. He was watching her, his expression intent and serious. She reached up and caressed his face and wondered what he was thinking about.

His eyes closed. He dropped his head to her mouth and slowly, gently—as if he had all the time in the world—gave her another goddess kiss. Then with a sharp intake of breath, he pushed himself inside her, stretching her and filling her. She lifted her hips urging him to thrust deeper. His sweet loving turned forceful as he drove himself into her again and again. They rocked together, arms locked tightly around the other's sweat-slicked bodies. Her desire broke against him in shudders that rolled through her body in one exquisite wave after another. She opened her eyes. Collin, his eyes black with passion, his face twisted with pleasure, was watching her as he came.

They held each other. His head rested against her breasts, and her legs were wrapped around his waist. Seneca listened to his breath slow and his body relaxed in her arms. He raised his head and gave the valley between her breasts a light kiss. "Good night." He slipped off her and turned away.

She stared at his back for a few moments. Sex with him was amazing. Must be chemistry. She frowned as she recalled what Collin said to her while he made love to her.

"How come the girl can't lead? How come the guy always ends up on top?"

The only response she got was a soft snore. He was already asleep.

It *had* been a long day. Who would have guessed when she got up this morning she would have the adventure of a lifetime, meet her father for the first time, listen to Poppy's house come alive with music and end up in bed with Collin. Nothing would ever be the same for her after today. She yawned and turned away from him, scooting backward in the bed until her bottom was touching his. Moments later, she was asleep, too.

Chapter 21

Seneca snuggled under the sheets, the soft brush of Collin's body against hers an irresistible temptation to stay in bed just a little longer. She listened to the sound of the wind whistle through the trees and rattle at the windows. She turned her head and pressed her nose into his shoulder, inhaling the scent of soap and sleep on his skin.

His regular breathing sputtered and his body stretched. His mouth moved against her neck, his breath warm and sweet against her tender skin, his teeth nibbling her earlobes as his hands explored whatever they touched.

"Good morning." The whispered words fluttered against her ear.

"Mmmmm."

"After I gave what I thought was a pretty awesome performance last night, I believe I heard someone complain as I fell asleep."

She twisted onto her side so she could see him. "I didn't complain. I made an observation." She smiled at him through half-closed eyes. "I thought it was nice, didn't you?"

He cocked an eyebrow. "Nice?"

She slid the palms of her hands up his chest, stopping for a moment on his pecs. "Okay. Awesome."

"That's better." He pressed his lips against hers and gave her a long good morning kiss. "So you want to be on top."

"If you think you can handle it, lieutenant."

"Try me." He rolled onto his back.

She propped her head on one hand and trailed the fingers of her other hand over his chest and down past his waist, stopping just short of his penis, which already stood erect. "This is hardly a challenge."

He growled and pulled her to him. She studied his eyes, already dark and glazed. "Have mercy on me, Sen."

She smiled wickedly. With her teeth she peppered his neck with little love bites before she slipped on top of him and straddled his hips. His hands cupped her breasts and fondled them. Seneca leaned over him, burying her mouth and nose in his hair. His mouth closed over each breast, and he kissed and suckled until her body throbbed with desire. She pulled away from him, lifted her hip, and took him inside her, enjoying the play of expressions on his face—concentration, desire, pleasure—as he watched her slowly descend on him.

"You're so beautiful, Sen."

His hand found the place where their bodies joined and he slid his fingers between them and caressed her. Her head rolled back and she closed her eyes, savoring the light press of his fingers against her. She loved being in control, and since this was payback for torturing her last night, she wasn't ready to give him what he wanted just yet. She lifted her hip and took him in her hand again, rubbing against him in a slow, teasing, circular motion. His hips bucked up but she held herself outside his reach.

With a deep, masculine growl, he rose up and flipped her over on her back. His knees wedged her legs apart. She surrendered, lifting her hips to him. As he plunged inside her, she wrapped her legs around his waist and met each thrust with her own until pleasure spiraled through her, and he stiffened and strained above her.

She looked up into his face. "You cheated."

His eyes gleamed. "Now you know why the guys get the top."

"Because you can't control yourselves?"

He dropped a light kiss on her lips. "Because we're stronger."

Contentment flowed through her like hot soup on a cold day. "I'm attracted to you something powerful, Collie."

"Me too." He kissed her again. "What are you going to do about it?" His expression sobered.

"My father asked me that same question last night."

"Your father?"

"He asked about you, or us, really. I couldn't lie. The Simms family has kept enough skeletons locked away in the closet." She tried to smile, but her mouth refused to turn up at the corners. "I told him about Michael. I may have also mentioned that I was attracted to you."

"What did he say?"

"He said I couldn't keep both of you."

"Your father is a master of the obvious." The butterfly bandages on his cheek stretch as his jaw muscles tensed. "What about Michael?"

"I don't know. It's complicated."

She watched his eyes turn icy blue. "I think it's pretty simple. Either you want to be with him or you want to be with me."

"I-I-I think I want to be with you, but the wedding—and-and the house. I won't have anywhere to live, and all my savings went into our home."

His grip on her shoulders tightened until her muscles ached. "So you would marry a man just to have a roof over your head? Is that what you just said?"

"No! Let go of me!" She pushed his hands away.

The anger on his face melted into defeat. He pulled the covers aside and sat up. "This was a mistake."

"Collie, wait."

His head dropped.

"This is hard for me."

"Do you think it's easy for me?"

She knelt up behind him and laid her hands on his shoulders. "It's not the house and the money. I swear on Momma's old bible."

"What then?"

"It's hard to find the right words to say how I feel."

Beneath her fingers, his muscles stiffened. "Try."

"Please don't be angry with me. Come back to bed."

With a deep sigh, he lay down and drew her into his arms.

She kissed his right pec. "I made a commitment to Michael. How can I look at myself in the mirror if I just walk away?"

"People break up all the time."

"We're getting married a week from Saturday. Would you respect me if I called off the marriage because I found this really hot guy that rocks my world in bed?"

His voice was tight. "That's all I am to you?"

She tried to nuzzle his chest, but he pulled away. She sighed. "I don't know what you are to me. I don't know anything anymore. I have a new father and a new lover and my dog got shot and I'm broke and my fiancé expects me to move in with him tonight. That pretty much sums up my current circumstances."

"Marrying Michael is the solution?"

"I admire Michael. At first the whole environmental movement didn't grab me, but he's convinced me it's worth devoting my life to."

"So what you're saying is you depend on Poindexter to give your life meaning."

"Why are you being purposely obtuse? That's not what I said."

"Sounded like it to me."

She pushed him away from her and sat up, pulling the sheet up with her to cover her breasts. "Michael is doing something important. He knows what he wants and he's not afraid to fight for it. I find that attractive."

"And you don't believe I possess those 'attractive qualities.'"

"*I* don't. Lots of people meander through life and never know what they want or where they fit in. Lots of people, including me."

"And me." He yanked the sheet out of her hands and pulled her under him again. He kissed her deeply and thoroughly. Her loins melted all over again. When he came up for air, he said, "Maybe we can help each other figure it out."

Outside, a dog that sounded like Peabody Hill began to bark.

Her father's voice called "Aida!" Then Henry Stiles shouted, "Hey, there!"

"Shit." Collin jumped out of bed, pulled on a pair of black boxer briefs and his desert camo pants, grabbed a tan tee shirt as he slipped his feet into a pair of battered topsiders and raced out of the bedroom. The door banged shut behind him.

Less than a minute later, Collin was in the yard below. "Mornin', Henry. Mornin' Tom."

She sat up and groped on the floor for her pajamas. She pulled them on and went to the window to see what was happening in the yard below. The three men were gathered at the fence, Henry on his side, Collin and Tom on the Simms' side. Seneca watched Collin nod while Henry talked excitedly. Her father huddled beside Collin. Finally Henry ran out of things to say. Collin began to speak. She watched his hands gesture with palms held open in supplication. She could tell he was begging Henry not to broadcast the news that Tom Simms was home. Whatever he said must have hit the right note for Henry. He nodded, then shook Collin's hand and went back into his house. Collin guided her father back into the house with a firm hand on his shoulder and Aida followed.

Seneca pulled out her jeans and grabbed one of Poppy's pale blue oxford shirts from the closet and put it on. The tails hung down to her thighs and the cuffs past her finger tips, but it covered her. She rolled up the sleeves and went downstairs.

Collin and her father were in the living room. Collin paced back and forth, covering the small room in three strides before he pivoted on the heels of his topsiders and strode back the way he came. She arrived just as he said, "We have to take things one step at a time, Tom." He spoke gently despite his agitation.

Her father sat on the sofa watching him mournfully. "Sorry."

When Seneca appeared, her father excused himself with a few mumbled words and ran upstairs to take his first shower in several dozen years.

"I'm leaving to check on Peabody Hill and make a coffee and breakfast run," said Collin. While I'm gone, you guard the doors. No one enters the house. No one leaves the house. That means knowing where you father is *at all* times. Are we clear?"

Seneca didn't much care for the raw recruit treatment, especially from her lover. She saluted him. "Whatever you say, lieutenant honey, sir."

She watched as he struggled to maintain a straight face, then gave up. "Come here." He slipped an arm around her waist, pulled her against him and soul-kissed her until her knees gave out. "Just keep an eye on him until I get back, okay?"

After he drove away with Aida in tow, Seneca lifted her father's guitar from Poppy's old easy chair and sat down. She propped the guitar against the end table and listened to the shower go off upstairs and her father's footsteps patter down the hall to his room. What would Poppy think about his son returning home. Did he know the police just wanted to talk to his son, not lock him up, or did he always believe his son would go to prison if he left his hiding place on Peabody Ridge?

Seneca picked at the wires of the guitar as she considered the imponderable question. The pings were metallic and strong. The vibrations flowed from her index finger through her body. Music was meant to live in this house. While she listened to her father play last night, the house had come alive around her, and Momma and Poppy's memories came alive too. She ran her fingers over the guitar wires.

"You play the guitar?"

She jumped. Her father had managed to get down the stairs and into the living room without making a sound. Lieutenant Atlee would be most displeased with her if he knew.

She snatched her hand away from the guitar as if it burned her. "No. Never have."

"Would you like to?"

"Not now." She would play music again. She would! But she wasn't ready.

Her father came around the chair and into the living room. Collin had lent him his razor so his face was freshly shaved, but his home-chopped hair hung down to his chin and even with a clean denim shirt from Poppy's closet, he looked like an escapee from the insane asylum. Her father was taller and thinner than Poppy so the shirt hung on him and the sleeves reached just past his elbows. The old denim overalls didn't help but none of Poppy's pants would fit him. He carried his violin and bow.

He caught her critical gaze. "I'm a sight for sore eyes, aren't I?"

"You just need some clothes that fit and a decent haircut."

"Yeah." He sat on the couch opposite her.

"I heard you play last night."

"What did you think?"

"I wished Poppy could hear it."

"Me too."

He bowed his head and concentrated on the braided rug at his feet. "The hardest part of being stuck up there was watching the fight drain out of him and knowing it was my fault and there wasn't a single thing I could do about it. When he told me he gave up music and joined the post office, I cried for a week." He tried to look at her, but his eyes shifted away. "I'd sight a rabbit for dinner and suddenly tears would start to leak out. Didn't eat too well for a time."

An uncomfortable silence filled the room. She rooted around in her head for something to say. "It was Bach, wasn't it? Last night. The music you played."

"Yeah. In A minor." He lifted his head and studied her for a moment. "Would you like me to play something for you?"

"Yes."

"What would you like to hear?"

The first time she heard him play, it had been the wispy

tendrils of Beethoven's "Ode to Joy" drifting down Peabody Hill like incense, and she'd inhaled deeply and known she had to get away from Peabody. She wanted to be moved like the first time. She was engaged to Michael and falling for Collin. Could her father's music could reach into her soul again and help her to make another hard decision? "Beethoven's Ninth."

He studied her, tilting his head to the side as he considered her request. "Of course, daughter."

He tucked the violin under his chin and drew the bow across the strings a few times, then the music began to rise from the violin in stormy waves as he played the first movement. She leaned back in the chair and closed her eyes. No thoughts disturbed her, no worries pricked at her. Her whole being, body and soul, listened to the music. The familiar three beat followed by a fourth downbeat began to emerge. She hummed under her breath, afraid to disturb the musical perfection of the composition in her father's gifted hands.

The music slowed, became more lyrical, and her father's low, warm voice sang the words. The final movement ended, the music faded, and there was silence.

Like the night before when he'd played the violin concerto, she was wrung out and damp with sweat. She drooped in the chair with her eyes still closed, her eyelids too heavy to lift.

"You're crying." He spoke gently, but he sounded as exhausted as she felt.

She brushed the tears from her cheeks and opened her eyes. Worry lines creased his forehead. "I'm fine," she said.

"Good." He bowed his head again and stared down at his feet. When he looked back up at her, he was a little nervous.

"What, Dad? Is it all right if I call you that?"

He nodded. "Play something with me, daughter."

"I haven't played in years. Not since high school. I probably don't remember—"

"I'll help you."

"I don't have a violin anymore."

"Old Maggie's in the kitchen. I tuned her up this morning." He hung his head and waited.

Seneca swallowed hard. "I-I-I'll make a mess of it."

"That's okay. I would just like to play with you."

She went to the kitchen to fetch Old Maggie. It sat on the table waiting for her. She ran her fingers across the strings. Her father had tightened them and replaced a frayed one. He'd oiled the wood case until it gleamed. As she picked up Old Maggie and slid it under her chin, a memory of her girlhood popped into her head.

She'd race into the house just before dinner, and Poppy called to her from the kitchen. *Don't forget to wash your hands.* She was starving so she ran her hands once under the faucet and wiped them on the back of her jeans. Then she sat down at the kitchen table to watch him fill their plates at the stove. He turned to her and smiled. *Hope you're hungry, Sen.* His smile faded when he saw her face. *Are your hands clean?* She shook her head and felt ashamed. Poppy set the plate on the counter and came to her. Her heart was thudding as she waited for his anger to rise. But instead of scolding her, he bent over and kissed the top of her head. *You're a good girl, Sen. Now go wash your hands.*

"I love you, Poppy." She whispered the words into the empty kitchen. Then she went back to her father.

He looked up at her as she sat down. "What would you like to play, daughter?"

"Daughter. It sounds odd."

"I'm the only one in the world who can rightly call you daughter. But I'll stop if it bothers you."

"It's fine." She studied him. "How did I get the name Seneca?"

"What did Pop tell you?"

She shrugged. "He said he just liked it—him and Momma."

The lines at the corner of his eyes deepened, and he almost smiled. "When I told him your name, he said, 'What kind of crazy hippie name is that?' But I liked it. We liked it. Your mother and I."

"No hidden meaning or anything?"

"I was a rocker. We had to give you a cool name. There's a lake in upstate New York named Seneca. A songwriter I knew kept a big place up there so Sonny and I and the rest of the band flew there a few times. It was peaceful and beautiful. We thought of Lake Seneca when we named you."

"That's a good story. I like it."

"Well, Seneca, what are we going to play?"

She laid Old Maggie on her lap. "Dad, honest, I haven't played in years. I'll probably shatter your eardrums. Plus I don't remember the notes to anything."

But her father was determined. "What about a hymn? Did you learn to play hymns in church?"

"After Reverend McAllister told Poppy he would be struck down by a thunderbolt for his stubborn ways, I was allowed to sing in the choir and play the organ on Sundays."

"Reverend McAllister." His father shook his head at an unspoken memory. "Does he still have the old Wurlitzer? Is that what you played?"

"Yes. You?"

He nodded. "My first music lessons were on that old pipe organ. "

"Mine too."

"How about *Amazing Grace*? Can you play it on the fiddle?"

"I'm not sure, Dad."

He settled the violin under his chin. "I'll play it through once. You watch me and finger along without Old Maggie, then we'll try the real thing."

The violin that just rendered a heavenly Beethoven filled the house with the triumphant hymn of salvation and thanksgiving while she imitated her father's finger movements. When the last notes faded, her father looked over at her. "Ready?"

"I can't promise I'll be any good."

"Watch my foot. I'll tap out the meter. Trust your ear, then let go and feel the music. Don't worry about mistakes. It's just the two of us."

"Okay." She slid Old Maggie under her chin.

"On the count of five. One. Two. Three." His foot began to tap. "Four. Five."

She drew her bow across Old Maggie's strings. She hit the first note, but she put too much pressure on the bow and the chord turned into a squeal. She looked at her father. His eyes were closed. "Keep going," he said without opening them. "Watch my foot."

She did. They were about halfway through the hymn before the music became part of her. She let her fingers move against the strings without thinking and her arm drew the bow across the fiddle as naturally as a breath.

When they finished, her father opened his eyes. "Well done. Do you know the words?"

She nodded.

"Again then. Play it through once, then we'll sing."

This time she pulled the bow over Old Maggie's strings without a squeak and kept up with her father's foot. They played the hymn. Their instruments complimented each other—her father's high and clear, Seneca's rich and deep. Then they sang and their voices blended like their instruments into the perfect bouquet of high and low, rich and clear. Their eyes caught and held as they sang. Seneca lost her sense of time and place.

They finished singing the final verse and played the last chord. She looked up. Collin stood in the hall staring at her. He held a tray of coffee and orange juice and a bag of breakfast food from the Mountain Mist. Beside him, Aida showed off her new pink collar with proper dog tags dangling from it.

He looked stunned. Then he blinked and his eyes narrowed into hers. "How can anyone who plays and sings like you do believe they were born to hug trees?"

"Hug trees? What are you talking about?" Her father looked confused.

Collin jerked his head at Seneca. "Ask her." Then he disappeared into the kitchen.

Chapter 22

The kitchen table was scattered with the wrappings from bacon-and-egg sandwiches, and empty paper cups with the dregs of orange juice and coffee. Collin, unaware of the sacrilege, lounged in Poppy's chair. Seneca brushed stray crumbs into the palm of her hand and shook them onto the waxed paper square in front of her. Tom wiped his mouth on a paper napkin with *Mountain Mist* printed on it and raised his eyes to Collin's.

"I have some money in L.A. If you would stake me a few bucks, I'd like to buy some things this morning."

"Dad! I'll give you money."

"I don't want to take money from my daughter. I just need a small loan."

Her father had lived on a mountain top for decades. Whatever money he once had was surely gone by now. She already owed Collin five hundred dollars, and now that she had her father to take care of, Poppy's money would have to keep a roof over his head until she could figure out what to do with him. As much as the idea irked the hell out of her, she would have to work out an installment plan with Collin. Owing money to a guy she was sleeping with gave her a sick feeling in the pit of her stomach.

"Dad, Collin's a retired soldier with his own business. He doesn't have—"

"Sen, it's no problem. I can afford to front Tom some cash. Okay?" He turned to Tom. "I saw a big shopping center out on the highway when we came in. I'll drive you out there after we clean up the table."

Her father nodded. "'Preciate it."

She glared at Collin. He must have felt the heat, because he turned and looked at her. Whatever he read on her face, he chose to ignore. "Your father needs to tie up some unfinished business with the LAPD."

"Am I going to be okay?" Her father's voice shook.

Collin turned his gaze back to Tom. "Seems like it, but you have to talk to them. Seneca has a friend in the Public Defender's office here in Peabody. While we're out shopping, she'll call Janie for advice.

Collin was issuing orders again! Steam rose off the top of her head. Who did he think he was? This was her home and her problem and *her father!* "Anything else, lieutenant?"

"Tom, why don't you grab your coat and meet me out by the Jeep."

Her father's gaze swept from Collin's face to hers and back to Collin's. "Right," he said and rose from the table.

"You had no right to say yes." The last 's' slipped off her tongue like a hiss.

"Why not?" Collin's forehead furrowed and angry creases framed the corners of his mouth.

"My father hasn't seen a bank statement in almost thirty years. He could be flat broke for all we know. Poppy's five hundred dollars may be all the money we have and I've already promised that money to you!"

"You're just speculating about him. And as far as I'm concerned, I can look after myself just fine without you. Whether or not you pay me or whether or not Tom pays me back, I will manage."

"Why are you doing all this?"

He stared at her, his expression thunderous. "You know something? You're a lot nicer when you're naked."

Her head was about to explode. "How dare you!"

He leaned closer to her. "How dare I what, Sen? How dare I try to help you and your father? How dare I not pillage Poppy's bank account? How dare I presume to give *you* orders?"

Her anger turned to regret. "I'm acting like a bitch."

His hand slid across her shoulder. "I'm not being charitable. There is something in this for me."

"Like what?"

"I don't want to leave you down here. I want to take you back up to Chicago with me."

"Impossible." She folded her arms and studied him though narrowed eyes.

He leaned in and kissed her. "Possible. I just need a little cooperation . . . and a few more days."

She bit her bottom lip and considered this. She was broke and had two extra mouths to feed—if you counted Aida. Her job would be hanging by a thread after she called in sick for the rest of the week. If he could help her father get settled and have her out of Peabody by the weekend, she might still be employed on Monday. Of course, she was returning to Chicago with a lover in tow and a fiancé waiting for her. Still, one problem would be solved. That was worth a little cooperation. She held out her hand. "Peabody Hill ate my phone. I will need to borrow yours to call Janie."

As the Jeep pulled out of the driveway, Seneca made two calls to Chicago on the cell phone. The first to her boss to request a few more days off for a family emergency. After ten minutes of shouting, it was begrudgingly granted. The second call, to Michael, also went as she anticipated—not well. He was a busy man, and his fiancée's unexpected absence was a major disruption in his life.

When he answered the phone, his hello was tentative.

"It's me."

"Seneca, is that you? Where are you? What's happening? Who the hell is Collin Atlee?"

That threw her. "How do you know Collin?"

"Hello. You're on his phone."

"Oh. Ah, just someone here in Peabody. He let me borrow his phone since the dog ate mine."

"Are you okay? You sound distracted?"

"I'm fine. It's just that I'm going to need a few more days here. Th-there're some papers I have to, uh, sign about the house."

"You are aware our wedding is in exactly eleven days."

"Of course." She tried to sound excited, but her voice shook. "Michael?"

"What?"

"I've been thinking about taking up the violin—"

"Seneca." He sighed dramatically. "Didn't you say after your father died that it was a distraction. Why do you need a hobby anyway? We have so much to do. I'm meeting with the mayor's chief of staff next month about lakefront erosion, and next year the state senate campaign will start. I'll need you out shaking hands and helping with organization. Isn't that enough?"

The campaign! Tom's story was sure to come out. "Hey, I have a question for you. A friend of mine from school is married to a-a-a guy who is going to run for something down here, and she just found out that the man she thought was her father isn't. Her real father was a famous, ah, writer and sort of disappeared for awhile after his wife killed herself. She was my friend's real mother. Do think this will hurt her, ah, husband's campaign?"

"Sounds ridiculous to me. Are you sure your friend isn't making this up?"

"Just answer me. What do you think?"

"I think no one will care."

She tried to feel relieved, but she didn't. If he'd been horrified, she could end the engagement with a clear conscience. "I-I'm sure she'll be happy to hear that. It's been bothering her."

"Whatever." He cleared his throat. "When, exactly, do you expect to be back?"

She remembered what Collin said earlier. "A few days."

"A few days. Can you be more specific? Thursday? Friday? Saturday? Shall I keep going?

"Saturday, Michael. I'll see you Saturday."

"Will you be back in time for the rally? It starts at two."

"I'll try. How's you speech coming?"

"Not good. I guess my mother will have to help me since you won't be back in time. She'll have to order the cake and pick up your beeswax candle too."

To leave the smallest footprint possible on the environment, the wedding would take place at the nature center before a dozen friends and Michael's family. She would carry a beeswax candle in lieu of cut flowers and wear a peachy, lace-trimmed dress they found at a thrift shop. Afterwards, they would celebrate over unfiltered fruit juice and a vegan wedding cake.

"I'm sorry. Truly. I'll be home Saturday, and we'll have a long talk." *What was she going to say to him?*

They said goodbye, and she made her last call—the one she dreaded more than Michael. But Janie was warm and understanding once she got over her initial surprise. She promised to clear her afternoon schedule for Seneca and Tom.

She hung up with Janie and stood in the front hall, absorbing the stillness that filled the house. After Poppy died, the silence was so profound, the house was like a tomb to her. But not today. Today the silence was peaceful and warm. She studied her father's violin, which lay face-up on the sofa where he left it when he was called for breakfast. Beside her, Collin's muddy field jacket hung from a hook by the door. She reached out for one of the sleeves and pressed it to her nose. His scent lingered in the rough fabric. She closed her eyes and inhaled. For a time she stood with his sleeve pressed to her nose, eyes closed, thinking of nothing. Then she became self-conscious and turned away.

The pocket doors to the dining room had been closed since early September when she'd slammed them shut. She approached the doors, slid her fingers into the familiar brass recesses and pushed both doors back into their pockets. With arms flung wide, she studied the room.

A wooden Valencia orange crate sat on the table. Poppy kept all his important papers in it. Scattered around the crate were piles of receipts and minor documents still stacked just as she left them when she'd discovered the second birth certificate. Freaked out, she stuffed the certificate in her purse and fled the house as if the ghosts of Thomas and Sonja Simms were chasing her.

She stepped up to the long oak table and brushed off a thick layer of dust with the sweep of her hand. Seven of the eight chairs were tucked under the table. The eighth lay on its back where it fell when she read the certificate and jumped up in shock.

No one had ever eaten in this room when she was growing up. It was the place where she did her homework and Poppy sat across from her when he paid the monthly bills. She studied the matching oak hutch. On its shelves, gaily painted plates and gold-rimmed goblets had sat untouched for a lifetime. Two tall brass candlesticks with faded yellow candles waited for the party that never happened. *How come we never eat in here, Poppy? Not without Momma, Sen. This was her special room.* The walls were papered with faded yellow-buttercup wallpaper and the chairs upholstered in worn yellow-and green-checked fabric. A thick film of dust covered everything, even the stacks of papers. It was time to clean away the old. Her father was home and he'd brought music back into the house.

She went to the kitchen, pulled out a dishtowel to tie back her hair and got to work. The dining room of her childhood began to emerge from the dust. She put away the orange crate—she'd found what Poppy intended—then dusted the furniture until it gleamed. She washed the windows, she vacuumed, she shined the candlesticks and washed Momma's plates and goblets. She moved on to the living room, wiping away months of grime and dust before tackling the kitchen. She'd just finished mopping the kitchen floor when the front door opened. Collin and her father were home, hauling a dozen shopping bags in their hands.

Her father's hair was cut just like Collin's, short on the sides, a little length on top. He was also wearing desert camo pants, a tan T-shirt and a leather jacket exactly like Collin. Seneca looked from her father to Collin.

"Really, Collin, how could you?" But she was pleased. Her father looked years younger.

Collin and her father looked at each other. "Told you," said Collin. He took stock of the clean house. "Looks like a different house, Sen. Nice job." Then he turned back to Tom. "Let's get the rest of your things in."

Her eyes widened. "There's more? Oh, Collin!"

One of his perfect eyebrows arched. "Cooperation. Remember?"

She sighed. "I remember." Saturday. She'd promised Michael she'd be home by Saturday. "I'll help unpack the car."

Collin and her father had gone on a mini-shopping spree. In addition to clothing, shoes, outerwear and toiletries, they'd bought an iPod, a laptop and a cell phone. They'd stopped for groceries, too—a dozen bags of staples, dog food, frozen dinners, plus chocolate bars and soft drinks. But the final item they pulled out of the Jeep made her squeal with horror.

"Collin Atlee! We can't afford that!" It was a widescreen TV.

"Don't worry, daughter. I have money in L.A."

"Dad—"

"Seneca." Collin's voice held a warning. She opened her mouth to respond, but he talked first. "Did you call Janie?"

"Yes. She seemed to think everything would be fine. We have an appointment after lunch."

"Wonderful." He reached out and brushed at a smudge on her cheek. Then he took her by the shoulders and turned her toward the stairs. "Why don't you go upstairs and get cleaned up? Tom and I will fix sandwiches."

She sighed again, this time in heavy forbearance. "Why am I the only one around here who has to cooperate?" But she went.

*

The interview with Janie proved to be routine and positive. Tom answered all her questions, and when Janie told him she didn't believe there were grounds for prosecution, he insisted she call the LAPD. He wanted resolution, he told her. He gave a lengthy statement to Collin's contact, answered a few follow-up questions, and he was a free man.

Afterward Janie walked them out of the building. "I guess we'll see you tonight, Sen."

That stopped her in her tracks. "Tonight?"

"Yes. Collin called just before you arrived and invited Jim and me and the boys for dinner."

Chapter 23

From the Simms porch, Collin watched Seneca back the Jeep out of the driveway and roar off to the County Building with her father. As soon as the Jeep disappeared over the hill, he pulled his phone out and checked the call history. She'd called Poindexter as he'd known she would. But their conversation lasted less than ten minutes, which didn't leave much time for pillow talk once she explained what had happened. His eyes narrowed. If she'd even explained anything to him.

Satisfied, he made a quick call to Janie and to Mush and invited them for dinner. The idea of hosting a small get-together came from Collin's time doing community relations in Special Forces. He'd seen how people who shared a meal grew close. Despite his assurances to Seneca, he wasn't convinced Tom would be ready to fly solo in a few days. Linking him back into the Peabody community so he had a support structure would help him live independently and free Seneca to return to Chicago to break up with Poindexter.

He stuck his phone in his back pocket and strolled over to Henry's. The front door swung open on his first knock.

"Collin!" Henry stuck his head out of the door and peered at the Simms house. "Where's Tommy?" he asked in a low voice.

"He and Seneca are running errands. They'll be back later. I came over to see if you and Katy would like to join us for dinner tonight. We're having a little welcome home party for Tom and Aida."

"Aida?"

"Tom's dog. She's Peabody Hill's sister. Anyway, it would be nice if Aida and Katy could be friends."

"Where's Peabody Hill?" He stuck his head out of the door again to study the Simms house.

"Had a little hunting accident but he'll be fit as a fiddle in a few days."

Henry shook his head. "Darn hunters."

"Yeah. Say, I was wondering if you could give me a hand. I need some help getting ready for tonight."

"Sure thing."

An hour later, they chugged into the Simms driveway with planks of plywood strapped to the roof of Henry's '95 Pontiac Bonneville. The trip to the lumberyard took a little longer than Collin anticipated because the Bonneville stalled out twice. But after a brief rest and a little coaxing, it started up again and got them home just a little behind schedule. They lifted the plywood off the roof and carted it over to the porch where Henry built a makeshift ramp so Mush could get into the house under his own steam.

Henry was pounding the last few nails into place when Seneca pulled the Jeep into the driveway. Collin, who held a plywood plank in place for him, straightened up. Seneca had fought him every step of the way on this mission. Was she going to fight him on the party too?

One look at her expression as she stepped out of the Jeep, and he had his answer. Yes.

"What are you doing!"

He girded himself for battle. "What do you mean?"

She stamped up to him, green eyes flashing, auburn hair flying, hands on hips, and he was in love all over again. "Are you serious? What do you think I mean? I mean what is *this*?" Her gaze swept down to the ramp, then back up to him.

"It's a ramp."

Anger stained her cheeks a bright pink, but she managed to keep herself under control. "I know it's a ramp, Collin. I can see it's a ramp." Her voice began to rise. "Why are you building it?"

Henry set down the hammer and removed the nails he held in his mouth for easy plucking. He was wide-eyed and looked just a little nervous. Tom, who stood just behind Seneca, stared down at his feet.

"I invited Matt for dinner. He needs the ramp to get in the house."

"Don't you think you should have talked with me before you invited people over? My father—"

"He talked to me. I thought it would be okay," said Tom. His apprehension clashed with the authority of the pale blue oxford shirt and trim gray slacks he'd worn to his meeting with Janie.

Seneca turned to her father. "Dad, are you sure you're ready for company?"

"I'd like to feel comfortable here in Peabody. Collin said he would introduce me to a few friends. I didn't think you'd mind."

"I-I-I don't mind." She looked confused and unhappy.

"I'm sorry, baby," said Collin. "I should have talked to you first." Not true since she would have given him a flat out 'no!', but he wouldn't embarrass her in front of Henry and Tom for the world.

Tom met his eyes and raised an eyebrow. Collin hadn't fooled him. But it mollified Seneca, and Henry, too, who popped four nails between his teeth and went back to work on the ramp.

Tom was full of surprises. He'd shed his shuffling, hermit-like persona with the enthusiasm of a man sprung from the penitentiary. At their first stop, an upscale men's store, he'd known his size and exactly what he wanted. Later, he'd made his way up and down the aisles of Wal-Mart as if he'd been shopping all his life. He'd insisted on changing his clothes in Wal-Mart and getting his hair cut. After the haircut, he'd thrown his old clothes into a dumpster behind the shopping center before dragging Collin into Best Buy.

Collin was alarmed by his rapid transformation. "Maybe you should slow it down a little, Tom." They stood in front of the iPod display where Tom had just asked him to explain what an iPod did.

"I never thought I'd get a second chance at life. But I have one now, and I don't want to waste it."

"Will you go back to California?"

Tom shook his head. "Not to live. If I'd stayed in Peabody I wouldn't have lost my values. I want to make music again, but no matter where I play, I'll always come home to Peabody."

"Not much happening here."

"I'll keep busy. Pop always worried that the old Appalachia music was dying out. Maybe I can do something to save it before it's gone for good. For Pop's sake."

That's when the idea of the party popped into Collin's head. Tom loved it. "What I missed most these past years was playing for other people. I suppose it's not cool to care whether anyone listens to my music, but the experience is more intense with other people around." Then he returned to his iPod inspection.

*

When Collin pulled out of the driveway to pick up Matt for dinner, the stars were spread across the sky like a blanket. Beneath them, the Simms house was shadowy and quiet. The few lights came from the bedrooms upstairs where Tom played his guitar and Seneca was changing her clothes. They were both a little nervous about the party. Had he gone too far? Maybe Tom—and Seneca—weren't ready to open their home to people yet. Would tonight turn into another Collin Atlee screw-up?

When he returned with Matt, he was relieved to see the house ablaze with lights and the Highsmith's minivan parked at the front curb. As he trotted around the side of the Jeep to help Matt, he saw Henry and Katy emerge from the Stiles house. He began to relax.

Matt was settling into his wheelchair as Henry and Katy came up the driveway.

"Evenin' Collin."

"Henry, I want you to meet Matt Peterson. Matt's an old

buddy of mine from boot camp. Turns out he and Seneca were schoolmates."

Henry extended his hand and shook Matt's. "Mighty nice to meet you, son. Got two grandsons in Afghanistan."

"God bless 'em," said Matt. "Hope they make it home safe and sound."

"I pray every day." Henry looked sad for a moment, then seemed to recall he was going to a party. "What are you up to in Peabody?"

"I work at the old repair shop across from the county building." Henry nodded.

"Matt's going to school in Jotham to study computers. He just needs to line up some transportation."

Henry's dark eyes were sad. "We should do a better job looking after our boys. I'd drive you myself, but my old Bonneville is on its last leg."

Matt's wide grin beamed up at Henry. "'preciate the thought." Then he slapped his knees with both hands. "Hey, is this a party or a funeral?"

"Sorry," said Collin. "Don't know how we got on this subject." But he did because he'd introduced the 'subject' just as he'd planned to do ever since the idea of the party popped into his head. "Let's go in. I'll grab the pizzas."

Matt spun his wheelchair around and saw the ramp. "Zowie, Hollywood! Did you do this for me?"

"Henry put it together this afternoon. He's mighty talented with wood and nails. You ought to see his house."

"Thanks, man," he said to Henry.

Henry nodded, and in the glow of the porch light, Collin saw tears fill the old man's eyes. "Glad to do it." He cleared his throat and looked down at Katy. "Come on, girl, let's go meet our new neighbors."

They walked up the steps to the house and Matt followed, rolling up the makeshift ramp under his own steam. Collin brought up the rear with a stack of pizza cartons in his arms.

Inside, the Highsmiths had made themselves at home. Little Jake sat on the living floor petting Aida's back and playing with her floppy ears while his baby brother slept in a baby carrier nearby. The Highsmiths must have brought refreshments with them because Seneca and Janie sipped wine from gold-rimmed goblets while Tom and Jim Highsmith held cans of beer. They stood in a half-circle near the front door.

Tom called out to Henry. "Hey, look at me!"

Henry's bushy eyebrows popped up in surprise. "Tom? Wouldn't have hardly recognized you from this morning."

Tom brushed a hand over his cropped red hair. He'd changed back into desert camo pants and a brown T-shirt. "Did a little shopping."

Henry studied him, then he glanced around, taking note of Collin's desert camo pants and Matt's desert camo field jacket. "Gonna have to get me some of those camouflage pants and maybe a jacket too. Look comfortable."

They all laughed. "Well, now," replied Collin, "you better be careful. Someone might mistake you for a soldier and ship you overseas."

"That would be okay with me. Wouldn't mind seeing a little action."

Everyone laughed again. Collin and Seneca made the introductions, then Seneca went to the kitchen to grab a few more beers for the newcomers, while everyone else—except for the sleeping baby—followed Collin and his pizzas into the dining room.

"Ordered the pizzas from Giovanni's," Collin said. "Henry told me it was the best place in town for pizza."

Tom grew misty-eyed. "I haven't eaten Giovanni's pizza since I was a kid."

"What can I get you, ladies?" Collin asked. He picked up a paper plate. "We have cheese, pepperoni, and deluxe."

"Cheese!" It was little Jake. He sat next to Janie on a stack of Poppy's ancient phone books.

"One slice of cheese pizza coming up." He handed the plate to Janie who set it in front of Jake and broke the wedge into bite-size pieces for him.

"Everyone, grab a plate and dig in." Collin's eyes swept the table stopping at Seneca who'd handed around the beers, then seated herself across the table from him. Her cheeks were flushed from the wine and her eyes glowed. He loved her so much, he ached with the knowledge. Janie, who sat beside her, leaned toward her and whispered in her ear. Seneca tilted her head back and giggled, and her eyes met his. She sobered. He suddenly felt exposed. Lowering his lashes, he gave her his sexiest smile.

The seven adults and one little boy demolished the four extra-large pizzas. Tom alone consumed five slices—one cheese, one pepperoni and three deluxe—amid much friendly teasing.

Henry patted his full stomach. "Thanks Collin." Haven't ordered from Giovanni's since my grandsons went away. "Still the best pizza in West Virginia. I'd stake Giovanni's against anything they make in Los Angeles *or* Chicago." As he said 'Chicago' he looked at Seneca. "Say Seneca, are you sticking around for awhile now that Tom's back?"

Seneca's smile faded. "I-I don't know exactly."

There was a clumsy silence, then Tom came to his daughter's aid. "Enough conversation. Before we call it night we should have some music."

"Great idea!" they all chorused. For a moment, Henry appeared confused, then he smiled. "Hope you remember *Barbara Allen*, Tom. No one could ever play it better than you."

"Of course, I remember it. One of Pop's favorites." He rose from his chair and one by one all the guests followed. Collin made a detour to the kitchen to make coffee. He listened to Tom and Seneca tune up their fiddles as he pulled a can of coffee out of a cabinet and dug around in the drawer for a spoon to measure the grounds.

"You got it pretty bad, don't you?" The voice was soft and low.

He concentrated on scooping the coffee into the basket. "I don't know what you're talking about."

"I think you do. I saw the way you looked at her during dinner." Janie took a few steps closer and lowered her voice. "I couldn't believe I forgot the name of my best friend's fiancé. So I checked my emails. You aren't her fiancé or at least your weren't engaged to her a week ago."

He poured water into the coffeemaker and turned it on. "It's not her fault."

"Fill me in. What's going on?"

He gave her a brief rundown—two birth certificates, hired to find out why, needed a cover story—omitting the more succulent details, but not much got past Janie.

"You left out the fact you're sleeping with her."

"I never said—"

"You don't have to. It's written all over your face and hers."

"You're angry."

She took a step closer and leaned against the counter. "Look at me."

He did. She was pissed.

"Just because this isn't a war zone and no one's out there shooting off guns doesn't mean people can't get hurt in the good ol' USA. There are invisible wounds too. Seneca's life hasn't been an easy one. Don't make it harder for her."

"I'm not." A searing pain roared through him.

"And Tom?"

"He knows about Michael and, er, me."

Janie's eyebrows popped up. "There's a man in Chicago tonight who believes he's marrying a faithful woman next week. What about him?"

In the living room two fiddles began the chorus to *Barbara Allen*. Beside him, the coffee dripped into the glass carafe. "I'm sorry. I didn't choose this. It just happened." Seneca and Tom's voices rose and intertwined.

In Charlotte town where I was born
There was a fair maid dwelling
And every youth cried well away
For her name was Barbara Allen

"How does Seneca feel about cheating on her—"

From the other room, Seneca screamed. Then Tom shouted, "Collin, Collin, come quick." Jake began to howl, and Jim let out a strangled shout. Collin raced out of the kitchen. Janie was right behind him. In the dining room, Jim held a tearful Jake in his arms. One of Jake's little hands was covered in blood.

"What happened?" Janie pushed past Collin to get to her son.

"He was running around the dining room table, and he must have grabbed the top of a beer can and cut his finger," said Jim. He was a big man, as tall as Collin, with the build of a linebacker. He looked pale and shaken.

"We should get him to the emergency room right away." Janie looked a little pale too.

"Let Collin take a look." It was Tom. "He's pretty good with this sort of thing. Practically saved Peabody Hill's life last night."

A gross exaggeration, but the group accepted this as hard fact and everyone relaxed. He looked around at the circle of faces. With the exception of little Jake, who screamed and writhed in his father's arms, and Matt, who appeared to be amused, everyone else looked surprised. His eyes went to Seneca's. She studied him as if she'd never seen him before. He knew she was thinking about the conversation in the parking lot. *I learned that night I wasn't anything like my grandfather so I dropped out of pre-med at Stanford.* He *wasn't* anything like Grandpa Collins. He *wasn't*. But how he'd loved helping his grandfather when he worked at the children's free clinic.

"I'll take a look."

Jim handed Jake to him.

He took the warm, squirming bundle in his arms, then lowered himself into one of the chairs. "Sen, can you run upstairs and grab my Dopp kit?" he asked over the little boy's agonized screams. She turned and raced up the stairs, taking the steps two at a time.

Jake's wails were ear-splitting. Drops of blood soaked through the leg of Collin's pants and stained the top of his shoes. But he didn't care. All his attention was on Jake. He knew exactly how he felt. It wasn't just the pain or the blood, it was the indignity of having the rug pulled out from under you just when you were having fun. He pulled the little boy close to him. "It's okay, son. Everything is just fine." He rocked the boy in his arms.

By the time Seneca appeared with his kit, Jake's wails quieted to soft, teary sobs. "What happened to your finger?" he asked Jake.

Snot dripped from Jake's nose. He pulled out his hanky and dabbed. Jake sniffed. "Hurts."

"I know it does, son." He cupped Jake's injured hand in his. "Is it okay if I see?"

He sniffed again, then nodded. "Hurts."

"I can tell." He kept his voice calm, his tone soothing as he repeated the phrases he remembered his grandfather using at the free clinic. "Sen, there should be some antiseptic in a clear bottle and sterile gauze. Can you get it out?"

She dug around in the kit until she found them. She handed a piece of gauze to him.

"Show me where it hurts, son."

Jake stuck the thumb of his good hand in his mouth and held out his other hand for him to see. He dabbed away the blood with a square of gauze and examined the pads of the little boy's fingers. There was a small scratch on Jake's middle finger. The cut on his index finger was deeper but not deep enough to hit any nerves.

Collin looked up at Janie and Jim. "It's not as deep as it looks.

With thin cuts like this, you sometimes get a lot of blood. Look, the bleeding's almost stopped."

Jake's parents breathed a sigh of relief.

"I'll just clean it and bandage it. He'll be fine." Collin tousled Jake's hair. "Right, son?"

Jake wasn't ready for the drama to end. "Hurts."

"You've been very brave." Collin applied the antiseptic to Jake's fingers.

The sting of the antiseptic took Jake by surprise. He stiffened and began to cry. "Oooh. Hurts."

"There now, it's over. Let's see if Aunt Seneca can find my special camo bandages. Those are the ones all the brave soldiers wear. Don't they, Matt?"

"That's right," said Matt as Seneca pulled an ordinary, flesh-colored strip out of the kit. "That's the only kind us soldiers will wear."

Jake, still teary-eyed, nodded solemnly. "Are you brave?" he asked Matt.

"Sometimes."

Jake nodded again. "Me too." Then he stuck his thumb back in his mouth, leaned against Collin's shoulder and closed his eyes.

The party broke up after that. It was past Jake and Henry's bedtime, and Matt had to work the next morning. When Collin pulled the Jeep back into the driveway after dropping Matt off, he was bone-tired. It had been another long day, and tomorrow would be long too. Peabody Hill was coming home. He thought about Seneca and wasn't quite so worn out.

The shower was running upstairs, and through the alcove, he glimpsed Tom perched on a kitchen chair strumming his guitar. A cup of coffee sat on the table in front of him. He looked up as Collin walked in the front door.

"Hey, Collin. Got a minute, man?"

He sighed. "Sure thing." He went into the kitchen, pulled out a chair and sat down. Too beat to sit up straight, he slouched and waited.

"Can I pour you a cup of coffee?"

The shower was still running full blast upstairs. He wished he was there. "Nah. Keeps me awake."

Tom nodded and ran his fingers along the guitar strings. "My daughter seems to be in some distress."

"I'm not sure what you mean." He grew wary.

Tom set the guitar down on the table and turned to him. "She wants to go back to Chicago, but she's afraid to leave me behind in Peabody."

"Look, this is between you and her."

"She'll say what she thinks a dutiful daughter should say."

The water went off in the shower. "She has a job up there, and I expect you've picked up on the fact money is tight for her. There's about five hundred dollars sitting in a bank account in Poppy's name plus this house, and that's about it."

Tom nodded. "She rolls her eyes every time I mention it, but I do have money. A few years back Pop told me my old manager called and wanted to know what to do with some accounts in my name. I told Pop to take it, but he considered it the devil's coin so he refused."

Collin nodded. A blow dryer whirred to life over his head. That would buy them an extra few minutes.

"Bottom line. What is the plan?"

"We want to leave on Saturday morning."

Tom's eyes widened. His hand closed around the neck of the guitar, and he pulled it onto his lap. His finger plucked out a tune Collin didn't recognize.

"Look, I won't leave you high and dry, I promise. My buddy is sending down a van so Henry can take Matt to Jotham, but it's for you, too. Henry will be able to drive you—"

He stopped strumming his guitar. "I can take care of myself."

"I know you can." He didn't sound convincing even to himself.

"Honestly. I already have some ideas. I told you about saving the music Pop loved. And I want to see if any of my band mates are still around. Maybe I can get some gigs."

Above them, the blow dryer died and the bathroom door opened. "I don't want to keep you."

"You didn't say why you wanted Seneca to stay."

"It's not about the money, and it's certainly not about being alone."

"Then what?"

"I've missed my daughter all these years. I just wish I could have a little more time to get to know her better."

"I'm sorry." And he was. Without his selfish plotting, Seneca would have stayed in Peabody for at least a few months. Now Tom would be deprived of his daughter, and she deprived of her father, just so Collin could have her with him. *Nice going, asshole.*

Tom leaned over and patted Collin's shoulders. "It's okay. Sometimes we just have to go with the flow and let life happen. It'll work out."

Seneca was waiting for him in the bedroom. When he opened the door, she looked up at him from the edge of the bed where she was perched. A thick towel was wrapped around her body. Her eyes shone.

"You were awesome with Jake."

"Yeah." He shrugged uncomfortably.

"Dad said you saved Peabody Hill's life."

"He's overstating what happened. I cleaned the bullet wound and drove Peabody Hill to the vet. He was never in danger of dying."

She tilted her head and studied him. "You're embarrassed, aren't you?"

He pulled his shirt over his head and unzipped his pants. "What I am is tired."

For a few excruciating moments, she continued to scrutinize him, then she shrugged. "Whatever."

He didn't like the sound of that. But then she stood and dropped her towel, and he forgot all about it.

Chapter 24

Tom sat on the porch steps and watched Seneca and Aida play fetch with an old tennis ball. It was a perfect autumn day in West Virginia—blue sky, warm southern breeze, a cardinal's song floating through the trees above, the rustle of dried leaves in the wind, a daughter playing in the sunlight. A man could get used to this.

He was content. His daughter had opened up to him with an eagerness that surprised him, and he'd seen in her acceptance the hungry heart inside her. He didn't know anything about Michael except that he was an environmental activist. Tom had a lot of respect for the tree-huggers of the world. But it was plain to him that Michael didn't fill the need inside Seneca. On the other hand, he suspected Collin did.

Tom watched Seneca struggle to pull the ball out of Aida's mouth. The dog understood the part of "Fetch" where she was supposed to chase the ball and trot it back to Seneca. She was having trouble with the "drop" command, and she refused to give the ball back. He smiled at Seneca's attempts to look stern when the dog disobeyed.

His smile faded as his thoughts returned to Collin. That boy was equal parts caring and smart, and remote and immature. Tom had glimpsed the hunger in his eyes when Seneca wasn't looking at him, and he'd watched his hunger turn into a 'come hither' look when she turned in his direction. Tom suspected he was in the habit of hiding his feelings behind his handsome face. Could his daughter see through that? He didn't think so, at least not yet. But there was no point in obsessing over their relationship. Either Collin would grow up or his daughter would move on. Tom was fine with either scenario. It was her artistic future that interested him. Whether her heart was full or not, he knew music could fill her soul as it filled his during his long exile.

Tom studied the shiny, new handicapped van parked in his neighbor's driveway. It arrived from the Brouchard Carworks this morning. Henry was overcome when he saw it. Tom suspected Matt would be too.

He considered the shape of his own future. He did have money. Enough to maintain Pop's house and live a simple life for many years, and a little extra left over to pay for his daughter to take up music. He'd used his new computer to locate Eddie Weiss, a former band member who'd collaborated with him on some songs in the old days. Eddie lived in Atlanta with his third wife and two young children. Next week Eddie was driving up to Peabody to meet with him since Tom didn't have a driver's license or car yet. Both were at the top of his to-do list.

Seneca giggled, and he looked up. She sat in the grass playing tug-of-war with Aida who held onto the tennis ball for dear life. She threw her head back and laughed as she strained to loosen the ball, and she suddenly reminded him of Sonny. She used to throw her head back just like that when she laughed.

"Seneca?"

She stopped pulling on the ball. The dog yanked it away from her with a twist of her head, but when she saw that Seneca wasn't paying attention, she dropped the ball and barked. Seneca scooped up the ball and threw it. As Aida scrambled after it, Seneca stood, brushing bits of dried leaves and grass off her jeans as she came up to the porch.

"Sit down with me."

She did.

"What time are you leaving tomorrow?"

"Collin wants to be gone before sun-up. I believe the last departure time I heard was four o'clock. Each time I ask, he pushes it back another hour."

Tom nodded. "I'll miss you."

Seneca studied her bare feet. "I'll call you every day. I promise."

He didn't want her to worry about him. "Not if I call you first."

She smiled.

Whenever he saw her smile, he thought of Pop. His daughter had Pop's mouth. "I want to send you some money each month so you can spend time playing music up in Chicago. You'd still have to work, but not full time."

She frowned.

"If you want."

She shook her head. "I don't know, Dad. I'm twenty-seven already, and the cost—"

He was caught off-guard by her answer. How could anyone who loved music turn down a chance to play? "Fuck your age! Fuck the money! Fuck anyone who stands in your way! One thing matters. Do you want to play music? Do you?"

She stared at him. "I've never seen you angry."

Collin pushed open the screen door and came out to the porch. He stood behind them, watchful and tense.

But Tom didn't care if he shocked them. "I'm angry because music matters more than anything else in the world to me. Does it matter to you?" He waited for her answer in silent misery, his heart in his throat, his hands so unsteady he was forced to grip his knees.

"I didn't mean to sound flip. It was an honest reaction."

"So?" He wasn't letting go of this.

She shifted her gaze from Tom to Collin and held out her hand to him. Collin came and sat beside her and held her hand. She turned back to Tom.

"Yes, Dad. I want to play music."

"Okay then," he said gruffly to hide his own emotions. "Go to the Chicago Conservatory when you get back home. They'll tell you what you need to study."

She nodded.

His emotional outburst had taken the peace out of the day. He gazed at the top of Peabody Ridge and tried to mentally transport himself out of the moment, but he couldn't manage it.

Collin stirred. "I was hoping Seneca would give me tour of Peabody. It's my last day here, and I haven't seen much but the county building and the vet's office.

God bless that boy. He had the instincts of a prize bloodhound. "Wouldn't mind a little tour myself if you don't mind some company."

Collin fetched a leash for Aida and checked on Peabody Hill, who was still too weak for a long walk. Then Seneca led them down Sleepy Hollow Road, pointing out various houses as they strolled along.

She waved her hand at a neat white cottage with a trellis of dying roses beside the front door. "That's the Nevins' house. Do you remember them, Dad?"

As they passed a two-story red brick house that looked like a relic from the Civil War, she said, "Oh, this is where Will Collier lived. He tried to burn down the principal's house when I was in school. Crazy, crazy boy." She smiled as she remembered the high school renegade.

Next door to the Collier's former residence was another cottage, this one was pale blue and sat behind a wide porch. "Mrs. Gabler lives here. Her niece was Miss West Virginia awhile back. She was so excited, she must have told everyone in Peabody about it ten times. I thought Poppy would bust a gut the tenth time he got told."

Tom half-listened, enjoying the company more than the guided tour. He held Aida's leash intertwined in his fingers. Beside him Seneca and Collin held hands. They turned the corner, and Tom saw the simple clapboard church where he'd spent his Sunday mornings as a boy. It was white-washed, shining brightly against the blue October sky. A bell tower had been added since Tom last saw the church and the sunlight reflected off a large brass bell. He realized with a sense of deep pleasure that he'd heard the bell peal every Sunday morning when he'd lived on the mountain.

As they passed the church, Reverend McAllister drove up. His black Chevy Impala squealed to stop beside them, and the Rev jumped out of the car as if the church was on fire. Tom was shocked at how much the Rev had changed. He'd been a young man when he was growing up. Now he was stooped and gray-haired. But Tom was no spring chicken himself, was he? The Rev's green eyes were as alert and wise as he remembered.

"Tommy Simms, is that you?" He jogged up to them. "Where have you been? We all thought you were dead!"

Seneca and Collin froze up beside him. But he'd already decided how he would answer this question. "After my wife died, I broke down and had to go away. I've been living alone not too far from here. But when I heard about Pop, I felt I should come back for my daughter's sake." That's all he intended to say. The rest of the story would remain forever between him and Seneca and Collin Atlee and Janie Highsmith. Period.

The Rev nodded as if this made perfect sense. "Good to have you back, Tom."

Chapter 25

Peabody Hill was supposed to stay with Tom but when Seneca and Collin carried their things out to the Jeep, they found the dog was snoring loudly in the backseat.

Seneca was already in a grumpy mood, and this made her grumpier. "The whole, entire purpose of this trip was to bring him back to Peabody!" Vapor rose from her lips as her heated breath hit the cold, predawn air.

Collin was being the stoic soldier. His expression was stony as he studied her. "Really?"

"Why do you always take everything I say literally?"

He arched his brow. "Just seems like a whole lot of interesting things have happened that had nothing to do with dropping off Peabody Hill."

"Do you have to end every conversation with a sexual innuendo?"

"Sorry." He dropped his head and stared at his boots. "Let him be. If you and—if you can't take him—can't take care of him, I mean, he can bunk with me."

"Fine." She turned away so he wouldn't see the sudden flush in her cheeks.

They'd been walking on eggshells since they woke up. No morning lovemaking, no banter, no discussion as they dressed and stuffed their clothes into bags. Today was the day when Seneca would have to decide what to do about her engagement to Michael.

She *knew* she couldn't marry Michael. Deep down, she *knew* it. But letting go was hard. He'd been so good for her. She'd miss the beautiful house in the woods they'd built together. She loved to sit on the warm ground under the trees with her head on Michael's shoulder while she listened to the birds. She'd felt connected to someone besides Poppy for the first time in her life. Michael gave her that.

Which brought her to the real problem. What to do about Collin. She wanted him like a fish wants water, but that was not the same thing as love. Besides, if she canceled her marriage to Michael and went right to Collin, could she live with herself? She wasn't sure. A broken engagement seemed like it required a mourning period

"Seneca? Come and say goodbye." Her father waited on the porch with Aida at this side. He wore Poppy's pajamas and a new plaid robe. His face had begun to fill out, and his eyes no longer shifted away from her face like they did his first day back in Peabody.

She went to him and let him hug her close. They held each other for a long time. She didn't want to be the first to let go, and maybe her father felt the same way. They released each other at the same moment.

"I love you, daughter."

"I love you, too, Dad."

He looked into her eyes. "Whatever you decide to do, you always have a place with me. You're a Simms. Love is a wonderful thing, but for us, it's music that fills our souls."

Maybe he was right, but for the moment love filled her thoughts. She hugged him quickly. "Thanks."

Then she spun around and hurried down the steps trying not to feel like the worst daughter ever for leaving him behind.

*

Collin was unusually quiet on the drive up to Chicago. Just before Louisville, he uttered his first words since they left Peabody. Talking over the chatter of Click and Clack on NPR's "Car Talk," he said, "Would you mind if we stopped for something to eat?"

"No, of course not." Her voice was several octaves higher than necessary.

"Thanks." He pulled into a McDonald's just off the Frankfort, Kentucky, exit and looked at her. His face was an unreadable mask. "I was going to do the drive-through unless you need a break."

"No, no. Drive-through is fine." Her voice was still too high. What was wrong with her! But she knew. She was torturing him. She didn't mean to, but she wasn't ready to say she wouldn't marry Michael because the next words out of his mouth would be "What about me?" She had no answer for him.

He ordered a sweet tea for her—she couldn't have choked down a sandwich if she was starving to death—and coffee and an Egg McMuffin for himself. Peabody Hill, still not quite himself, slept through the brief McDonald's layover.

Those were the last words either of them uttered all the way through Louisville and around Indianapolis, then up through central Indiana. They were thirty miles outside Chicago when she forced herself to say the words Collin was waiting for.

"I can't marry Michael."

Tears filled her eyes, and she stared unseeing through the windshield, accepting the pain of her loss and the seismic shift in her universe as she let go of her old life.

Beside her, Collin shifted his weight, and she realized he'd barely moved or breathed since he finished his coffee and sandwich two hundred miles ago. He flipped on the turn signal, pulled over onto the shoulder and put the Jeep in Park. His hand circled her arm. "Are you okay, Sen?"

She shook her head, afraid if she spoke, she'd begin to sob.

He rubbed her arm. "I'm sorry."

She shook her head again. "No you're not." The words popped out of her mouth like little sobs.

He didn't argue. He just rubbed her arm until other parts of her body warmed up. Maybe he sensed her desire because after awhile he stopped rubbing and restricted himself to a sympathetic gaze.

She swallowed hard to push back the ache in her heart. "I'm okay now. Let's go."

He didn't move. "Where is he?"

"Do you honestly expect to drive me up to the house and wait outside while I drop the bomb on poor, unsuspecting Michael?"

"Yes. Where is he? Let's get this over with."

"Collin, I am not going—"

"Don't you think he deserves to know now? Or are you going to string him along until *you* get up the courage to tell him? I thought you were better than that, Sen."

He was right. But . . . "Don't you think it will be harder on him if you're waiting outside for me?"

"Harder for him or harder for you?"

"Please. Drop me off at my apartment. I'll drive myself."

"No. I'll drop you off down the street if you want and park around the corner."

He could wait out on the shoulder of the road at the foot of their drive. The gravel driveway wound through the woods for at least a quarter-mile. Michael wouldn't be able to see Collin or the Jeep from the house, and she didn't really want to go alone. She didn't know how Michael would react, and even worse, she didn't know how she would work up the nerve to break the news. Bringing along back-up might be a good idea.

"Okay." She turned and looked at him, but there was nothing to read in his sapphire eyes but caution. "This does not mean anything as far as we're concerned. I-I've got to get through this first. Okay?"

His head spun away from her, and he shifted the Jeep into gear. "Of course."

At the end of the driveway, he pulled along the shoulder of the two-lane country road. Beside them lay an empty cornfield littered with dried corn husks. In the distance a prosperous brick farmhouse and modern white barn sat in peaceful solitude beneath the browning leaves of three giant weeping willow trees. She wished she were there right now.

On the wooded side, a thick forest of trees stretched for miles. Mailboxes marked the ends of driveways at one-mile intervals as far as she could see. The handmade pine mailbox painted in festive orange letters announced 'Michael Berger and Seneca Simms.'

Seneca climbed out of the Jeep, and Collin stepped from the car too. Peabody Hill woke up and raised his head. Collin was supposed to wait in the car. "Why are you getting out?"

"Just stretching my legs." He opened the passenger door and helped the dog out of the Jeep, cushioning his jump so he wouldn't land on his shoulder. "Peabody Hill needs to pee."

"I mean it, Collin. You have to stay here. You can't follow me. It's bad enough I'm leaving Michael at the altar, he doesn't have to know he's been cheated on too."

"The zoo has an altar?"

She narrowed her eyes, then spun on one foot and marched across the road.

A late fall color scheme of gold and brown adorned the woods. *Their* woods. The trees had shed most of their leaves, but even in the dead of winter, the woods were so thick, it was nearly impossible to see the house from the road. Above her, a dozen starlings began to screech from the top of a maple and a flock of wrens rose from deep in the trees and flew toward the south.

Seneca covered the first hundred yards keenly aware of Collin's gaze on her back. She looked behind her, as she passed the mailbox. He slouched against the Jeep's hood dressed in his jeans—she'd patched the knee for him—boots, black T-shirt and leather jacket. His arms were folded across his chest as he watched her. The dog sat beside Collin. His chocolate eyes watched her too. She turned her back to them, then stooped down and picked up a handful of gravel. She squeezed the sharp pebbles in her fist before she deposited them in the pocket of her jacket as a keepsake. That would give him something to chew over while she talked to Michael.

Since Collin was watching, she forced herself to walk at a normal pace. But with each step, her heart beat faster and her stomach twisted along with the dregs of the sweet tea she'd choked down back in Indiana. She reached the 'Purple Martin' curve in the driveway with relief and with one long step disappeared out of Collin's sight. The 'Purple Martin' curve circled an apple and pear orchard they planted last year. In the center was a Purple Martin house where a mating pair came every spring to raise their young. The fruit trees were still too immature to bear fruit, but in a few years, they hoped to put up jam. *They.* She had looked forward to canning jam from their home-grown fruit. Now Michael would share that pleasure with someone else.

She stopped. Behind her, Collin waited. A few feet further on, the driveway straightened, and she would be visible to Michael if he was home. She stood in the sanctuary of the hidden curve, stared up at an apple tree sapling and pondered her approach with Michael. She wanted to exonerate him from all blame—that was the least she could offer him—but she didn't want to be the villain either. But how to hit the right note? The faint tinkling of dog tags from the main road broke into her reverie. Collin would not wait out of sight forever. At some point he would grow impatient and come after her.

She began to walk again, rounding the edge of 'Purple Martin' curve, blinking as a ray of dull autumn sunshine bounced off the glass wall of the house and hit her eyes. Through the trees, Michael's ecological wonder sparkled like a diamond. He designed the house himself as a tribute to Mother Earth, choosing thick, insulated glass walls with endless views of the woods in every direction and a roof of solar panels angled southward like sun worshippers. Pale, eco-friendly bamboo floors glistened under recessed lights and the creamy white inner walls, which hid the mechanical core of the house, radiated tranquility.

Seneca raised her hand to her brow and squinted into the light. She took short, tentative steps up the driveway as the gravel shifted beneath the thin soles of her ballet flats like the shifting tectonic plates of her life. She stuck her free hand into her pocket and grabbed the pebbles, rolling them between her fingers as if they were precious stones. She'd reached the house clearing when the front door opened and Michael stepped out, zipping up his jacket as he emerged. He ran down the steps and hurried toward her.

"Seneca!" He stopped before he reached her and frowned. "Are you all right? You look sick."

"I'm fine." She stuck her hands in her pockets. "I came here to tell you something."

His expression turned to alarm. "What is happening, Seneca? Where's your car? What the hell is going on?"

Just say it, she told herself. "I-I-I can't marry you. I'm sorry. Really and truly."

He stared at her like she'd just grown two heads.

"Michael? Are you okay?"

He took a step back. "Why?" The word sounded like a gasp.

Her heart ached, but she plain didn't have enough love for him to last a lifetime. Plus, what her father taught her over the past few days was her true passion in life was for music, and Michael, her single-minded, visionary Michael, would never understand how music could mean more to her than the environment. Then there was the fact she couldn't very well marry one man when she couldn't keep her hands off another one. "I-I will always care about you. Truly. But I-I don't deserve you."

He stared at her. "What are you talking about? I don't understand any of this!"

Through the trees came the tinkling of dog tags and the crunch of heavy boots on gravel. This meeting was about to go horribly, terribly wrong. *Please, God, keep Collin away.* But the Lord Almighty did not listen. She was afraid to turn around, although based on the recognition dawning in Michael's eyes, she knew what she'd see. A man and a dog on a mission.

Michael's jaw dropped. "This is the guy—and-and that's not Rory—" His eyes were cold and angry. "I thought you were a virgin when we—" He took a step closer and pushed his words through gritted teeth. "You are nothing but white trash with the morals of a jack rabbit." Then he slapped her across the cheek hard enough to make her teeth vibrate and bring tears to her eyes.

Stunned, she pressed a hand to her throbbing cheek and tried to catch her breath. Before she could blink, Collin was beside her. His right arm exploded from his shoulder and his fist connected with Michael's left eye. Michael spun backwards and landed on his rump.

"Didn't anyone ever teach you not to hit girls?"

Michael looked up at him. "That's assault. I'm calling the police and pressing charges."

"Then I would have to explain to them I just witnessed your assault on this lady and came to her rescue." He took Seneca's arm. "Come on, Sen. It's done." He slid his arm around her shoulders and half-pushed, half-dragged her up the driveway.

Peabody Hill growled. "Come on, boy," said Collin. "He's not worth it." The dog's tags clinked as he turned and followed them up the drive.

As he turned the Jeep toward Chicago, Collin turned talkative. "Has he ever hit you before?"

The shock of Michael's assault was wearing off, leaving anger in its wake. Thanks to Collin, Michael thought she was a slut. "No, Collin, no one has ever hit me before in my life, including Michael, and if you had respected my request to remain *in* the car, it wouldn't have happened today."

"Are you blaming me?"

"I am blaming you for sticking your nose in my business."

"Your business? None of this has anything to do with me? Is that what you're saying?" He looked hurt, and Seneca felt a little guilty. Then she remembered Michael.

"Please take me home."

"What about—"

She raised her hand. "I don't want to talk to you."

"Ever?"

"For chrissake, Collin! I just broke up with my fiancé one week before my wedding. A fiancé you just slugged. I do not feel like talking to you right now. And maybe tomorrow I won't feel like talking to you. And maybe if I'm lucky I won't feel like talking to you every day for the rest of my life." She folded her arms across her chest and stared at the windshield.

When he pulled up in front of her apartment, she jumped out of the Jeep and helped Peabody Hill down. Then she grabbed her things out of the back before Collin could help her with them and stalked off. With pleasure, she noticed even the dog didn't look back before they both pushed through the front door, leaving Collin standing alone beside the Jeep looking bleak and weary.

Chapter 26

"This is it," Seneca said to Peabody Hill. She climbed out of her Ford Focus and opened the back door. The dog dropped to the pavement. With tail wagging and nose to the ground, he began to explore his new home.

She studied Collin's townhouse from the curb. It was a classic Chicago townhouse, tall and narrow, dark brown brick, high windows. It sat in the center of a tree-lined block of elegant, turn-of-the-century townhouses, each with its own postage-stamp square of grass. His house looked dingy compared to the others on the street. Its brown trim was faded, its windows grimy, the shrubs along the foundation were overgrown and leggy, the grass weedy. A black wrought-iron fence as tall as Seneca with sharp spindles on the top of the posts surrounded the house and yard. Not exactly welcoming,

She debated with herself on whether to drag her bags up to the door and hope he'd let her stay, or ring his bell and ask first. If he slammed the door in her face, she and her dog would be officially homeless, since the student who sublet Seneca's apartment arrived at seven o'clock this morning to move in. She left her things in the car. It would be hard to throw herself on Collin's mercy encumbered by suitcases.

"Come on, boy."

She pushed open the heavy metal gate. It groaned and squeaked, and the hair on the back of her neck stood up. The dog raised his sad, brown eyes to her as if to say, "Are you sure about this?" But he followed her across the overgrown brick path. Seneca stared up at the tall front door and took a deep breath. She pressed the tarnished brass doorbell. A deep chime echoed through the house. Utter silence followed. She glanced behind her. Collin's Jeep was parked by the curb. But she hadn't talked to him since she stormed off last Saturday, so he could be out of town or anywhere. She pressed the doorbell again. Same echo followed by the same silence. Seneca took another deep breath and pressed the bell again. The door swung open, and there was Collin looking rumpled and sleepy and gorgeously sexy in a pair of gray sweatpants slung low on his hips.

He didn't seem pleased to see her. "What time is it?"

Seneca lifted her chin and tried to act more confident than she felt. "Eight. Can I come in?"

He stepped aside to let Seneca and Peabody Hill into his house. The interior was as gloomy as the exterior. Carved walnut paneling lined the entryway walls. A wide staircase rose opposite the door, its balustrade fashioned from the same heavy walnut as the paneling. Halfway up, as the staircase turned, a stained-glass window with squares of gold, red and blue cast murky light on the worn burgundy carpet lining the steps.

Collin closed the door and leaned against it. He observed her crossly. "To what do I owe the honor of this visit?"

"Well, as you may recall, I, uh, sublet my place because I thought I was getting married today. So I need a place to stay until I can find an apartment." Her face was burning but she forced herself to meet his eyes. He was waiting. "Or, uh, if you could at least take Peabody Hill, I can stay at a hotel." Which would cost a fortune since it would take her at least a month to sign a lease for a new apartment.

He didn't move.

"I'm sorry for yelling at you last week. I was having a very bad day, but that was no reason to take it out on you the way I did."

His eyes narrowed as he considered her apology. Then he nodded. "I'm sorry, too. I shouldn't have followed you." He bent over and patted Peabody Hill's head. "Okay, you can stay."

"Thanks. You've saved my life. Truly. And I don't want you to think I'm asking for charity. I insist on paying rent. Just tell me what you think is fair." She stopped as his eyes widened. "I know this is a little awkward. We left things unresolved—" She considered her next words carefully, but there was no way to put this delicately. "I need my own room."

"Do you want permission to date, too?"

Irritation pricked at her. "Coming to you like this after everything that happened is hard for me. Why do you have to make it into a joke?"

"I'm taking it seriously."

"Exactly what about this are you taking seriously?"

"Everything."

"Name one thing, Collin."

"I don't know."

"See? I'm right."

"You." He muttered the word.

Her irritation evaporated. She blinked. What the hell did that mean?

He pulled himself off the front door. "Let's see if we can find a room that's up to your standards."

A dim, narrow hallway ran the length of the second floor. Closed doors lined the corridor, except for the one at the far end. He nodded at the open door. "That's my room." He stopped and studied the closed doors. Then he opened the one next to his. "Maybe this room. It was my mom's when she was growing up. I think there's still some sheets for the bed if they haven't disintegrated, and the guest bathroom is across the hall.

Seneca peered into the room but all she could make out were pale, shadowy objects undulating in deep gloom. Collin felt his way through the murkiness, shuffling forward so he wouldn't run into the furniture. He tugged up a shade. Morning sunlight burst through the window and filled a bright, spacious bedroom. At the far end a white brick fireplace yawned and two stuffed chairs covered in red-and blue-flowered chintz sat at cozy angles. Near the door a double bed topped by a white canopy waited. Its bedspread and dust ruffle matched the chairs. A white armoire and dresser were arranged against rose-colored walls and a pale blue carpet covered the floor. When she was a little girl, Seneca dreamed of being a princess and sleeping in a room like this. "Oh, Collie, it's unbelievable!"

"Glad you like it." But he didn't sound glad at all. He turned to leave. "Give me a few minutes to get dressed. I'll get your stuff out of the car for you."

She didn't want to inconvenience him. "I can do it."

He stopped at the threshold but didn't look back at her. "I'll just be a few minutes. We can unpack the car together. In the meantime, why don't you see if the sheets in the armoire are still usable." His feet padded down the hall, then his bedroom door closed.

A dozen photos taped to the edges of a tall mirror over the dresser demanded further study. Seneca crossed the room to look at them. Near the top of the mirror someone had taped a small black-and-white photo-booth picture of the most beautiful teenage girls Seneca ever laid eyes on. One girl had dark, sleek hair, almond eyes and pouty lips. Beside her shimmered a blond angel with long dark eyelashes, winged brows and high cheekbones. She had to be Collin's mother.

In a formal portrait stuck on the other side of the mirror, Collin's mother smiled with bright eagerness in a maroon-and-gold sweater and short, pleated skirt. Her hands held maroon-and-gold pompons. There were two faded snapshots of her in a skimpy white satin majorette uniform as she waved a baton and marched on a football field, one of her in nurse's scrubs with a stethoscope around her neck and a few with an older man, who became thinner and grayer as she progressed through her teens and twenties. His intelligent sapphire eyes, so much like his daughter's and his grandson's, crinkled at the corners. His warmth shone through in the pictures. Seneca touched his face with her finger and smiled back at him.

A photo stuck into the bottom of the frame caught Seneca's eye. She slid it out so she could study it without bending over. It was a picture of Collin's mother with her head resting against the shoulder of a dark-haired man who must be Collin's father. His mother's eyes were half-closed, and her lips were curved into a blissful smile. The man's features were chiseled and handsome, and he looked like he was about to burst with pride as he stood straight and tall with his arm around the slender waist of the beautiful blonde girl at his side. They both looked so young and happy and hopeful, Seneca couldn't imagine them as the rich snobs Collin described. Seneca slid the photo back into the mirror frame and straightened up.

She remembered the sheets and went to the armoire. The baton from the photo was propped against the side of the armoire, as if its owner set it there and would return for it any minute. A chill ran down Seneca's spine. Inside the armoire on the top shelf maroon and gold pom-poms lay alongside a maroon sweater and skirt wrapped in tissue paper. On the middle shelf were three sets of sheets—pale blue with the initials MLC embroidered in white—which she judged to be in decent condition. She'd have to wash them first. She hoped Collin had a washing machine and dryer that worked. She pulled out a set and laid them on the bed before crossing the hall to inspect the bathroom.

The walls of the guest bathroom were tiled in pale cream. The floor was covered in tiny hexagons of black-and-white. The sink, shower, and tub fixtures were thick white porcelain with "Hot," "Cold," and "Waste" stamped on them. Old-fashioned, a bit dusty, but otherwise clean. Inside a cupboard by the sink, black towels faded to gray were folded in neat piles. She opened a drawer and found a toothbrush with yellowed bristles and a half-empty toothpaste tube. She tried to press her finger against the tube but it was as hard as a rock. Fossilized toothpaste. Time had come to halt inside this house. Probably on the day Collin's grandfather died. Seneca shivered again.

"Ready?"

Seneca jumped. Collin was standing behind her. "Yes."

Collin looked down at the drawer. He snatched up the toothbrush and toothpaste. "If I'd known you were coming, I would have cleaned."

"No problem." But she didn't see how a quick run through the house with a vacuum and a dust rag could clean away the ghosts that lived in this house.

With Collin's help, she managed to cart her meager possessions into the house and up to her room in one trip. As Seneca unzipped her suitcase, Collin settled himself on the bed to watch.

"Can I have some privacy, please?"

He gave her his sexy, sapphire-eyes-through-the-eyelashes look. "I've seen your panties before."

He wasn't buying into the separate bedrooms. Unfortunately for him, she knew just how to press his hot buttons. She shrugged, bent down and pretended to rifle through her suitcase. "What does MLC stand for?"

"What?" He looked blank.

"The sheets I pulled out of the armoire have MLC embroidered on them. What do the initials stand for?"

"Those were my mother's initials before she was married." He stood. "I've got some things to do downstairs."

"Aren't you going to answer my question?" Seneca persisted. He stared at her, and Seneca stared back, wide-eyed, daring him to retreat. "Well?"

He dropped his gaze and spun out of the room. As he strode off, he mumbled, "Martha Louise Collins I'll be downstairs if you need me."

Collin's mother's room brimmed with mementos of her girlhood. When Seneca pulled open the dresser drawers, she found a neat stack of oversized T-shirts and yellowed bobby socks Martha Louise Collins must have slept in before she was married.

In another drawer, two moth-eaten cardigans were folded beside a faded pair of bell-bottom jeans. The closet was stuffed with garment bags, and when she unzipped one of them, the stiff skirt of a cornflower blue tulle and silk gown popped out. Seneca stuffed it back in and zipped up the bag. She pushed the bags to one side of the closet until she made enough space for her meager wardrobe.

She pulled open the bedside table to stow her cell phone charger and found old ticket stubs, a dried rose corsage, a program from the original production of *Hair*, a torn piece of notepaper with a phone number written in neat block letters, and matchbooks from long-forgotten restaurants. A plastic bag filled with sand and sea glass caught Seneca's eye and she lifted it out of the drawer. It was tied with a bright green grosgrain hair ribbon. Another scrap of notebook paper was taped to the side. Seneca squinted to make out the faded writing—*Met Richard Atlee today. I'm in love. Oak Street Beach August 9.*

From downstairs, Collin called her name. Seneca dropped the bag of sand and sea glass back into the drawer and ran to the stairs. She skipped down a few steps so she could lean over the balustrade and look down. He wore his jacket, and Peabody Hill had a leash hooked to his collar. They gazed up at her.

"What?"

"I said, what are you doing up there?"

"You know what I'm doing."

"You can unpack later. Come on."

"Where are we going?"

"We're going where lovers always go on Saturday mornings."

"And where might that be?

"You've lived a sheltered life, haven't you?"

She felt another prick of irritation. "We're not lovers."

"I'm backing into it. Come on. I'll buy you breakfast."

The morning air was crisp and sweet, the sun bright against

the cloudless sky. As she scrambled to keep pace with Collin and Peabody Hill, Seneca couldn't enjoy these simple pleasures. As callous as it was, she'd barely spent more than a few minutes this past week worrying about Michael or how hurt he must be or how his eye was healing. Most of her waking hours—and more than a few of her sleeping ones—were haunted by Collin. She missed him so much it made her heart ache.

Her father had counseled caution. "Take it slow, Seneca. There's no need to rush into anything with him." He'd paused, then added, "I wonder if Collin has a little more growing up to do."

After that conversation, Seneca spent time thinking about Collin's maturity. Did he have any idea what he wanted out of life? Did he really want a serious relationship or just a bedmate? Was he the marrying kind of man?

"When you said you were serious about me, what did you mean?"

A shadow crossed Collin's face. "Just that."

"I-I mean are you serious about sleeping with me or are you serious about having a relationship together?"

He hesitated. "Both."

"Do you remember what we talked about in Peabody? Just before my father and Aida wandered out of his house and Henry discovered them?

"Who was going to be on top?"

"Not funny, Collin." He turned away, then jumped aside for a jogger who came up behind them. After the jogger passed, Seneca tried again. "We talked about how we didn't know how we fit into the world. Just before Aida started to bark, you said, 'Maybe we can help each other figure it out.' Do you remember?"

"Yeah." He waved to a girl in workout clothes across the street. "Morning Melanie." The girl waved back.

She stopped, forcing him to pull up short. Peabody Hill looked from her face to Collin's and laid down on the grass for a nap.

Collin's gaze slid across her face before his eyes locked on hers. There was nothing for her to read in the opaque depths, but she sensed his interest so she went for it. "Are you sure you want me? Because if you don't, say so now. Just so we're clear, I want the real thing with you. Not the 'I only kind of, sort of love you, but we get along really, really good' relationship like I had with Michael."

His face was closed. "I get it."

Did he? "I'm just going to lay it on the line here."

"Okay."

"I haven't gone more than five minutes this whole week without thinking of you. I want to have you in my life. All of you. Not just the hot you, but the you inside. Are you ready to open up and be close with me? If you're not, say so. Sure, I'll be hurt at first, but—"

"Okay."

"Okay what?"

"Okay, I'm in."

"That's all you have to say?"

"Tell me what else you want me to say."

She sighed and gave up. Her father's advice to go slow seemed wise. "Nothing. Let's go eat."

Collin stopped in front of a neighborhood café around the corner from his house. A green neon sign with the word "Trudy's" written in script hung above the door. Blue checked café curtains rippled in the windows and through the plate glass, blue checked tablecloths peeked out. As Collin tied the dog to a tree in front of Trudy's, the café door swung open, and Rory stepped out with his arm around the waist of a young woman teetering on three-inch, baby blue stiletto heels.

"Collie! Seneca! What are you two doing here?"

Collin straightened up and he and Rory did their ritual double fist bump, then Collin hugged the girl with Rory. "Hey DeeDee. Don't tell me you're giving this S.O.B. another chance." She flashed Collin a pretty smile, arched her neck and laughed. Her breasts seemed to pulse. To his credit, Collin managed to keep his eyes on DeeDee's face.

Rory proudly introduced DeeDee to Seneca. "Seneca, I'd like you to meet DeeDee Landman. DeeDee, this is Seneca."

DeeDee was eye-candy. A mane of curly platinum blond hair, china blue eyes, cute little dimples on her cheeks, and a perfect bow-shaped mouth. Her jeans were so tight Seneca didn't see how she could breath and her vee-neck blue sweater dove low enough to expose a deep valley between perky breasts. She wished she'd changed her T-shirt or at least put on some lipstick before she left Collin's house.

"Very nice to meet you," DeeDee drawled.

Rory studied Collin and Seneca. "How's the case going?"

"Solved," said Seneca.

"Oh?" He turned to Collin. "So what's happening, Bro?"

Collin looked nervous. Collin's eyes slid sideways and met hers. She arched her brows.

"Seneca and I are dating." He apparently didn't expect any congratulations because he slipped a hand around Seneca's arm and began to pull her toward Trudy's. "See you later, Bro."

Rory didn't move. "*You're* dating?"

"What's wrong with that?" He sounded defensive.

"Well nothing, I guess." He frowned at Collin then swung his gaze to Seneca. He was about to say something to her when DeeDee interrupted him.

"We gotta run along, sweetie pie, or we'll be late for my manicure." She waved her frosted pink talons at them. "I'm switching to an autumn color."

Rory glanced down at her small white hands. "Of course, honey." He turned back to Seneca and Collin. "Take good care of Seneca, Bro. Okay?" He didn't sound convinced this was a given.

Collin's jaw widened, and his eyes flashed with anger. He

nodded to DeeDee. "Welcome back." Then with firm pressure on Seneca's upper arm, he escorted her into Trudy's.

"What was that about?" she asked once they were seated.

He glanced up from his menu. "He's being an ass. Forget it."

"Collin—"

"Have you decided what you want?"

She sighed and opened her menu.

*

"You uttered two words all through breakfast, and those were 'bacon' and 'eggs.' On the walk over here, I shared my feelings with you and all I can get out of you is 'I'm in.'" She said the words in a deep, gravelly voice that mimicked his. "Something is bugging you or making you mad. Something I did."

He dropped his eyes to his plate.

"Collie. If you don't talk to me about what you feel, we can't have a relationship, can we?"

He didn't raise his head. "You're playing me again."

"Playing you? I don't understand."

"Maybe I'm way out of line here, but . . ." He trailed off, looking uncertain.

"It's okay, Collie. Just tell me."

"You slept with me every night in Peabody but you still kept me hanging the entire time before you told me you were breaking up with Michael. You dumped Michael and told *me* you never want to see me again. This morning you come to my house and say you are serious about me but you won't sleep with me. Can you explain what's going on so a regular guy like me can figure it out?"

He looked wounded. She reached across the table and squeezed his hand.

"I'm sorry I haven't looked at this from your point of view. That was selfish of me. But I feel like we put the cart before the horse back in Peabody, and I want us to slow things down a little so we can get this right. I don't want to start living with you before we're both sure we-we-we're serious about each other. We haven't even had an official date if you think about it."

The stubborn expression on his face said he didn't agree.

"Could we compromise?"

His eyes glittered suspiciously. "Compromise?"

She lowered her eyelashes, smiled at him and pressed another hot button. "If you give me one month of celibacy, I will give you a night you'll never forget."

A perfectly shaped, dark eyebrow popped up. She had him. "One week," he said.

Seneca figured he would haggle so she'd started high. "Two weeks from today and it's a deal."

He nodded.

"But you have to communicate with me the entire time."

"You can count on it, baby."

It was on. She knew just what she would do for his unforgettable night.

Chapter 27

Collin closed his office door and locked it. Night had already fallen across the city although it was just past five. He was supposed to shadow a client's husband who always had to "work late" on Wednesday nights, but never answered the phone when she called the office. If Collin didn't follow him tonight, he would have to wait an entire week for another opportunity. But he didn't care. Not tonight.

Outside he zipped up his jacket and turned up the collar against the cold. Steam rose from the sewer grates and writhed up toward the 'L' tracks above the street. A young man with a scruffy beard and backpack burst through a curtain of steam and bumped into him. Collin muttered an apology and walked on. He blew on his hands to warm them as he turned the corner and found his Jeep. He didn't turn on the radio as he wove through the rush hour traffic. Music, people, food, anything good irritated him today. He shouldn't enjoy any of it. Ever. He should be dead.

Peabody Hill was waiting for him in the dark townhouse. Seneca had her voice lesson tonight, then she would stick around and jam with the students and teachers at the conservatory until the building janitor kicked them all out at eleven-thirty. He let the dog outside then filled his bowls with kibble and fresh water. When the dog barked at the back door, Collin let him in again. With a deep sigh, Collin shrugged out of his jacket and retreated to his grandfather's study under the stairs.

He never used this room. He paid bills at a desk in his bedroom and used the family room attached to the kitchen for watching TV and entertaining. But when he needed to be alone with his thoughts, he came in here. His hand patted the wall beside the door until he found the light switch and flipped it on. One lone bulb came to life in the ceiling fixture, illuminating his grandfather's huge mahogany desk in the center of the room. He kept meaning to change the burned out bulbs in the chandelier, but he always forgot until he came in here. But the last bulb cast enough light so he could read the brass nameplate on the desk: *Benjamin Collins, M.D.*

He couldn't see the walls of the study through the heavy darkness but he didn't need to see what he knew by heart. Built-in bookcases stuffed with his grandfather's books covered two walls of the study. Half of the volumes were medical books, and Collin remembered how he loved to thumb through them when he helped his grandfather research a medical condition. There were other books too. History, philosophy, science and his grandfather's favorites—westerns. He had read every book in his grandfather's library by the time he graduated from high school. He could recite the titles of the books on the shelves by heart, starting from the top of each wall and going down. He reached out and smoothed his fingers down the spine of an old edition of *Grey's Anatomy.*

On the far side of the room, beneath heavy window drapes sat a plush red velvet sofa. Grandpa took a nap every afternoon on that sofa. "Refreshes the body," he told young Collin, who didn't understand how anyone could sleep when it was light outside. Against the last wall an old examination table from his grandfather's first office stood ready for the next patient. Beside it hung a genuine human skeleton. Grandpa used the skeleton— named Mr. White—to teach him the names of all the bones.

He crossed into the study and went to his grandfather's desk. He slumped into the worn leather chair behind the desk to brood. *Armistice Day. Veterans Day. Collin Fuck-Up Day. Alex Menendez's Death Day.* His hand closed around a bronzed stethoscope paperweight his grandfather received when he retired. He pressed the cold metal against his cheek. God, he missed Alex. Alex was the Hispanic version of Collin. Tall and handsome, dark where Collin was fair, strong and fast, smart. Alex had everything going for him except one thing. He was a sergeant in Collin Fuck-Up Atlee's detachment.

"Are girls allowed in the bat cave?"

He set down the stethoscope and looked up. Seneca stood in the doorway. She wore her coat and carried her violin case. She was studying him.

"Why aren't you at your lesson?"

"I switched it to Saturday."

"Why?"

She slipped into the room and approached him. "I was worried about you." She set her violin case on the desk beside the stethoscope, then shrugged out of her coat and laid it on top of the case.

"Worried?"

"You were a little melancholy this morning when I left for work. I thought you might need company tonight."

He had been looking forward to a night of brooding. Couldn't a man just be alone with his thoughts now and then without the whole world fussing over him? "I'm fine."

"Which is why you're keeping company with yourself in the dark."

She perched herself on the edge of Grandpa's desk and looked down at him. She was dressed for the office in a black V-neck sweater and gray slacks. A tiny diamond on a thin gold chain shimmered at her throat. With one hand, she tucked her auburn hair behind her ear, and his heart contracted with love.

"Come here."

She slid off the desk and onto his lap, settling herself against his thighs. He wound his arms around her and held her close. Burying his nose in her lemon-scented hair, he closed his eyes, and for a long time he thought about nothing, just let himself feel her closeness. Then he lifted his head. The rows of books rippled in the darkness.

"Three years ago today, I killed my best friend." He waited for Seneca to pop up and protest, but she remained curled against his chest. He kissed the top of her head. "There was this kid, Abdi. He spoke English. We met him in one of the villages north of Baghdad, and he offered to be our interpreter. Our mission was to recruit for the new police force. But we spent more time ducking bullets and detonating suspicious objects. It was slow-going, hotter than hell with all the gear we had to wear and the civilians wouldn't have anything to do with us."

Seneca stirred in his arms, then settled against him again. "So I was grateful to have Abdi. He became sort of an ambassador for us in the villages, and we got two candidates because of him. But Alex—that was my friend's name—didn't trust Abdi. He tried to tell me, but I didn't listen."

He closed his eyes again and remembered what Alex said. "He's too eager, Coll. Why aren't any other villagers volunteering? It doesn't make sense. Did you know he disappeared again last night?" Collin dismissed his concerns. With Abdi's help, he was getting some traction in the area.

"Then one day—today, three years ago—Abdi came and told us he'd found another recruit in a little town at a crossroads about five miles away. So we followed him. Right into an ambush. The whole town was maybe ten mud huts. There was no one on the street, not even a stray dog, which was unusual. But Abdi was with us, so I didn't worry. Then Abdi just melted away, and I realized Alex was right. I turned around to warn my men. That's when it happened, Sen."

"A bullet?"

He shook his head, then pressed his mouth against the side of her face. "No." He forced himself to tell her the rest and prayed he wouldn't die of shame.

"Roadside bomb. IED. Alex was killed on the spot. There were maybe a dozen insurgents hiding in the huts, and they began to fire at us so we dove for cover."

When he poked his head up from behind a low wall, he'd seen the young soldier with the leg wound still crawling toward cover.

Hopped up on adrenalin, he opened fire on the insurgent position as he darted from behind the wall and dragged the soldier back to safety. One of his men radioed for back-up as Collin bandaged his soldier's leg. *Just a little metal. You'll make it back to base, Davis.* He wrapped up the wound with gauze and surgical tape he always carried with him and turned back to the street.

"Alex's body was lying in a ditch by the road. We could tell from his injuries he was dead. But those fuckers starting shooting at it anyway. And we heard them laugh."

"You went back for the body, didn't you?"

He looked down at her. "How did you know?"

But she didn't say anything, just curled her legs up and snuggled close to him again.

She was right. He'd die before he'd leave Alex's body to be desecrated. His men gave him cover, and head down, heart beating like crazy, he sprinted the longest twenty yards of his life. He slung the body over his shoulder and ran like hell. When he returned to Baghdad, they gave him a bronze star for bringing the rest of his detachment back to base in one piece and putting himself in the line of fire to save his wounded and retrieve Alex's body. As if he could have done anything else.

He sat in the dark with Seneca for a long time. They listened to the traffic in the street die away and dinnertime turned into late evening and late evening into bedtime. He was content to hold her as a salve against the pain of Alex's death.

Then she lifted her head and looked at him. "It's almost midnight. If you wanted to stay with me tonight, it would be okay."

Even on day one of their celibacy period, he suspected it wouldn't be too much of a challenge to get her in bed. But he was enjoying the anticipation of her "unforgettable" night. If she showed up in his bedroom in her bra and panties, it would be enough to please him, and yet she had a way of throwing him off just when he'd figured her out. He didn't expect to be disappointed on Saturday night.

"I'll wait for my night of shock and awe. Speaking of which—" He bussed her lips. "If you go to the conservatory on Saturday, will you have enough time to prepare?"

She was not the least bit intimidated. Her beautiful green eyes were twinkling with laughter as she slid her arms around his neck. "I don't think I'm the one who needs to prepare, lieutenant."

His brow popped up, and he smiled despite himself. *Damn, he liked her.* "Thanks for brooding with me tonight, Sen."

She rose from his lap. "Hey, I have an idea. How about a memorial service for Alex? Wait here."

She spun around and hurried from the room. A moment later she returned with the American flag he hung by the front door on holidays. She propped it against the bookcase before the desk, then opened her violin case and pulled out her instrument. She stood beside the flag, tucked the violin under her chin and closed her eyes as she tuned up. Then she began to play "The Battle Hymn of the Republic."

He rose from his grandfather's chair and stood at attention. The strains of the music tightened around his body like his old dress uniform. He closed his eyes. When Seneca's clear voice began to sing the words, he hummed along with her and said a prayer for all the good men and women who never came home from war.

Chapter 28

Collin turned and inspected his room one last time. It was the biggest bedroom in the house after his grandfather's, which lay entombed at the opposite end of the hall. When he came back from his first stint in the army, he painted the walls in this room white and bought a second-hand bed, dresser and desk, plus a new mattress, extra firm. No paintings hung on walls, no curtains covered the metal blinds on the windows, no photos sat on his desk or bedside table. It was Spartan, a soldier's room, but Collin felt comfortable here.

He wanted Seneca to feel at home here too, so when she left for her make-up lesson at the conservatory this morning, he'd cleaned it until it could have passed an inspection by the sarge. Collin smoothed a little wrinkle out of the clean sheets on the bed. If he dropped a quarter on the thick brown blanket, it would bounce.

He was still fuming over his earlier confrontation with Rory, who was supposed to be his friend. Three minutes after Seneca left for her music lesson this morning, Rory rang Collin's doorbell. Collin had just thrown his sheets and towels into the washing machine and grabbed the old Hoover from the utility closet in the kitchen. He figured Seneca forgot something, so he pulled the front door open, his hand still gripping the vacuum, and Rory stood on his doorstep dressed for a day of wheeling and dealing in dark slacks, a blue dress shirt and buttery leather blazer.

"What do you want, Rory?"

Rory eyed the vacuum in Collin's hand. "You know, my cleaning lady has an extra day. This place would look so much better—"

"If the dust bothers you, leave."

"You're in a bad mood."

"I wasn't until you showed up. I'm busy right now. Why don't we meet for lunch next week? You pick the place, I'll buy."

A pair of pale pink house slippers attracted Rory's attention. "Is she staying here with you? Shit, Collie, what are you thinking? Seneca's classy. She's a *nice* girl."

Collin set down the vacuum and scowled at him. "What is that supposed to mean?"

He didn't back down. "It means you are an ass and you treat women like tramps."

"I do not."

"Then why did your last girlfriend try to run you over with her car?"

"I forgot her birthday, and she overreacted." He'd gotten cold feet and forgot on purpose, but that wasn't the point.

"*You* invited her out to dinner for her birthday and stood her up."

Seneca was different. He loved her. "Look, I promise to treat Seneca like the lady she is. Okay? Will you go now?"

Rory narrowed his eyes. "You hurt her, and you're not my bro. *Capiche?*"

Collin's temper caught fire. "*Capiche.* Now get the hell out of my house." He opened the front door. Rory had no choice. He stormed out, and Collin slammed the door behind him. Then he dragged the Hoover upstairs to clean his room for Seneca, but a little of his excitement had ebbed away.

Collin tried to push the whole Rory episode to the back of his mind as he inspected himself in his bathroom mirror. The cut on his face was healed. There was just a thin pink line where the hickory branch sliced his cheek. He'd gone for a haircut this afternoon and treated himself to a shave. Gray sweatpants hung low on his hips so Seneca would have plenty of lean, muscular torso to salivate over. Plus he didn't expect to be wearing clothes for long, and these were easy to pull off.

Earlier tonight he'd taken her out for a romantic dinner at a little bistro a few blocks away. They'd chatted through dinner about little things. He'd found himself describing how he'd played Cyrano de Bergerac to Rory's Christian in high school, penning overwrought poems for Rory so he could impress the girls. Seneca was curious.

"I'd sure like to read one of your poems sometime, Collie."

Her cheeks were pink from the wine, but also excitement. She'd been invited to sing a solo with the conservatory choir on Christmas Eve. He promised to come and cheer her on.

Not once during the dinner did she betray with a single word or expression that she was thinking about the unforgettable evening, or that they would make love before the end of the night. To borrow a word from Rory, she acted classy. Collin squirmed when the word popped into his head. *Damn Rory!* When they got home from the restaurant, she smiled up at him and said, "Give me a few minutes to freshen up, okay?" before she skipped up the stairs to her room.

He glanced at the clock radio beside his bed. He'd given her more than a few minutes. Fifteen to be exact. That should be enough time for even a classy lady to slip out of her dress, shouldn't it? He opened his door and went down the hall to her room. Her bedroom door was still closed. He knocked.

"Seneca?"

There was a rustle on the other side of the door, then the knob twisted, and the door opened. He blinked. "What are you wearing?" She was dressed as a peasant girl in a rose-colored, full skirt that fell to the middle of her bare calves. A thin white chemise, cut low and tucked into the waistband, veiled her tawny nipples and a black corset tightened across her ribs. The tops of her small white breasts mounded over the chemise.

She inspected him critically. "I could ask you the same thing, lieutenant." She cocked her head. "I thought a marauding soldier like you would have no trouble recognizing a village maiden when you saw one. Although if you are invading villages dressed like that, the farmers are probably running you off with their pitchforks before you get close to the maidens."

Amusement burst inside him. He loved her more than he ever thought possible. He took a step backward and gestured toward his room. "I, ah, better get dressed for marauding."

She tilted her chin up and raised a brow. "I guess you better. I'll be in my mean little hovel stirring the dinner porridge and praying I don't get ravaged by a marauding soldier tonight." Then she closed the door.

Still smiling, he hurried back to his room and put on his camo pants and his field jacket. He skipped briefs and a belt. What else? He glanced down at his feet. A soldier needed boots. He pulled on his combat boots and laced them halfway up. Then he marched down to Seneca's room in search of a maiden to ravage. He twisted the knob on her cottage door and opened it a crack. With his combat boot, he kicked it the rest of the way open just to demonstrate he was in the game. It banged against the wall. Seneca, standing beside the fireplace, jumped. Her hand went to her throat.

"Who are you?" Her eyes were sparkling, and she didn't look the least bit frightened.

"Lieutenant Atlee. I'm in charge of the Marauding Soldier battalion in this area."

She pressed herself against the chimney bricks. "What are you going to do to me?"

He strolled in, hands clasped behind his back, and proceeded to inspect her "cottage." He saw a silver baton leaning against the armoire and picked it up. He slapped it across his palm. "That depends."

"On what, sir?" She pressed her hand against her ribs, and his eyes dropped to her half-exposed breasts.

"On how cooperative you are." He lowered himself into one of the chairs in front of the fireplace and tried not to smile. "Come closer."

"Oh, sir. Please."

"Do as I say or I'll have to go out to your barn and ravage your cow."

Her mouth curved into a smile, and she bit her lips to hold back her laughter. "Not poor Bessie!" She shuffled forward.

He shot her his sexy, through-the-eyelashes look. Then he ran the tip of the baton down her creamy white shoulder and across her breasts. "Do you have any weapons under there?"

"No sir."

"Come closer so I can check." He rested the baton against the chair and spread his legs so she could stand between them. "Lean down."

He looked up at her face. She'd stopped laughing. Desire replaced amusement. He cupped the sides of her face with his hands and kissed her deeply. She tasted of wine and chocolate mousse. She braced herself against him, pressing her hands against his chest. He tried to concentrate on the game. "Let's see what you have in your blouse." Her lips brushed against his hair as he pushed down the top of her chemise and suckled each of her breasts. Her breath quickened, puffing against his forehead in soft gasps.

His erection scraped against his zipper. He grimaced, then pulled her chemise back up and covered her breasts. "No weapons there."

He set her away from him and closed his legs to adjust himself before retrieving the baton from the side of the chair. "What about here? Any weapons under here?" He lifted the side of her skirt with the baton, exposing shapely calves, slender thighs and a bare flank.

She licked her lips. "No, lieutenant, sir."

"Sit on my lap so I can check." He straightened up a little and held out his arms.

She took the baton from his hand and tossed it behind him. "I get nervous when you have a weapon." Then straddling his lap with her knees hugging his waist, she looked up at him and said, "Like this?"

"Exactly." He'd meant the word to sound gruff, but it came out like a choke. But Seneca seemed to have lost interest in the game. She brushed her mouth against his. Her tongue traced the shape of his lips. She pressed her half-exposed breasts against his field jacket and French-kissed him.

Her fingers fumbled at his neck and unbuttoned his jacket. Then her hands slipped further and she unbuttoned his pants. "Going commando tonight, lieutenant?" she whispered as she slid her fingers inside and touched him. He smiled despite the damn zipper, which felt like a thousand tiny pins every time it rubbed against his penis.

"Seneca," he gasped. He reached for the zipper, but she pushed his hand away.

"Let me. That's what village maidens are for, aren't they?"

He knew he should say something clever, but he couldn't think of anything. Seneca raised her hips off his lap, released his zipper carefully and pulled his pants over his hips. She lifted her skirts and lowered herself on him. He was buried deep inside her.

"Collie," she whispered as he slipped his hands under her skirt and caressed her bottom, her thighs, her desire. She moved on top of him, in slow motion at first, then faster. He opened his eyes and saw her head thrown back, her eyes closed. One perfect breast popped out of the chemise. She said his name again. *Collie.* It excited him more than anything she'd said or done all evening. His own pleasure came, so intense he could have died happy in the next moment.

He opened his eyes and looked up at her. She leaned into him, kissed his cheek and nibbled on his ear. "This counts as being on top, doesn't it?"

He thought about how perfect she was and how much he loved her.

*

Seneca was proud of herself. She could see by the expression on Collin's face she'd pleased him. She was gripped by an emotion that grew more intense as she held him. He stirred beneath her. She slid off his lap and stood. Her legs wobbled. He stood too, adjusting his pants and gingerly zipping them halfway up. He grinned at her. "Come on."

"Where?"

"Where you belong." He scooped her into his arms and carried her down the hall to his "barracks," which is what Seneca called his room. She'd poked her head in once when he was off on a "reconnaissance" mission. The man hadn't even laid a carpet over the worn wood floor. And a brown blanket? White sheets? Jeez! Fortunately, the sexy resident of these barracks made up for the complete lack of decoration.

But he was proud of himself as he carried her in and set her down beside his bed. They pulled their clothes off and threw them in a pile on the floor. A few moments later they were in each other's arms under his crisp, fresh-smelling sheets.

"So what did you think?" She propped her head on her elbow so she could look down at him.

He smiled into her eyes, his own sparkling like a million sapphires. "Definitely memorable." He kissed her. "Although you could have walked into my bedroom, taken off your clothes and climbed into my bed, and for me, it would have been memorable, too."

That was sweet. "You're easy to please, Collie."

A shadow flitted across his face. What was bothering him?

"Sometimes," he said. He traced her jaw with his finger. "My turn?" She nodded as he pushed her back into the mattress and brushed his lips against hers, soft as a feather. The goddess kiss. *He loves me.* He's telling me he loves me with his lips. An emotion that was almost maternal rose inside her. Instinctively she knew he never allowed himself to be vulnerable. At least not since his grandfather passed away. It was going to be hard for him to be in love when he didn't know how to lower his guard.

"I love you." She whispered the words against his lips.

His eyes popped open in surprise. She read uncertainty and fear in his face. His mouth tightened. "Don't say that. You don't know anything about me. Not really."

She reached up and caressed his perfect face. "You're right. There are a million things I don't know about you. Like your middle name. I am in love with a guy and I don't even know his middle name."

"Richard." He mumbled the word.

"Or your birthday."

"First of February." He relaxed just a little.

"I don't know your favorite color."

"I don't have one." His eyes darted away from her. "Maybe green. Like grass in the spring."

Seneca laid her hand against his chest. "Look at me." His heart thumped beneath her palm. "What I do know about you is what's in here. That's what I love."

Their eyes met. Collin looked scared to death. "I-I have a-a-a thing for you, too."

She wanted to laugh, but instead she stroked his hair. "You make me feel like a pepperoni pizza."

He studied her. A large hand slid across the sheet and closed around her breast. "I guess I love you too." He bent his head and kissed her. "No more talking," he whispered.

Chapter 29

Seneca pushed the heavy front door closed until the latch clicked. As she adjusted her eyes to the gloom of the townhouse, a brass key spiraled through the air and landed on the carpet by the toe of her boot. She looked up. Collin glared down at her from the landing.

"A girl dropped off your old apartment key. She said you can move back in anytime."

Seneca's heart sank. Every morning for the past week, she'd told herself, I'll talk to him today. I'll tell him how I feel. But she knew he would take it badly so she kept finding excuses to put it off.

Seneca unbuttoned her coat and shrugged it off. "Let's talk."

"About what? You're breaking up with me. Just pack your things and get out."

The hall was tomb-like in the shadowy twilight of the December evening. A cracked China lamp sitting on a small chest in the curve of the stairs did little to cast out the darkness. The squares of colored glass in the window behind him were opaque, and through the clear panes bare branches swayed in the sharp winter wind and light flakes of snow spun past in thin waves. She crossed the worn carpet so she could see him clearly. "I'm not breaking up with you. We agreed when I moved in it was just temporary."

"Bullshit. I never agreed."

"Please listen." He stood ramrod straight on the landing wearing his jeans with the patch Seneca stitched on them. She'd sat at the kitchen table in Peabody, Momma's old sewing basket at her feet and Collin in Poppy's chair across from her. He described his breakfast with Henry until she was belly laughing and stuck her finger with the needle. It seemed like a million years ago.

"Please." She began to climb the stairs toward him.

He threw back his shoulders and tensed.

How could she make him understand? "Almost a month ago, I looked you in the eyes and said 'I loved you.' And what did you say to me? 'I have a thing for you too.' I don't have a thing for you, Collie. I have a deep and abiding love for you." It felt good to say the words again. To tell him she loved him even if he didn't want to hear it. After their 'unforgettable night,' he did everything to keep her at arm's length but muzzle her. He knew when she was about to go mushy on him. He'd kiss away her words before she could speak or, in what was now a familiar ritual, he'd mutter 'no more talking' in a husky whisper and take her in his arms. It was getting old.

"I said it back." He sounded defensive, but even when saying the word 'love' could mean keeping her here with him, he couldn't say a simple 'I love you.'

"You said you *guessed* you loved me."

His jaw hardened. "What do you want? Do you expect me to go all romantic on you? Should I get down on one knee and confess my everlasting love like we're starring in a lame chick flick?"

She breached the last few steps and stood in front of him on the landing. It was past time to have this out. She wanted an adult relationship, marriage, and family. But she couldn't force him to want those things too.

When she told her father how she felt, he'd said, "Collin is stubborn. That's a good quality for a soldier, but a bad one for a lover. He can't be pushed or pulled, daughter. You have to give him space to work through his hang-ups. Hope for the best." For a man who'd lived most of his life on a mountainside, her father was extraordinarily wise.

She folded her arms across her chest. "Yes, Collie, that's exactly what I expect. Without sexy looks or jokes, just look me straight in the eyes and be there in every way, including romantic. One-hundred percent."

"You're being ridiculous. I don't think you-you-you care about me at all."

"I do care about you, but you're not ready for the kind of relationship I want, Collie. You're still finding your way." She tried to reach out and touch his arm, but he backed away from her.

"What the fuck does that mean?"

Her eyes filled with tears. "It means all this." She raised her arms and took in the townhouse. "You live in a mausoleum. Every time I turn a corner, I expect to run into a ghost. You're the smartest, bravest man I've ever met. You're a natural healer. But how do you make a living? Spying on cheating husbands and dishonest store clerks. You refuse to make amends with your parents and despite all your noble talk about doing them a favor, I think you're afraid of what they'll make you feel, and how much it might hurt."

His eyes were cold blue glass. His face chiseled in stone. "Why can't people just accept me for who I am? Why is everyone out to change me?" His words sounded rough, and there was a dismissive edge to his tone. He was not talking much longer.

It made Seneca angry. "*We* do accept you for who you are, Collin. The only person who can't accept you for who you are is *you*."

He was done. "Get out. Go back to your-your cramped little shoebox. I hope you're very happy." He pushed her aside and started down the stairs.

Her anger melted. She was losing him. "I'll wait for you."

"Then you'll wait until hell freezes over."

His combat boots thumped on each creaky stair as he raced down the steps and slammed into his grandfather's cave-like study. He shut the door with such force, the staircase railing shook. The flag, which had remained propped against the bookshelves, clattered to the floor. Then the chair behind the desk creaked. Seneca pictured him brooding alone in that dark, dusty room, another memorial to his grandfather like so many other rooms in this house, and it made her sad.

She climbed the stairs slowly, each footstep heavy and miserable, and went to her room to pack. It didn't take long to gather her things together. When she finished, she looked around to see if she'd forgotten anything. Her eyes settled on the baton, which was back in its proper home beside the armoire. She crossed the room and picked it up. Her eyes filled with tears again as she remembered their unforgettable night. She'd been so happy, so hopeful, so in love. But as the weeks passed, she'd become less and less sure Collin was ready for more than a bed-warmer and occasional dinner companion.

As she dropped the baton into her backpack to take as a keepsake, she saw the plastic bag she used to hold her Berger Woods pebbles. Another memento of something that was dead. What better place to lay it to rest than this townhouse filled with mementos of people and events long past. Seneca opened the drawer beside the bed and pulled out a blue satin ribbon that matched Collin's eyes. Perfect. The note she wrote was simple. *Chose Collin today. I'm in love. October 24.* Seneca tied the ribbon around the bag of pebbles and thrust the note into the knot before she dropped the little package into the drawer beside the bag of sand and sea glass. Then she gathered up her things and left.

Chapter 30

Collin rubbed his eyes and stretched his back. The numbers on his computer waved and split. He focused his aching eyes at the wall in front of him until they glazed over. This office reminded him of a prison. Bare white walls, steel gray industrial carpet and a second-hand desk with peeling oak veneer. Funny, it never bothered him before. But he'd never spent so much time here.

Damn Seneca! Why did she have to call his house creepy? He could barely stand to sleep there anymore. He'd just wanted to preserve his grandfather's memory. Since when did that make him ghoulish? But it was more than the house. He missed her like crazy. He hated coming home at night to his dark, empty house. He'd never felt like such a failure in his life.

After a week of dark fury, he'd admitted—to himself at least—she was dead on about the detective agency. He was wasting his time. He'd made up his mind to do another tour with Special Forces. They'd probably send him to the Middle East again, but at least he'd do something important. If Seneca found out he'd re-upped, would she think better of him?

A shadowy head moved on the other side of his office door. A murky hand rapped on the glass.

"It's open," he called, grateful for a visitor. He hadn't talked to a living soul since he stopped for gas a few days ago.

Rory came into the office wearing in a tailored wool overcoat. His cheeks were pink from the cold, and snowflakes melted in his hair. "Merry Christmas, Bro."

"Christmas isn't for a couple of days." Collin hated Christmas, which he'd spent alone last year when he came back from Iraq. This Christmas would be worse than the others because he'd not only be alone, he'd be alone missing Seneca.

"Tomorrow's Christmas Eve."

"So it is." He tried to sound like he didn't care. "Big plans?"

Rory grabbed a chair and sat. "Funny you should ask. I am getting engaged tomorrow night."

"Engaged? To DeeDee?"

Rory grinned. "Of course DeeDee. Who else would I ask?"

"Gee, Bro, isn't this kind of sudden? You've only been back together for a few months." It irked him that Rory was still with the girl he loved while Collin's girl walked out on him after a month.

"Not really. I love DeeDee, and she loves me. I want her to be my wife." Rory smiled and leaned forward. "Collie, you are going to love this. I have come up with the greatest proposal idea ever."

"Proposal idea? Don't you just sort of ask?"

"What's wrong with doing something special to honor DeeDee? Why shouldn't I tell the whole world how awesome and wonderful she is and how much I love her?" Rory looked hurt.

Collin's forehead began to throb. He rubbed it. "So tell me about your great proposal idea."

Rory leaned forward. He smiled and his eyes glittered with eagerness. "Okay. So tomorrow night the club has the Christmas Eve dinner. I wish you could come with us, but your mom and dad didn't go to Florida for Christmas this year so they'll be there, and I—"

"I get the picture." As if he would have shown his face at Arrowhead Country Club even if his parents were out of town. The members would ask him what he was up to, and he'd be forced to tell them he lived in a mausoleum and spied on cheating husbands for a living, to quote a certain lady he couldn't stop wanting. "Go on."

Rory blinked. "Right. So where was I? Oh, yeah, so right after dinner when everyone's having their coffee and stuff, it's going to happen."

Was Rory proposing in front of the entire membership of the Arrowhead Country Club? "What exactly is happening?"

"I hired this guy to dress up as Santa. He'll come into the dining room with a sack that's supposed to be filled with toys. And he'll say something like, 'Ho, ho, ho. I've come to deliver a very special gift to a very special lady. Where's DeeDee Landman?' So DeeDee will raise her hand, and Santa will come over and pull out a little ring box. My mother is going to wrap it in gold paper. Oh!"

He grabbed his coat and dug around in the pocket. "Here, Bro, you have to see this stone. It's unbelievable. One of a kind." He pulled out a Cartier ring box and lifted the lid. Nestled inside was the biggest diamond Collin had laid eyes on since he left Lake Forest.

"Wow!"

"Yeah, isn't it awesome? It's five carats, plus there's all the little diamonds on the band. Do you think she'll like it?"

He pictured DeeDee waving her frosted fingernails in the autumn air. "Yeah, she'll like it."

"I think so too. As soon as I saw it, I thought of DeeDee." Rory snapped the lid shut. "Where was I?"

"Santa has arrived at the club and asked for DeeDee."

"Right. So he pulls the ring out of his sack and hands it to her, and that's when I go down on one knee and propose."

"In front of everyone?" He couldn't understand why his friend would do such a thing. He would open himself up to ridicule or rejection while the whole country club watched.

"Of course in front of everyone. That's the point."

"What if she says 'no'?"

Rory's face dropped. "Why would she do that? She loves me. I love her."

"Sorry, Bro. Just feeling a little jealous, I guess."

Rory studied him. "After I propose, we're driving down to the city for midnight services. Seneca is singing."

The solo. He hadn't forgotten about it, but he couldn't show his face there now. Not after the way he'd treated her. He should have just said he loved her. Told her what she wanted to hear. But he'd tried so hard to keep everything friendly and cool. Deep and abiding love? That was nothing. Try a love that squeezed you so tight you couldn't take a full breath. Once he let that out of the cage, she would run for cover.

"Her dad is singing in Peabody for Christmas and she's singing up here, so she's sort of alone too. She's okay about it though. She's heading home for New Year's. You could come with DeeDee and me to hear Seneca."

"Nah. I'll probably stay in and watch *It's a Wonderful Life*." He grinned and tried to make it sound like a joke, but Rory didn't see the humor.

"Sure you will, Collie." He leaned forward and looked Collin straight in the eyes. "I predict you'll be a lonely old man someday. But don't worry, Bro. You'll always have me and DeeDee to lean on." He cleared his throat and went back to being happy. "DeeDee and I are eating Christmas dinner with my folks. I'm sure my mother would love to have you come too."

"Thanks, but I have plans."

Rory looked skeptical. "Staring at your walls?" Then his expression rearranged itself into alarm. He jumped up from the visitor's chair. "Oh my god! What time is it, Collie?"

"Almost seven. Why?"

"DeeDee's meeting me at the Cadillac Theatre in fifteen minutes. I'm taking her to see *Jersey Boys*. I can't be late!" He reached across the desk and fist bumped Collin. Then he grabbed his coat. "Merry Christmas, Bro," he said as he pulled open the door.

He stopped and turned around. His expression was tentative. "I, uh, almost forgot. Your father is having bypass surgery right after Christmas. That's why your folks aren't going to Florida for the holidays this year. Anyway, thought you'd want to know." He stepped into the dusky corridor and yanked the detective agency's sticky door shut behind him.

Collin rose from his chair as Rory's head disappeared. The elevator door screeched open, then closed again with a clank. He was too numb to move. This was his nightmare from Peabody Ridge when he'd told Tom about Poppy.

He collapsed back into his chair and a cold sweat broke out on his forehead. His father's heart was bad. He was having open heart surgery. Who would sit with his mother while his father was in surgery or relieve her while she kept a vigil at his bedside? Probably his father's two snobby sisters who would find a way to blame his mother for his dad's clogged arteries. What if his father died? Seneca's anguished words came back to him. Was he afraid to face his parents? Lieutenant Collin Atlee, Special Forces, afraid? He thought about the argument that started it all, and from the distance of years, his father didn't come off as the embodiment of all things evil that he seemed at the time.

It happened right after Grandpa Collins' funeral. He moved back to Lake Forest where he laid on his bed all day hating himself. After a week of being holed up in his bedroom, there was a sharp rap on his bedroom door and his father walked in before he could say, "Go away." Behind him, his mother huddled in the doorway, bleary-eyed and wilted.

"Collin. Collie. Are you okay?"

His father glanced back at Collin's mother and dragged a chair over to the bed. He sat down, crossed his legs and adjusted the crease in his trousers—a gesture Collin had seen him do a hundred times and suddenly despised.

"Son, you have to quit beating yourself up over your grandfather."

Collin stared at him. His father cocked an eyebrow and stared back. Finally, Collin broke the silence in a voice rusty from disuse. "I killed him, Dad. Fine doctor I would have made." Over his father's shoulder, he saw his mother blink away tears and turn away.

"He was eighty-seven years old, Collie. He had high blood pressure. You know that."

"It doesn't matter. He would still be alive if I hadn't been so selfish."

His father studied him. "What are you going to do?"

Collin shrugged. He knew what he wasn't going to do. He wasn't going to go to college, and he wasn't going to be a doctor. He'd done enough damage to humanity.

"Don't know."

"School starts in less than a month."

"Dad, I'm not going. I've already informed Stanford."

"So the school admissions counselor told me when he called. I instructed him to hold your place." His father paused. Then in a gentle voice, he said, "Collie. You have your whole future ahead of—"

"No!" The word exploded out of his mouth, and his jaw hardened into stone. "Don't you even care that the greatest man in the world just died and it's my fault? I'm not made of ice like you. I can't just act like nothing happened!"

His father was accustomed to obedience. Handling defiance wasn't one of his skill sets. He rose from his chair and glared down at his son, his dark eyes flashing with anger. He stabbed a finger at him.

"Three weeks from today, you will pack your bags and you will get on a plane to California and you will enroll at Stanford. Do you understand?"

Collin sneered at him. "Or what?"

"Or," said his father, "you can get the hell out of my house."

So Collin had gotten the hell out of his father's house.

As he sat in his office recalling the fight with his father, he couldn't even remember how he felt then. He'd been a spoiled brat who thought he would teach his father a lesson. But he'd done all the learning since then. Were there a couple of more lessons he needed to master?

He sighed. It was getting late, and he had a job to tie up tonight. A woman with three small children at home discovered her husband was leaving work early when he told her he was working late. She wanted to know what he was doing. Collin followed him for the past two nights to a bowling alley. Last night, he followed the man inside and discovered he worked a second job at the shoe rental counter for Christmas money. He could have called her to report on what he found, but he wanted to deliver the news personally. It beat going home to an empty mausoleum. He pulled on his jacket, turned off the lights in his office and locked the door.

*

"Thank you, Mr. Atlee." His client brushed a tear from her eye. "Merry Christmas to you and your family."

"Thanks, ma'am." No point explaining he didn't have a family.

Collin sprinted across the street and jumped into the Jeep. As he slid the key into the ignition, he saw the not-so-errant husband scurry up the front steps of the modest brick bungalow. Through the wide front window, two little girls with dark ponytails pounded on the glass with their small fists and waved. The man waved back. The girls turned away from the window and a moment later he stood behind them. The little girls leapt into his arms. Their father wasn't a big man, half the size of Collin, but he managed to lift them both up together and kiss them soundly. Collin shivered. He reached over to the passenger seat and groped for his coffee. It was cold.

Once the girls were back on solid ground, the man bent down. When he straightened up, he held a little boy wearing a blue shirt and diaper. He hugged the boy, then tussled his brown hair. Collin wanted to have a little boy of his own to love.

Collin's client came into the front room. She was a pretty woman with a dark ponytail like her daughters. She wore jeans and a red sweater with a green Christmas tree on the front. She hugged her husband and the little boy. The girls began to jump up and down and tug on the man's coat. The man and wife smiled at each other. Then the girls were caught up in a family hug.

The little group dispersed, and the homecoming seemed over. He'd slipped the Jeep into Drive when the man came back into view dragging a Christmas tree. The three children followed close behind him, skipping and chattering with each other. Collin put the gear back into Park and leaned back in his seat. He told himself he'd just watch for a few more minutes then call it a night.

Collin's client appeared. A stack of boxes teetered in her arms. As he watched, the little family set up their Christmas tree and began to pull lights and ornaments from the boxes. He should leave. He had no business spying on this private family time, but he couldn't tear his eyes away. He held his breath when the little boy reached up too high to hook an ornament on a branch and the tree teetered. The man steadied it, and they all laughed.

In the darkness and cold of the Jeep, he stared into the bright front room of the bungalow. If Seneca was sitting beside him now, he would slip an arm around her shoulders and pull her close. He would tell her how he really felt. But he'd blown his chance, hadn't he? He turned back to the bungalow.

He watched as the client's husband lifted the little boy high in the air. His chubby little arms stretched up to the top of the tree and set a gleaming silver star on the highest branch. Collin's client and the little girls watched and clapped. Collin would have given anything to be in that room. With Seneca. He frowned as the realization struck him. He could have this too. It was within his reach. She'd said she would wait for him. If he was willing to change, she would give him a second chance.

He thought about Rory. Hiring Santa might warm the heart of DeeDee Landman, but he doubted it would have any effect on Seneca Simms. He remembered the orange vest and the surprise in her eyes when she nearly tripped over him on the gravel trail. Her bright hair swinging from side-to-side as she stormed off after breaking up with Michael. He heard her violin playing "The Battle Hymn of the Republic" on Alex's death day. He tasted the sweetness in her voice when she told him that she loved him.

He would have to do this the hard way. Soldier-style. One-hundred-percent, just as she said. He'd need a list of targets and a battle plan. Timing would be important. Final negotiations would be delicate . . .

He had a lot to do. He twisted the key in the ignition and the Jeep roared to life. The happy family in the little bungalow didn't notice the dark Jeep pull away from the curb as they hung candy canes on the tree. Collin headed home to draw up plans for the most important mission of his life.

Chapter 31

Seneca sat on her blue sofa fingering a new Gibson six-string acoustic guitar she bought herself for Christmas. She couldn't play her violin in the apartment without disturbing the neighbors, but the low register of her guitar didn't penetrate the walls the way her violin did. She was absent-mindedly plucking out the tune to Jingle Bells, feeling just a little sorry for herself because she was alone and it was Christmas Day, when someone rapped on her door.

"Open up, Sen."

Collin. Since he'd finagled himself into the building already, there was no point in ignoring him. Not that she wanted to. She missed him so much, she'd considered moving back in with him, but as her father pointed out, "You'll be back at square one. And how long will it take you to get tired of the situation again?"

Seneca set her guitar down and let Collin in. He loomed over her in the doorway dressed in camo pants tucked into combat boots, a black tee shirt and his leather jacket. The effect was a combination Hells Angel and regular infantry. Not exactly festive. "Merry Christmas."

"Same to you." His eyes moved down her body past her ratty green sweater and jeans, to her bare feet. "Get your shoes on. Let's go."

"Go where?"

"Lake Forest."

"Lake Forest? I don't understand."

A tiny muscle quirked under his left eye. "Hell just froze over."

Lord Almighty. Was he going home? "Can you please be more specific?"

"You'll see when we get there."

"Collin—"

"Please, Sen. For once in your life, will you just cooperate?"

She studied him for a moment. His face was pale, his body tense, his expression closed like the afternoon he stormed Peabody

Ridge. If he was storming a certain mansion in Lake Forest, he'd need backup. She looked down at her old jeans and stretched-out sweater with the little fuzz balls on the elbows. She was not going to Lake Forest dressed in her oldest clothes. "I have to change."

"You look fine."

"I am not appearing in Lake Forest looking like a refugee."

He sighed. "Just hurry. We'll wait downstairs." He looked down at Peabody Hill who sat at attention awaiting orders. "Move out."

"Collin, no! He'll drool all over everything."

They stared at her as if she'd just blasphemed the Lord himself. "I'm not going in without my battalion."

She put her hands on her hips and inspected his military getup again. "You're not armed, are you?"

His eyes narrowed. "No." He turned and opened the door. "Hurry up." Then the door closed behind the Peabody Battalion of two.

If they made it past the front door, Seneca wanted to make a good first impression on the Atlees. She chose a black turtleneck sweater dress in soft wool, black tights and suede boots. She looped a red scarf around her neck and slipped the emerald studs her father sent her for Christmas in her ears. She looked out the window to see what Collin was up to. On the sidewalk below, he was hunkered down in front of Peabody Hill, talking earnestly to the dog as he rubbed his neck. Well, whatever his flaws, no one could ever call Collin boring. She grabbed her jacket and headed out.

After a futile attempt to drag the battle plan out of Collin, they spent the trip to Lake Forest in silence. Christmas carols played on the radio, but neither of them listened. Seneca gazed out the Jeep window at the tall apartment buildings along Sheridan Road, which gave way to beautiful old homes on tree-lined streets. Beside her, Collin was wound up so tight, the air in the car crackled, and even the dog found it impossible to relax. He sat on the backseat behind Seneca, nose thrust out into the frigid December air, and slobbered on the back window all the way to Lake Forest.

A sign beside the road announced 'The Village of Lake Forest.' Collin's hand groped for the radio and turned it off. A few miles further on, past the quaint little downtown, he flipped on his signal and turned into a narrow lane. He pulled the Jeep onto the dirt shoulder.

"Sen." He was turned away so she couldn't see his face. Her name sounded like an apology on his lips. He took a deep, cleansing breath. "I don't know what will happen. Rory and Ray think—but I don't know. I may get the door slammed in my face. They could be angry I stayed away so long. I don't know."

Seneca reached across the seat and pressed her hand against his arm. Beneath her fingers, a muscle flinched. "Whatever happens, we'll face it together. The way we have everything else these past few months. Okay?"

He nodded, and the car rolled forward again. Mansions that could have held ten Simms households sat on woody lots the size of city blocks. On the east side of the road, the icy waters of Lake Michigan and a gray winter sky peeked between houses and trees. Beneath a thin layer of winter frost, weedless, manicured lawns awaited spring.

The Jeep slid around a gentle bend, and a yellow streamer tied around a gate post whipped in the wind. Another ribbon, still tied in a neat bow, circled the opposite gate post. Beside her, Collin said, "What?" Then he accelerated the Jeep, squealing into a wide cobblestone driveway, and screeched to a halt halfway to the house. Seneca's shoulder belt locked, and poor Peabody Hill nearly lost his snout before he caught his balance. He barked at Collin, but Collin was gaping at a sea of yellow ribbons and didn't notice. Every tree, every bush, every lamp, every fence post was tied with a yellow ribbon. One hundred yellow ribbons just like the song. Would there be exactly one hundred if she counted them?

"Oh, Collie." Then she couldn't think of anything else to say.

He opened the door and pushed out of the car. He stood beside the Jeep, leaning against the door, and his eyes roamed over the lawn. When he moved, it was to pinch the bridge of nose. Then he began to walk toward the sea of yellow.

Seneca leaned over his seat and pulled his door shut, then turned off the Jeep and dropped the keys into her pocket. She looked back at the dog. His nose was out the window again, and he was sniffing up Lake Forest air like it was the most expensive in the world. She got out of the car and opened the door for Peabody Hill. They stood by the car and watched Collin wander across the lawn, touching the trees and fingering the ends of the ribbons as if he'd never seen trees or ribbons before in his life.

A movement caught the corner of her eye, and she turned toward the stately Tudor-style mansion enthroned on a grassy rise. The front door opened, and a tall, gray-haired man came out on the front steps and studied Collin. Even from halfway down the long circular driveway, she recognized the high forehead, aristocratic nose and prominent cheekbones of Richard Atlee. His mouth moved and she thought he said, "Collie," but she couldn't be sure. He took a step backward. Her heart nearly stopped. Was Collin right? Was his father going to shut the door in his face? But he stuck his head back in the house and shouted, "Marti, come here. Hurry!" Then he spun around and stepped down the gracefully curved front steps.

Collin heard his father too. He turned and faced him, standing alone on the wide lawn, a sea of yellow undulating behind him, penitent and exposed. For the first time since Seneca met him, he looked vulnerable. In stoic silence, he watched his father cross the driveway and walk across the lawn to him. The walk seemed endless, and she wondered if Collin felt the same way.

When Richard reached his son, he stopped. Collin bowed his head and said, "Dad." Then his father took the last step and pulled him into his arms. Collin's arms closed around his father's shoulders. The two men embraced, holding each other so tight, she couldn't tell where one began and the other ended.

A scream from the house broke the tension on the lawn. A slender woman with shoulder-length blonde hair and blue eyes framed in long, dark lashes stood on the steps. She was pure elegance in winter white wool slacks and sweater, but expensive clothes couldn't contain the former pompon girl inside.

"Collie!" she cried.

With apparent reluctance, Richard released his son and turned. The woman screamed again. She kicked off her doeskin high heels, sending each spinning high in the air before they clattered to earth against the cobblestones. Barefoot, she skipped down the steps and raced across the frozen lawn, arms wide open, face twisted with emotion. She threw herself into Collin's arms with such force, he had to take a few steps backward and spin her to keep his balance. Her body shook as she clung to her son's neck, and when he spun away from the Jeep, Seneca saw she was sobbing. Collin held her tight against him, and once he'd steadied himself, his father stepped close again, put his arms around his wife and son and hugged them.

Collin stirred first, releasing his mother and straightening up. He turned to Seneca and held out his hand, and she walked across the lawn to him, slipped her hand into his and squeezed it tight.

"Mom, Dad, I'd like you to meet Seneca Simms."

His father's smile was warm enough to heat the entire state of West Virginia. "Welcome, Seneca. I'm Richard." He slid an arm around his wife's shoulders. "This is Marti." Richard's smile faded. His dark eyes focused on Peabody Hill, who'd just sauntered up. "Who's this?"

Collin grinned. "My backup."

Richard's gaze slid to his son's camo pants and combat boots, then back to the dog. "Preparing to take on an army of rabbits?"

Collin laughed. Marti giggled. Seneca smiled. Collin's sense of humor was an inheritance from his father.

Richard's eyes traveled around the group, then he said, "Why don't we go inside and talk." Everyone nodded. He led them inside, stooping to pick up Marti's shoes. After settling Peabody Hill on a very expensive-looking carpet in the two-story entry, they followed Richard to a cozy family room near the back of the house. Seneca tried not to gawk at the magnificent rooms or the twelve-foot Christmas tree in the foyer. A fire was crackling in the fireplace, and newspapers were scattered on the floor. She judged it was professionally decorated. Hunter green silk covered the walls and a sofa and loveseat were upholstered in prints that picked up the green color. Every stick of furniture fit perfectly.

Richard gestured toward the loveseat. "Please sit." Collin and Seneca sat down, and Marti settled herself on the sofa and tucked her feet under her.

"Can I get anyone a drink?" Richard asked.

Collin shook his head. "Not right now." Seneca and Marti shook their heads, too.

Richard sat down beside Marti and gathered her in close to him. "I imagine we all have things we want to say." He looked at Collin. "But I'd like to go first if that's all right with everyone." He didn't wait for permission.

His dark eyes were solemn, and they never wavered from Collin's face. "I am sorry, son. My thoughtlessness has caused you and your mother a great deal of pain, and I never intended for that to happen."

Collin nodded.

"As you might remember, I'm not much for conversations about feelings, but there are a few things you need to know. I'll say them now because I want to be sure we're clear, then I'll probably never mention them again. But I'll always be thinking them."

Collin nodded again. His eyes never left his father, but he squeezed Seneca's hand so tight, her fingers ached.

"First, your mother and I have followed your military career and life in general through Rory. He's been kind enough to bring us news. We are so proud of—" Richard's voice broke. He cleared his throat. "We are so proud of you, Collie. Of everything you've done for the country and everything you've done in your life."

Seneca's fingers began to tingle as Collin's grip on them tightened.

"Second, and this is my most important point." He broke his gaze from Collin for just a moment and looked at Marti. She nodded, then dabbed at her nose with a tissue. He turned back to Collin. "I love you. We love you. We want you in our lives no matter what. If I ever get angry with you again or we fight, please remember this." He reached up and pinched the bridge of his nose. The gesture was exactly like his son's. "That's all I have to say."

Collin bowed his head. "I'll remember." He released Seneca's hand. Then he leaned forward, propped his elbows on his knees and stared down at the floor. "My turn." The silence in the room thickened. She listened to the fire crackle and breathed in its woody perfume while she waited. Then he tilted his head up and looked at his parents.

"Since I left Ops, I haven't been living up to my potential. I've been accused of living in a mausoleum and wasting my time with the detective agency." He stopped and glanced at Seneca. Her face reddened. She hadn't meant to be cruel, but that's how it sounded on Collin's lips. She glanced at Richard and Marti. They were studying her. Collin turned back to his parents and went on. "She also said I was afraid to come here. She was right on all three counts."

"So I've decided to go to medical school. I want to be a pediatrician like Grandpa Collins. I'll take the exam next month. I'd like to practice in West Virginia. That's where Seneca is from, and I think I could be useful there."

His father tilted his head. "Are you and Seneca, ah, planning a future together?"

Collin stared at his father. "I don't know." He took a deep breath, exhaled, then slid off the loveseat, falling on one knee in front of her. He took her hands in his and raised his eyes to her. They were filled with love. "I love you, Sen. I love you so much I want to spend the rest of my life with you and have a family with you and-and make you proud. I promise to give you one-hundred percent every day. Would you do me the honor of being my wife?"

For a split second, Seneca tore her eyes from Collin's to assess Richard and Marti's reaction to this new turn of events. They both looked shocked. Nothing like being dropped into the middle of your son's life. Maybe a little perspective would help . . . plus she'd make Collin squirm a little. Which he deserved. Battle plan, indeed.

She looked back at him and squeezed his hands. "Collie. You are truly a wonderful man. You have a kind heart and a special way with people. You found my father for me and helped him get back on his feet. You spent your own money to help Matt go to school. You gave me and Peabody Hill a place to stay when we lost our lease." A slight frown marred his face. He was growing impatient. She got to the point. "I love you, too, Collie. I would be honored to have you as my husband."

He smiled. "Good." He released her hands and unbuttoned the back pocket of his camo pants. He dug around for a moment until he pulled out a platinum ring with a modest, square diamond. "Mined in Canada. No blood." He slipped it on her finger. "It's not as big as the one DeeDee got, but I'm just a retired soldier so I hope you will accept this ring as a token of my love."

"It's beautiful, Collie."

He lifted himself off the floor and sat down next to her again. He looked at this father. "I guess we're officially planning a future together."

Richard's eyebrow quirked up. "I don't know when marriage proposals went public, but the practice is beginning to grow on me." He stood. "Well, I better get the champagne."

*

It was late when they said goodbye to Richard and Marti. The clouds had lifted, and the sky was filled with stars. The waning winter moon sat high above the Atlee mansion. Collin and Seneca strolled down the cobblestone driveway with Peabody Hill while Richard and Marti watched and waved from the steps. Collin was returning in a few days to take his father to the hospital and sit with his mother. After his father recovered, Marti would come to Chicago to help them clean out the townhouse. Then there was a wedding to plan, although Collin made it clear he wasn't waiting long so Seneca and Marti better keep it simple.

After Collin helped Seneca and Peabody Hill into the car, he turned one last time to wave goodbye to his parents, and his gaze traveled to the yellow ribbons waving brightly in the moonlight. He strode into the stand of trees again, stopping at a tree with a large bow. He reached into the breast pocket of his jacket and pulled out his pocket knife. Then he cut the ribbon off the tree and stuffed it in his pocket. He waved again to his parents before trotting back to the Jeep.

*

Michael Berger settled back in his ergonomic chair as he listened to his new girlfriend putter around in the kitchen as she cooked the lentil patties for dinner. He took a sip of green tea and opened up the local paper. He usually skipped the *Engagements and Weddings* page, but something caught his eye. He sat straight up, righting himself so quickly, he nearly spilled his tea.

Simms–Atlee

Collin Richard Atlee, son of Mr. and Mrs. Richard Atlee of Lake Forest and Miss Seneca Simms, daughter of Thomas Simms of Peabody, West Virginia, were married on May 1 at the Peabody Community Church. Reverend Asa McAllister officiated. The Matron-of-Honor was Jane Highsmith of Peabody and the Best Man was Rory Brouchard of Chicago. The bride, wearing an ivory satin Vera Wang gown, was escorted by her father. The couple honeymooned in Paris and Vienna. Collin Atlee will attend medical school in the fall. Seneca Simms Atlee will divide her time between her musical career and her directorship duties at the Simms Center for the Preservation of Appalachian Music in Peabody.

When did that little cheater take up music? And wasn't her father dead? And how had she managed to meet the son of Richard Atlee? Vera Wang? Paris? Vienna? So much for her commitment to smaller footprints. Her wedding cake was probably made with eggs and butter.

Thank god he'd gotten rid of her. He'd always suspected her devotion to the environmental movement wasn't genuine, and the closer the wedding came, the surer his conviction that their relationship was a mistake. It had been painful, but he'd been forced to call the engagement off at the last minute. Good luck to the Atlees. At least she wasn't *his* problem anymore.

"Michael! Dinner is ready."

"Coming, Lindsey." Lindsey was a true believer. She worked at the nature center and had her masters in environmental science. It was a match made in heaven.

"Michael! I'm not cooking anymore if this is the thanks I get." He threw down the paper.

"Coming, dear."

Epilogue

Dr. Atlee, please report to Obstetrics.

It was his third page, but he'd been with a nine-year-old boy who'd just finished his first round of chemo, and he couldn't leave until he was sure the boy and his family were okay. Collin's pediatric residency would end next month, but he knew he'd come back to the university hospital in Charleston, West Virginia, to visit the boy until he was well enough to go home. Collin and Seneca had moved to Charleston for his residency, and they'd seen that many more children needed medical care than there were doctors to go around. So they'd decided to stay. They'd bought a house, joined a church and built a circle of close friends.

He said goodbye to his young patient's family and promised to look in on them tomorrow. As soon as he was out of Pediatrics, he began to sprint, sidestepping wheelchairs and gurneys. Just as he was paged for the fourth time, he hit the Obstetrics floor. He burst into the waiting room, and a little ballerina in a pink tutu and purple sneakers jumped up from the couch.

"Daddy!" He caught her up in his arms and hugged her.

"Lulu-belle. How's my girl?"

She kissed his cheek and hugged his neck. "Oh, Daddy, I love you so, so much!" At four, Louise Martha Atlee—Lulu—was the image of his mother. She had blonde hair, blue eyes framed in dark lashes and a flair for the dramatic.

He examined her blue eye shadow and pink lipstick. Then he sighed and looked at his mother who sat on the waiting room sofa with a solemn, auburn-haired girl beside her. "Don't you think Lulu is a little young for make-up, Mom?"

"We were just trying some new looks when Seneca's water broke." His mother and father were babysitting the Atlee children while Seneca was in the hospital. Tom was in Europe, but he was cutting his tour short and would be in Charleston in a few days as well. Then his family would all be together.

He set Lulu down and held out an arm to his other daughter, Sonja. "Hey there, Sunshine, how about a hug for your dad?" Six-year-old Sonja stood. "Only if you call me Sonja. I'm not a baby anymore." She was so much like Seneca, it made his knees weak sometimes.

"Okay. How about a hug for your dad, Sonja."

She came to him and hugged his waist. He put an arm around her shoulder. Sonja Simms Atlee had "the gift" as Tom liked to put it. She was proficient with the piano and the violin, and Seneca had begun to take her to Peabody, a hundred miles south of Charleston, when concerts were scheduled at the Center so Sonja would learn to appreciate Appalachian music. Sonja loved the trips. She wanted a fiddle for her seventh birthday.

"Where's Alex?" Alex Richard Atlee, his oldest, was seven going on forty. He was dark-haired and green-eyed with a winning smile and the Atlee family talent for convincing other people to do his work for him. He was destined for a boardroom in Chicago someday, although for now Alex was mostly interested in soccer and baseball.

"He went with Richard to the driving range."

"It's forty degrees outside."

"You know your father. He's obsessed with golf. Besides, they won't be long. We have reservations at Le Havre at six."

Collin rolled his eyes. "Please tell me you're not taking my three children to the fanciest restaurant in Charleston."

His mother raised her chin. "Their table manners are impeccable. Why shouldn't they enjoy fine dining?"

"Because they prefer Chicken McNuggets." Collin looked down at Sonja for confirmation of this fact. She gazed up at him, her bright blue eyes clouded with worry. "Our baby brother's coming, Daddy."

The baby! "Look, I gotta go," he said to his mother. "Eat wherever you want. But don't be surprised if Le Havre bans us for life after an evening with my kids." He disengaged Sonja's arms from his waist and Lulu's from his leg. "Don't order the escargot," he called to his daughters. "They're dead snails." Accompanied by their girlish squeals, he ran for the delivery rooms.

A few minutes later, washed and gowned, he found Seneca. Her hair was sticky with sweat and her eyes were bruises in her small face.

"You're an awful coach, Collie. The baby's head just crowned."

"Sorry." He lifted her hand to his lips and kissed it. "Are you okay?"

She smiled at him, then brushed at his cheek. "You have lipstick right here. Were you chasing the nurses?"

He rubbed his face. "A ballerina with a sticky mouth attacked me in the waiting room."

She started to laugh, then grimaced as a contraction gripped her body. He placed his hand on her abdomen and felt her muscles harden. "Push, baby."

She did. A few minutes later their fourth child, a second son was born and laid on Seneca's chest. He was fair-haired and blue-eyed, like Collin and Lulu and his mother and Grandpa Collins.

Seneca always knew what he was thinking. "He looks like your grandpa, doesn't he?"

He nodded.

"We'll name him Benjamin Collins."

"But we've already agreed on Thomas."

"No, Collie. Ben."

He thought about how his true journey in life started the day his grandfather died, and how it had spun him out of his boyhood home and to places far away, then brought him back to this perfect moment, surrounded by love and family. His grandfather would be proud. He leaned over and kissed his wife's damp forehead.

"Thanks, Sen."